'Amanda Lohrey is one of the best novelists in Australia, and if you were of a gong-giving disposition there are good reasons for saying she is the best of the lot.'

Owen Richardson, *Sunday Age*

'A novel about the difficulty of choosing between fateful alternatives, particularly when reason dictates one path and desire and instinct another. Lohrey is pressing firmly against a bruise on our modern psyche.'

Good Reading

'*The Philosopher's Doll* reads as an almost voyeuristic snoop into the intimacies of a marriage.'

Rita Feldman, *Big Issue*

'This intelligent study of a marriage in crisis will engage everyone who's ever contemplated parenthood.'

TravelLink

'Lohrey is about the finest fiction writer currently working in Australia...devastatingly skilful in the passionate and thoughtful detailing of individual lives.'

Helen Elliot, *Limelight*

PENGUIN BOOKS

the philosopher's doll

Amanda Lohrey was born in Tasmania in 1947. Her previous novels are *The Morality of Gentlemen*, *The Reading Group* and *Camille's Bread*. The latter won the Association for the Study of Australian Literature Gold Medal, and the Victorian Premier's Literary Award for Fiction.

AMANDA LOHREY

the philosopher's doll

PENGUIN BOOKS

PENGUIN BOOKS

Published by the Penguin Group
Penguin Group (Australia)
250 Camberwell Road, Camberwell, Victoria 3124, Australia
(a division of Pearson Australia Group Pty Ltd)
Penguin Group (Canada)
10 Alcorn Avenue, Toronto, Ontario, Canada M4V 3B2
(a division of Pearson Penguin Canada Inc.)
Penguin Books India Pvt Ltd
11 Community Centre, Panchsheel Park, New Delhi – 110 017, India
Penguin Group (NZ)
Cnr Airborne and Rosedale Roads, Albany, Auckland, New Zealand
(a division of Pearson New Zealand Ltd)
Penguin Books (South Africa) (Pty) Ltd
24 Sturdee Avenue, Rosebank, Johannesburg 2196, South Africa

Penguin Books Ltd, Registered Offices: 80 Strand, London, WC2R 0RL, England

First published by Penguin Group (Australia), a division of Pearson Australia Group Pty Ltd, 2004
This paperback edition published by Penguin Group (Australia),
a division of Pearson Australia Group Pty Ltd, 2005

1 3 5 7 9 10 8 6 4 2

Text copyright © Amanda Lohrey 2004

The moral right of the author has been asserted

Design by Debra Billson © Penguin Group (Australia)
Cover photographs by Getty Images and photolibrary.com
Typeset in Centaur by Post Pre-press Group, Brisbane, Queensland
Printed and bound in Australia by McPherson's Printing Group, Maryborough, Victoria

National Library of Australia
Cataloguing-in-Publication data:

Lohrey, Amanda.
The philosopher's doll.
ISBN 0 14 300133 7.
I. Marriage – Fiction. I. Title.

A823.3

www.penguin.com.au

Contents

Duck

1

On the day that Lindsay Eynon is to beget a child, he is extremely hungry. It is worth describing this day because it will reveal the contents of Lindsay's head, and it is appropriate to focus on his head since, as a philosopher, this is what he values above all else. To espouse the head above the heart is deeply unfashionable — unfashionable, at least, in the realm of public sentiment — but in his view a great deal of woolly talk about the heart is little more than weak camouflage for prejudice, laziness and stupidity. If he has any role as a teacher it is to show how and why this is so, to instruct his pupils in the arts of Reason.

This part of his life is relatively straightforward.

Relatively? What does that mean? Not absolute, that's what it means. Not absolute, or existing by itself. So the professional part of his life is straightforward in relation to the rest of his life where, just lately, he has felt himself drifting into the ocean of the becalmed. Some insidious virus of banality has found its way into his bloodstream.

It's something to do with being no longer young, only youngish. It's something to do with being married long enough for the excitement to have evaporated. Each day he knows, more or less, what will come out of his wife's mouth. Not that she is a dull woman, far from it. She is a remarkable woman, in many ways stronger than he, with a fierce, robust animality about her that sometimes dismays him; not mere sensuality, but something verging on a vital coarseness, a force-field that will have its way.

And now, he fears, she would have her way about babies.

He can almost see them, those two little ovaries glowing in the dark. In the thick tangle of her pubic hair there is a homing device that will send his sperm inexorably to their target.

Her target.

Their bed is a radar field.

When did they begin to argue about this? When did it begin to curdle their blood? Did she raise it first, or could it have been him? No, it must have been her. Why would *he* raise it? He was happy. He had plans.

Downstairs in the kitchen he begins to prepare his breakfast. First, the freshly squeezed orange juice from the new Baal machine, a gleaming, stainless-steel press with a kind of clinical beauty that is a joy to contemplate. Then the muesli with yoghurt and thickly cut sourdough Vienna toast with cream cheese and marmalade. Perfect. On a good day this preparation is a happy ritual, both precise and thoughtful. Today, however, is not a good day.

Kirsten has already left for work, skipping breakfast as usual. She will eat an apple in the car and drink too much coffee all morning. He has known her to go all day without eating and be none the worse for it. Fiery creature that she is, she seems able to live off the very air. He, on the other hand, though methodical and even-tempered, is hungry most of the time.

It must be his metabolism.

Every morning he walks from Ruckers Hill in Northcote to High Street, where he catches the tram. He and Kirsten have mortgaged a freestanding, two-storey Edwardian house in a prime position with good aspect, even if most of the rooms are dilapidated and dark. Not yet gentrified, their street is in poor repair: a patched road with humps and cracks in the bitumen, narrow footpaths that slope away underfoot, kerbs that crumble into gutters strewn with pizza boxes and crumpled soft-drink cans. In many of the small front gardens lemon trees are in delicate white flower and gardenias shed flurries of pink and white petals onto the street. When first they came to live here he was enchanted by these and would stop and pick off a blossom, sniffing at its luxurious scent before slipping it into the pocket of his jacket.

Before long he is in his room on campus, working at his desk beside a window that faces out onto the large courtyard and its Japanese garden, a small sea of fine white pebbles with a single maple tree. And directly opposite, on the mellow sandstone of the west wall, someone has scrawled an enormous piece of graffiti in white paint: DO ANIMALS HAVE SOULS?

The defacement has been there for months now, with no effort made to remove it, and he wonders if the authorities find it amusing. It wasn't so long ago that undergraduate graffiti was all about politics, sex, drugs and police brutality in custody. In so material a tradition, a little metaphysics can seem almost whimsical.

After he has opened up his email and scanned his messages, he begins to trawl through some research sites on the Web, looking for material on the obscure Scottish phenomenologist Edward Craigie, who studied under Heidegger in the thirties. Then it occurs to him that he would be better occupied in revising his notes for the first-year lecture on Rationalism that he is due to give at noon. He gets up and moves across to the filing cabinet, rummages among his old notes and becomes increasingly irritable when he can't immediately locate what he knows to be there. Is he more than unusually impatient today? Yes, he is. There is a tremor in his blood — he can feel it — like an unseen tide, a kind of slipperiness in the pulse. He is finding it difficult to settle to any one thing, and a tautness at the back of his neck suggests that a head-ache is looming. Flick, flick, flick through the drab olive files – ah, here it is. Good. Maybe he can have some fun with this. At the very least it will give him an opening to talk about one of his favourite characters from this or any other era, the outrageous Enlightenment *philosophe*, Julien Offroy de La Mettrie.

'Come in!'

It's a student, Ben, wanting to deliver a paper in person; wanting to talk about nothing in particular; wanting to satisfy an abject craving for recognition, some acknowledgement, however fleeting. At such times Lindsay looks directly into their eyes and gives them 'the gaze', says quietly and earnestly, 'Thank you very much, Ben.' And shuts the door.

Once again he attempts to settle at his desk, but phrases from last night's argument with Kirsten are rising in his head like flares. 'One more year,' he'd said, 'one more year and we can renegotiate the mortgage and complete the renovations. After that we'll be ready.'

That's when she'd screamed at him. *You'll never be ready!'* (investing that word 'ready' with particular venom). Then she'd picked up the alarm clock and hurled it across the room. Fortu-nately it was the cheap plastic variety and made only a small dent in the plaster.

Where was he? La Mettrie. From the moment he read his

first account of La Mettrie he had warmed to him as an uncompromising figure with a genius for deploying extremity like a scalpel. A physician whose main interest was medicine, not philosophy, La Mettrie had outdone his mentor, René Descartes, by offering a wholly materialist account of the mind. His infamous work, the provocatively titled *L'Homme-Machine*, had outraged the traditionalists. In it he argued that Man, like the beasts, is a machine. The soul and the mind both are illusions produced by the interplay of the physical components of the body: they are the reflex activities that arise out of the mechanistic principles of stimulus and response, and Man, as such, is no more than a peripheral and transient accident of material evolution. 'The ethical consequences of such a philosophy' (Lindsay can hear his own voice now, amplified by the subtle acoustics of the lecture room) 'was an outright hedonism which La Mettrie did not fail to embrace with vigour. He lived heartily in the spirit of his work, dying of indigestion at the age of forty-one after gorging himself on a pie of pheasant and truffles.'

At this point he will pause, and take pleasure in describing the agent of death. 'Death from a dish of red meat, hung to the brink of rotting; hung until it was the deep purple colour of a bruise; soaked for an hour in a bowl of sweet wine and then for a further hour in a tureen of warm milk; braised in a rich burgundy sauce laced with slivers of black truffles and lusciously encased in a buttery pastry, its golden dome glistening with a patina of egg yolk and adorned with a pastry *coq*.'

A gross death. A legendary death. An appropriate death for a materialist and a freethinker.

Of course, no-one could possibly die from a single bout of indigestion. An early instance, no doubt, of urban myth.

He lifts the file out of the cabinet drawer and carries it back to his desk. Then he looks at his watch. Only nine twenty-five. Could the day go any slower?

Something is unsettling him, a kind of indigestion of the spirit. But this in itself is not the problem: the problem is that he is unconscious of what *exactly* it is. The fight with Kirsten, yes, but something more. If he knew, he could address the issue: turn it over in his head, consider alternatives, rehearse arguments or rejoinders, go for a walk, polish a riposte or two, take out a loan. But no solution to his restlessness can be contemplated because the cause itself has not yet surfaced on the rippled pond of his awareness. Only the symptoms are there, hovering like march flies. Tiny missiles in search of a target.

That argument late last night about when they should have a baby – it's a scene they seem to be repeating more and more often and he can't for the life of him understand why. It's as if just when they are settled, just when they have their life in order (well, almost), she wants to disrupt things. His own argument is a simple one: since they are happy as they are, why risk change until they are both ready? It's not as if she is that old, only thirty-six.

And what about the mortgage? They can scarcely afford the house they've got, dark and run-down as it is, and it was only the legacy left to him by his aunt that enabled them to mount a substantial deposit; otherwise they would have had no hope of ever buying into the inner city. Now their combined incomes barely straddle the repayments. And they like to go out, and to eat out; they like movies, a season ticket for the film festival. They like to sleep in at weekends, to make love spontaneously on Saturday afternoons, to go off overnight to the coast. One day he would like the freedom to own an investment property, or a holiday house where they could escape the city. And it's not about greed, it's about being in control. This might sound selfish, but selfish in relation to what? Aren't there more than enough children, and neglected children, in the world already? Okay, it's a hackneyed question, but it holds nevertheless. Better they send money to sponsor one of those kids in Africa than add to the population burden.

Not that he said any of this last night. All he'd argued for was delay, to wait until they were in a better financial position. It was a matter of timing. Timing was everything. But whenever he tries to be reasonable and lay it all out on the table, Kirsten becomes hysterical and abusive; accuses him of living in a bubble, of being phobic and unable to make a decision.

How can he tell her that the very idea of a baby fills him with dread? That what's really eating him is a dizzying sensation of metamorphosis, of becoming his own father? And how could he put this into words, even if he wanted to? Instead he comes up with these trite codicils of reason. And the strain of it all needles him into tormenting her.

Where was he? Ah, yes, the question of animal soul. He will begin his lecture by taking his cue from the graffiti opposite his window and speculating as to who might have written it, and why. It is in any case a subject he is at home with, having written a chapter on it in his doctorate. Animal rights is a favourite topic of undergraduates, and why not? Hadn't Descartes declared the question of animal soul to be of comparable order to the quest for the philosopher's stone? In the seventeenth century it bothered the dreams of all the leading thinkers of the day, indeed was *the* great divide between the man of religion and the man of science. Take the household dog, that affectionate creature, so loyal and unwavering: could it be no more than a clockwork box of tricks? Or, to put it another way, a machine that bled? Did it have more than a robotically programmed consciousness, and if so, of what kind? And to what degree? These were questions that seemed then to lie at the very heart of whether or not we live in a meaningful world, or – more terrifyingly – in a universe of chance.

He begins to read through his old notes. 'It was Descartes, in the seventeenth century, who cut the cord and severed the link between animal and man. *From the very perfection of animal actions we suspect that they do not have free will,* Descartes wrote.' And this is one of Lindsay's favourite sentences in all of Western philosophical thought. Perfection is not compatible with free will and so, before we are even born, we are, as it were, excused. 'But the animal is a sensate automaton; a beast-machine. Soul is synonymous with reason, and animals, clearly, do not reason. Can we imagine an animal making a mistake? Of course not. And the most solid proof of their lack of reason is their absence of speech, with its infinite potential to conjure up options. For lack of just such a facility, beasts do not progress; they do not innovate. Thus the first spiderweb, for example, is no less perfect than the last.'

Unlike the automobile, he thinks, or any other man-made machine.

'Descartes likened the natural functioning of an animal to that of a clock, a sensate clock. As a young man, he was so intrigued by the possibilities of mechanistic system that he proposed the invention of a man-machine to be actuated by magnets. He also proposed the construction of two machines that would simulate beasts, one a flying pigeon and the other a pheasant hunted by a spaniel.'

The pheasant again, an animal of great interest to the

philosophes, not least because they liked to eat it. This pheasant, he tells his students, could well serve as a motif of Reason. Phase one of the Great Enlightenment: Descartes tries to engineer the real. Phase two: La Mettrie chokes on it.

But even better than the mechanical bird was the mechanical doll. Sometime after his death, Descartes' enemies circulated the story that he had kept in his possession a life-size mechanical doll in the shape of a woman. The doll was said by some to resemble his mistress, while others claimed that, in an access of grief, Descartes had named it after his illegitimate daughter Francine, who had died of cholera at the age of five. The eminent philosopher (a bachelor) was said to have taken the doll everywhere with him, and to have slept with her encased in a trunk at his side (centuries before the plastic blow-up model). In his definitive biography of the great man, Stephen Gaukroger dismisses this story as a calumny disseminated by the anti-materialists. But, Lindsay tells his students, we should read this fable of the mechanical consort – this female machine – as another of the phantoms of urban myth, a seventeenth-century version that expresses the sense of enormity men began to feel at the idea that the body, the human body, might be no more than a machine that bled.

Wait a minute, he's used that phrase already.

Sometimes he wonders why he continues to purvey this dubious narrative, but at least it keeps them awake (and he likes to remind them that the robot Maria from *Metropolis* and the replicant Rachel from *Bladerunner* had early antecedents). They need their philosophy enlivened by the cheap tricks of narrative, by gossip and scandal, and he maintains a fund of these in reserve for that pedagogical moment when he senses he has lost them — those restless first-years, lured to enrol in philosophy by a fervent hope that, within a few semesters, they will be able to rebut the sombre and oppressive logic of their parents. But when the dull penny drops, when they realise that this will be a long, drawn-out apprenticeship — that there is no strategy that will guarantee them a quick rout — their earnestness begins rapidly to fade. Ten minutes into any lecture the minds of all but a few unflinching note-takers will have drifted, on a tide of hormones or heroin, to the contemplation of some love object, and it's then that their eyes become warm and cloudy with the inner reality of the daydream. At this point he might drop in the story of La Mettrie.

Death from satisfaction, and how to achieve it.

Another knock on the door and a shiny bald head above a bow tie appears in the doorway. That odious fool Hunter, tiptoeing about in his patent-leather shoes.

'Leonie and Klaus can't agree about the restructuring of first year. There's a department meeting at one.'

'Thank you, Alan, I noted that on my email.'

'I never use it, dear boy. I prefer word of mouth.'

It's the archly salacious way he says 'word of mouth' that seals it. Lindsay looks out the window, rudely, to indicate that he does not wish to pass the time of day, and waits for Hunter to take the hint, which he does, closing the door in his soft, conspiratorial way.

Three-twenty in the afternoon, and the day has not improved. An honours seminar on Metaphysics: Option B, Negativity, a departmental meeting at lunchtime with only a soggy salad roll for consolation (he'd thrown half of it away), and a strong impulse to abandon the afternoon and go to the movies. Some action dick-flick with terrorists, exploding cars, men wielding thick tubes and spraying foam at a wall of fire. Then coming out of the plush darkness into the bright light of Bourke Street and the yellow McDonald's signs and the jangle of the pinball parlours and slinking home with a cranky feeling of disorientation and flatness and saying he'd been working all day on his paper for the conference in Boston on Mind.

No.

He will stay in his room. He will work on the paper.

But first he needs to clear his head of administrative trivia. On the broad window-ledge next to his desk he keeps a portable

CD player, a stack of discs and some headphones for exactly that purpose. The music will help him to settle. Something with clarity and order. Vivaldi's Concerto for Harpsichord – that should get him going. Adjusting the headphones against his large, prominent ears, he prepares to move into alpha state, to shut off from the – from the what? From the banality around him, that's what; its slovenly formlessness, its tepid casuistry. What he needs is a dose of pure classicism, and he begins to hum along with the music . . . But no. In the still, dead hum of mid-afternoon the Vivaldi jangles like a fire alarm, buoyant with a brassy, trumpeting optimism so schematic, so evangelical, it sets his teeth on edge. Jerking the headphones off, he tosses them onto the desk and lapses into staring out the window.

And there, perched on the outer windowsill, is some kind of small furry creature. At first he thinks it's a balled caterpillar – or is it one of those huge bumble bees lately arrived from New Zealand? Leaning forward in his chair to get a closer look, he sees that it is not one but two creatures, in the act of copulating. The female, much larger than the male, is immobile, with her beady head almost against the window. The male is mounting her from behind and the curious thing is this: no part of him is touching the sill, he seems to be riveted to her by his penis. His back legs are rigid in the air while his front legs are tucked in under the rim of her wings. All the while he is jigging up and down in slight movements, his feelers twitching with the effort of it, and on every seventh jig he gives an extra thrust so that her back momentarily arches and then subsides. This goes on for some time, as if he is delivering each sperm individually rather than shooting his load in one lightning rush. The female is lying completely passive. Any observer might think her dead, if not for the occasional tremor of her front right feeler. On further observation he sees that the male, who had appeared to be clinging to her back, is not, as he thought, unsupported. His wings are propped behind him on the windowsill, and despite their apparent fragility, their amber fineness, they are in fact the source of his equilibrium.

And, oh, what superb wings they are!

At last the female stirs, lurching her consort sideways and askew, and as he struggles to regain his purchase she turns away from him so that in an awkward grappling they stumble about until she manages, with one back leg, to break free of him. For some seconds they stand alone, stunned by their exertion, rear ends heaving. Then, as if nothing has happened, suddenly she flies off, leaving him pulsating, and alone, on the windowsill. As Lindsay watches, fascinated, without warning the male tumbles off the sill, hurtling out of sight in free fall.

Five p. m. And he has done no more than tweak his notes. By now the muscles on the left side of his neck are rigid, like a brick column, and he fears that he might be on the brink of a migraine. And he's hungry, damn it. He opens the top drawer of his desk and rummages around looking for pain-killers, for the packet of codeine tablets he keeps there, but all he can find is a litter of spilled paper clips, loose filing cards, fragments of silver foil and a mini-pack of condoms wrapped in a handkerchief. And the letters.

Oh, God.

The letters.

What is he going to do about these? For eight days and nights he has managed to put them out of his mind, but he knows he ought not procrastinate any longer. Last Wednesday he had arrived at work to find a second pink envelope nestling on the carpet behind his door, and even then his first instinct had been not to read it. But of course he had to. And, like the first, it was from Sonia Bichel, one of his postgraduate students, further elaborating on her erotic obsession. With him.

In words at once absurdly lofty, sentimentally abject and yet charged with erotic yearning, she had written of her overpowering compulsion to appear naked before him, 'mentally, physically, spiritually and in every other way'. Fortuitously, he has not seen her since, having sent her away to do a long stretch of work on her thesis. And anyway, he would not be tempted. She is not the sort of girl he would normally give a thought to, never mind encourage. She is not striking in appearance and has no personality; is a reserved, hesitant girl with glasses and mousy brown hair. On the other hand he cannot fail to be aware of her acute self-consciousness; a ripe, insinuating shyness of the kind that suggests she is quietly brimming inside with some simmering juice that might at any moment spill over and wet the floor. In other words, exactly the kind of woman most likely to discomfort him.

In the era of hi-tech, a hand-written letter was such an old-fashioned gesture, quaint almost. Or might have been but for its clumsy, pornographic contents in which, he, Lindsay, had been conjured into being as some kind of monstrous phallus on stilts. And he recalls, with distaste, their first interview; how she had arrived at his door in a red skirt and a black lace top, but with an old-fashioned granny cardigan wrapped incongruously around this vamp outfit so that the effect was jarring and uncertain. Peering at him nervously over her glasses, she outlined her proposed research on rhetorics of the heart, a comparative survey of philosophical and medical discourses on the idea of the heart as both a physiological organ and a metaphorical centre of the emotions. It was unorthodox, something attractively novel and possibly even virtuous, in a scholarly sense – that is, if she could pull it all together.

They had spoken for quite a long time. When she talked she seemed to lose her unease, to submerge herself in a flow of words, like a fish that might lumber about awkwardly on the rocks but could glide effortlessly in water. It was, he told her, a most unusual proposal and many would not approve it. He, on the other hand, was prepared to give her a semester to see what, if anything, she could make of it.

He remembers how she suddenly became silent and stared at him with a kind of mesmerising passivity, like an animal caught in headlights, and he'd wondered if she was one of those unstable, neurasthenic types who would never complete.

Meanwhile he knows what he should do with these letters. He should show them to the dean immediately. To cover himself. And in the next day or two, he tells himself, he will.

But not now. Now he must get out of here.

It's almost twilight as he walks along the path beside the library and on towards the weed-filled ornamental pond with its shabby modernist sculpture perched in the middle: a rust-encrusted iron sphere made up of interlocking rings, an abstract and now dated representation of the revolve of the world.

A light rain has begun to fall. He walks the few blocks to Lygon Street and pauses there to peer into the fug of steam and exhaust fumes that hovers above the wet tar. Absentmindedly he strokes his right temple, hoping that any minute a vacant cab will cruise into view, that he will not be late, even though the traffic is congested. Up and down the street the cars glisten like a line of wet-backed beetles and the drizzle turns into a steady rain. Now he feels his irritability level rising, not because he is damp – he likes the rain – but because he will be late, and he cannot bear to be late for anything. Indeed, he is obsessively punctual. It's part of his love of order. To his wife's annoyance he is often early, and they have quarrelled over this in the past, in a low-key, bickering kind of way, and he is beginning to lose himself in recall of the last time this occurred when – at last – a dilapidated Falcon breaks out of the line of traffic and swerves into the kerb.

Lindsay opens the door of the cab and sticks his head into the stuffy interior. The driver is a Sikh, his radio tuned to what must be an ethnic FM station, blaring out some nerve-scraping banshee wail accompanied by an exotic string instrument of the kind that sets your teeth on edge. For a second he hesitates, wondering if his headache can bear it, but in this weather he can't afford to knock back an empty cab.

Before they have travelled four blocks in the slow-moving traffic, the wail has keened into hysterical crescendo and the pounding in his head is in overdrive. After what seems an age of bumper-to-bumper honking, alternating with sudden swerves into potentially faster lanes, they take a left-hand turn out of the congestion of Toorak Road and glide at last into the quiet, leafy streets of South Yarra. It is now completely dark.

In the marble and brass foyer of the Bistro L'occident Lindsay brushes the rain from his trenchcoat and looks around for his wife. The huge entrance is sumptuous but cold, with a high-domed ceiling that makes it look like a Roman basilica, though it's hardly an inner sanctum — more like an upmarket pick-up trough, buzzing with young suits of both sexes.

Service at the bar is brisk, and a gin and tonic is before him while he is still looking around for Kirsten. And with the first mouthful, sweet and astringent, it suddenly occurs to him, with a mild pang of anxiety, that while she is often late she is not normally this late. But he isn't anxious, not yet. There's something earthy and indestructible about his wife, a quality both sensual and sensible. A deep intuition that she will outlive him, that he will not be left alone, is one of the reasons he married her.

And this is their Thursday night together, by now something of a ritual. Sometimes these nights are merely pleasant, but now and then they attain the sublime. It's when the evening does work that they have their best sex, the kind that can leave you feeling loose and mellow for days. He still recalls with pleasure a meal they had earlier in the year which had been quite magical: a delicate gnocchi, quail braised with fennel, a gorgonzola mousse. They ate at a new restaurant on Jacka Boulevard at St Kilda, out on a wide, white terrace looking down on the water. There was no breeze and the last of the evening light cast a sheen on her bare shoulders. All through the meal the surf broke whisperingly and insistently against the sand, until at last he felt himself merging into a perfect moment.

Ah, but just lately this Thursday-evening ritual has begun to pall. They talk too much, or rather they talk too urgently, and always about the wrong things. It comes out of nowhere – an ambush. They'll be discussing something mundane and safely utilitarian, like their mortgage, or the possibility of trading in their car, or whether to holiday in Noosa or Bali, and suddenly she'll take a deep breath and utter the *baby* word.

Uh-oh, he'll think, here it comes.

And so eating out has begun to lose its charm, because for some reason she rarely springs this on him at home where it's more intimate. No, it's always over the starched white table linen and the polished silver. Wham! Right between the eyes.

'Well, what do you think?' she'll say.

'What do I think about what?' (Raising his guard.)

'About maybe planning to get pregnant in twelve months' time?'

Or she'll say, as if in casual afterthought to a suggestion he's made, 'That would be all right except for . . .'

Long pause.

'Except for what?'

'Except that if we had children it wouldn't be practicable.'

One of her favourite stratagems is to adopt a pseudo-reasonable tone and say she isn't sure she even wants to have babies but that she – they – need to talk it through. As a philosopher, she teases him, he is adept at laying out all the many paths of reasoning, for and against. Why not indulge her? As therapy? He sees the mechanism of the trap opening even as she activates the spring.

And the traps abound, everywhere. One night, reading the newspaper, his eye was caught by a heading in the Lifestyle section: 'Putting it on Ice'. A married couple in London, in their early thirties – she a marketing executive, he a dentist – were agreed that they did not want a baby now. Their dilemma was this: what if they waited too long? After all, the body could not be relied upon. Bodies age at different rates. One man's sperm may be motile into his eighties; another's begins to tire and slow at around thirty-five. Afraid of risking infertility in their late thirties – and with it the horror of thwarted possibility, some niggling sense of lack – the London couple had arranged for their embryos to be frozen in a storage bank until a more convenient time.

Reading this, Lindsay had almost laughed out loud. Now, *there* was a variation on the futures market. For a moment he contemplated reading the article to Kirsten, but thought better of it. It was only the thought of leaving it too late that was making her obsess about a baby now, he was sure of that. It was some kind of genetically programmed female panic.

Not that he is attracted to the ice option. For one thing, he's not sure he likes the idea of offspring-in-waiting. He can see them now, two little icicled seahorses – what do they keep them in, an icecube tray? – waiting for him to drop by and fill out the withdrawal forms. It's the kind of thing that could haunt you; a potential that, in the end, would demand to be fulfilled simply because it was there. And what if it weren't fulfilled? Would they bury them with you? He had a mental image of himself laid out in a coffin, in the ground, with two defrosting seahorses nestling in his hair ...

Feeling a hand on his shoulder, he turns, and it's her, breathless and a little pale, but with that hazy, reddish-blonde radiance that so captivates him, even on a night like this. And he sees that she is well disposed towards him, despite last night, and suddenly all his mental agitation falls away. Already he is in a better mood, just seeing her, and he bends and kisses her lightly on the lips.

'Sorry I'm late,' she says. 'A last-minute admission.'

'That's okay. They make a good gin and tonic here.' He says this partly because it's true, partly because he wants to distract her. He doesn't want to hear about the last-minute admission – or anything to do with her work – he wants to look at her, to savour her, like the sweet dish she is. Despite the headache, despite his gnawing hunger, he can feel the sap rising. He wants to cup his hands around her breasts, here, in public; wants to kneel and eat her sweet brown nipples off a plate. The white flash of that image is so startling it almost unbalances him, and he grasps her arm a little tighter than usual to steady himself.

'Are we friends?' he asks, gazing intently into her eyes.

She laughs, and gives him that frank, amused look she wears when something has put her in a good mood. 'Of course we are.'

That's another thing about Kirsten: she's fiery but forgiving.

At that moment a young waiter comes over and indicates a small table in one corner, well away from the noise of the bar. Lindsay nods approvingly and they make their way around the edge of the rowdy throng.

Tonight, he observes, she is wearing that gold silk shirt that is so becoming and seems to reflect the lustre of her skin. With her dark, red-blonde tresses there is something Botticelli-like about her – a rounded Botticelli, since she has put on weight. He had thought the stress of her work might wear her away to a fine stick, but in fact the opposite has proved to be the case. He can see her turning in a few years into a handsome but over-ripe matron with a faint choleric flush and high blood pressure.

Settled, they begin their serious appraisal of the menu.

'Linz?'

He blinks. 'Yes?'

'What's the matter?'

'Nothing.'

'You're miles away.'

'Not really. I've got a headache.'

'Have you taken anything for it?'

'No. Have you got something?'

She reaches into her handbag, that enormous black leather tote in which she seems to enfold the known universe, and comes up with two capsules in foil casing.

'Thanks. I knew I could rely on you.' He takes them grate-fully, and pours them both some water. 'What are you having?'

'The duck,' she says. 'I've had a miserable day and I feel like something rich and sweet. What about you?'

'I'm starving. I think I'll try the squid-ink pasta in fish broth with mussels.'

'What about entrée?'

'The yabby salad sounds good.'

'Too much seafood gives you indigestion.'

'You're right. I'll have the five-fungi roulade.'

'Good. I'll have the yabby salad.'

He laughs. This is what he loves about Kirsten, these little games. They lead on to other and better games, usually between the sheets.

The waiter arrives at their table, one of those slim young men with black hair cropped close in a chic stubble and chalk-white skin the colour of urban angst, worn lightly. This one has the manners to go with it: condescending, but not in the studied way of head waiters, more offhand than that, as if he has something better to do – play *Hamlet* at The Playbox in spring, perhaps – and will be out of here soon.

Kirsten is licking her lips in absentminded anticipation. He likes it when she does this, likes the way her face blooms with appetite, how she leans forward intimately at a slight angle across the table and a glaze comes over her eyes. Dining out is one of their passions, the perfect preparation for Eros – the body replete, cheeks flushed with wine, hands interlocked on the walk to the car, her fingers caressing the inside of his thigh on the drive home. He can't wait.

'What?'

'I said, What do you think of the clientele?'

He sits back in his chair and looks around him, taking in the scene. Tonight could be one of their best nights in a while. It's been weeks since they had a really good time together. Five months, in fact. It's five months from when she started work at the rehabilitation centre, and since then she seems always to be upset about something. More than once he's come home late to find her sniffling in front of the TV, or crying in the kitchen, chopping coriander, pounding lemongrass or slicing eggplant, her eyes watery and her lips smudged, and he knows it's been a bad day. Sometimes she's just angry and she gets that look, that black smouldering look that could kill. If things don't go her way she can combust.

'The clientele is fine. It's the service I'm worried about. I'm starving.'

'There's our waiter. I'll try and catch his eye.'

It was when she had begun to get restless in her old job — she was a counsellor in a suburban high school — that she had first started in on the baby thing. It occurred to him that something new might offer her more satisfaction and he had encouraged her to look around. But then, typically, when finally she decided to make a move she had gone for broke, taken on a job as a case-worker at a detention centre for wayward and abandoned boys. This was Rundle House, a Gothic pile out towards Warrandyte, some colonial banker's mansion left to charity by its owner and now revamped from an old-fashioned orphanage into a cluster of 'family' cottages, with house mothers or house fathers and five boys to a cottage. All very civilised in theory, but in real life a cauldron. To begin with he had encouraged Kirsten to scale back on her enmeshment in the lives of others, but somehow the reverse had occurred – she had jumped out of a small frying pan into a blazing bushfire; opted for the nth degree of difficulty, the backward flip with triple somersault and pike.

'Linz?'

'Yes?'

'You've drifted off again.'

'No, right here. Do you think we might actually manage a bread roll?'

'It's crowded. They look as if they're flat out.'

'It's expensive. They should have more waiters on.'

She sighs. 'It *is* slow.'

There follows a brief silence, while he waits for her to ask him about his day. She doesn't. Instead she starts in on the gold-fish. Again.

Oh, no, he thinks, not the *gold*fish.

A few weeks ago she'd got herself into a state over a dispute about a fish. One of the newly admitted boys had wanted to bring his pet goldfish – the only thing he seemed to care about, according to the case report — into care with him, but had been refused permission. No pets — absolutely no pets — was the policy of Rundle House, because somewhere in the not too distant past some boy had kept a cat and some other boy had chopped off its paws. Kirsten had remonstrated with the chief administrator, a woman called Mairéad McGuinness, but she had been adamant. No pets. The directive had been issued to the boy's mother, but someone's wires had got crossed, or else the mother was bloody-minded — perhaps weak — because on admission day the boy turned up with his suitcase, his comic books *and* the goldfish, darting around in its pathetically small plastic bowl. The admissions clerk had explained that it would have to go back with the boy's mother, but in the official bustle of admission, not to mention the tears of farewell, the goldfish had got left behind, still in the care of its twelve-year-old owner, Joel.

Joel. That was the boy's name, Joel. He, Lindsay, can tell you *every single detail* of this case because he's heard it all, every bit of it, over and over and over again, ad nauseam.

The very next day, the goldfish was confiscated and placed in the tea-room of the main administration block while an absurd debate ensued as to what to do with it. Kirsten had argued the case for returning it to the boy. 'These children come from homes where they are not adequately loved or cared for,' she pleaded. 'We can expect that when they grow up they will most likely be unable to love either themselves or anyone else. They come here with the one thing they're attached to, and through which their affectionate and nurturing side can develop, and we take it off them!'

'Look, Kirsten,' and Mairéad had sighed with her more-in-sorrow-than-in-anger sigh, 'you know as well as I do how long that goldfish will last.'

'All right. So someone flushes it down the toilet, puts it in the boy's sandwich or smothers it under his pillow. We replace it, and we keep on replacing it.'

'Well, I'm sure the boys would just love that little game, wouldn't they? Waiting to see who'll crack first? How many goldfish will the state welfare budget stand?'

'There is a difference, Mairéad, between another child massacring your fish and people in authority, who are supposed to be in charge of your welfare, beating them to it. There's a different kind of message there, don't you think?'

Lindsay can imagine this scene all too vividly. He almost feels sorry for Mairéad. Kirsten could be icily eloquent when roused, and the goldfish has become something of a test case; a crucible, she says, of everything she is on about with these boys. Just lately she has begun to brood on it out of all proportion, describing the confiscation of the fish as heartbreaking. She even had a dream that she was bathing some goldfish in the sink when suddenly she noticed there was no plug, and the water was running away and the goldfish, bloodied like embryos, were sliding down the plughole. She woke sobbing.

And now she's telling him that the goldfish is dead. 'It died last night,' she says. 'I knew it would.'

What can he say? Is the bloody goldfish going to blight his evening? He takes a deep breath. 'Well,' he ventures, 'I suppose that's *that* problem done with.' (Hoping that now they can get off this topic once and for all.)

'Not quite. I haven't broken the news to Joel yet. Luckily he was out on an excursion and not due back until after dinner. I'm hoping I can tee up a replacement.'

'How?' (He shouldn't ask.)

'At the staff meeting this morning I made sure everyone knew about it, not that they cared. Mairéad just slid into her phony "Oh dear" routine. "They're notoriously fragile pets," she says,' and here Kirsten, always a good mimic, slips into a passable version of Mairéad's portentous delivery. '"For some reason, children always want a goldfish, not a common or garden fish – oh no, it has to be a goldfish, and they're the hardest to keep alive in captivity." And then of course Marcus has to chip in. "Even in a good-sized pond, never mind in a tank," he says.'

Marcus is a genial Anglican priest who functions as Mairéad's echo. Lindsay has met him at a staff dinner, where he took an instant dislike to him.

'"A goldfish *is* a common or garden fish," I said, "and I think it's incumbent on us to replace it." Well, that set them right off.'

Lindsay is smiling, despite himself. Kirsten can be very funny. 'So what happened?'

'I was overruled. For now.' And then: 'I'm fed up with them both. But they haven't got the better of me yet. I rang a couple of pet shops and asked about goldfish. One guy told me there's a particularly hardy species that survives against most odds and is therefore suitable for incarceration in almost any tank, anywhere, anytime. I wrote down its biological name and looked up its habits in a reference book. I'll write a short report on the little beast and put the case again next week.'

Her husband gives a sharp, mirthless laugh. Pet shops! How characteristic her response. How dogged but politically obtuse. She must be driving them nuts. 'You might have to concede on this,' he says.

Kirsten raises her eyebrows and gives him her 'Oh, yeah?' look. She is already on to her second glass of wine and they haven't sighted so much as a bread roll.

Now his stomach is rumbling. 'I can't believe how bad the service is here.'

'I need to go to the loo. I'll look for our waiter and ask for some bread rolls.'

He watches her make her way around the tables, her handsome hips just that little bit wider than the ideal. She has a good carriage, though, and can look very imposing. She's at the bar now, having a word with one of the waiters. He sees her point to their table, sees the waiter nod and then move to turn away – he is clearly busy, pressured even – but she beckons him back and says something else. He looks a bit miffed. Perhaps she's chipped him about the rolls. Overstated her case. At times she does go on. In fact she can be bloody unrelenting, to the point of unreason. She gets a bone between her jaws – or a goldfish – and won't let go.

But here she is, back at the table. 'I cancelled the entrées,' she says.

'You *what?*'

'The service is so slow, Linz, and in a place like this the entrée is going to be two mouthfuls and a rocket leaf and then we'd have to wait aeons for the main course while we died of starvation.'

He is speechless. Isn't that just like her? God, she can be peremptory, so black and white. She might have consulted him first. He can see the logic of it, but has to stifle a grimace nevertheless. He was looking forward to that roulade, something creamy and unctuous, something to lubricate his desire. Right now, though, he'd settle for a simple crust.

'I'm sorry I was so late,' she says again. 'We had the police turn up, out of the blue, with this kid.'

Oh, no, he thinks, here we go again. Frankly, in his heart of hearts, he's beginning to get fed up with all this ... all this *anguish at one remove*. Little Johnny's elder brother molested him and set fire to him in the garage; someone else's mother was pimping for him in a respectable suburb. One case history runs into another, like a series of tabloid caricatures, and it's not that he's unsympathetic. He's happy to pay taxes for the upkeep of these institutions but he does not want to feel, on a daily basis, that something is being demanded of him — some mechanical jerk of the heart-strings; some emotional tithe, like a tax on the heart.

And can't she see what this does to him? To them both? Can't she see that it's *inappropriate* to go on about it now, that it works like an anaphrodisiac? And that the main course, to which he's been looking forward inordinately (he thinks of that limp salad roll), is going to be drowned in the pathos of yet another case history? It's the detail that gets to him, an excoriating tangle of trivia, a thicket of pointless facticity, the detritus of anecdote. Get to the point, he wants to say, if there *is* one — and if there is he can usually see it coming a mile off, which is more than he can say for his main course. Another ten minutes and he'll get acid pain just beneath his ribs. And the codeine still hasn't kicked in. The frustration of being in a restaurant and denied food is a peculiar torment, one might almost say one of the torments of affluence: everything poised for the satisfaction of your appetite, everything glistening and ready –

'Linz?'

Uh-oh. He's wandered again and she's caught him out. He begins to fidget impatiently, flipping his knife. Are they being ignored because they're not regulars?

'I asked you a question.'

Had she? What was it? 'I'm sorry,' he says. 'It's this headache. And probably low blood sugar.' He rubs his temples, for effect. Out of the corner of one eye he can see a waiter, bearing plates and coming in their direction.

'Am I boring you, Lindsay?' Now she's staring at him pointedly, her fine dark eyebrows raised in two devilish arcs.

'It's not that,' he says, pausing while the waiter (at last!) sets two elegant-looking dishes before them and tops up their glasses. Unable to contain his hunger for another second, he lifts his fork eagerly and takes a bite from the black strands of ink pasta.

'It's not what?'

'Hang on, can I get a mouthful of something here?' He knows he sounds petulant but hunger has put him in a desperate ill humour. And not just hunger but the sense of yet another evening collapsing in his face. He chews on the mouthful of pasta – and could almost spit it out. Aaargh! The noodles are undercooked, chewy in fact, and a meagre portion at that. Well, that does it!

'If you must know,' he wipes the fish broth from his lips, 'I get sick of these lurid stories, these ... these case histories! Actually,' warming to his theme now, 'it's the case-history aspect of it I most object to. A whole lot of dismal stories, none of them going anywhere.'

'Really? And where would they go *to*, Lindsay?'

'There's no need to be snaky. It's a question of what you *do* with this information. Frankly, Kirsten, you could do with more detachment, you need to stand back from this.' Ugh, there's sand in the mussels. He pauses to remove a fragment of shell from his tongue. 'If we talked about some general principle it could be interesting, instead of all this harping on the particular.'

'What do you mean, harping on the particular?'

He lays down his fork, abandoning the undercooked pasta, the mussels overloaded with grit. 'I'm interested in cause and effect, not especially in Joel or Jason, or whoever. That's just anecdote. Anecdote is only meaningful to the subjectivity of the persons involved. You'll say that's callous, but your obsessing about the details of individual cases is a cul-de-sac. You'll end up crying into your duck and you won't see the wood for the trees.

Surely, when you studied psychology, they gave you a set of guidelines, of first principles. I'd be interested in a discussion along those lines — models of family dynamics, and so forth. A discussion that would take us somewhere.'

'Like where?'

He shrugs irritably. 'I don't know.'

Kirsten sits for a moment, motionless, her shoulders slumped. Her eyes are lowered, her mouth sags at the corners. She's tired, and he's wounded her. For a little while she stares at her plate. Then she picks up her knife and begins, methodically, to slice at the dark meat of the duck. Slowly. Eating in silence.

Another blasted evening.

What can he do? Grimly he picks at his own food, impaling a pallid mussel on his fork and lifting it out of the broth. A few strands of sticky noodle cling to his tongue in a smudge of glutinous black soup.

'How's the duck?'

'Too salty.'

'Too salty?'

'Yes, too salty!' she snaps.

'Can I try some?'

'Don't you believe me?'

'Of course I believe you. I'm just curious. I've never had it before. What is a *confit* of duck, anyway?'

Listlessly she pushes the plate in his direction and he stares down at the remains of the duck, which look brownish-grey and unappetising. Here it is, then. Another unhappy evening. A pretentious meal that will cost them a small fortune and when they get home he'll need a toasted cheese sandwich to fill up on. They should have stuck to their favourite Thai restaurant. Or Italian. At least with Italian, you know you've eaten.

Kirsten is staring, in silence, at the table. Then she lifts her head and says, 'That's all very well, Lindsay, that's how *you* approach things. Fine. But I'm working with particular boys, not general ones.'

Oh, no, he thinks, she's going to go on with it.

'You don't see them. It's like they've come up out of hell, into the daylight, and the frightening thing is that they think that hell is normal. It's the daylight that's freaky. Rundle House is freaky. I'm freaky.'

Okay, okay, he'll see if he can take this somewhere. 'Do all of them think that?'

She reflects on this. 'No, not all of them. Some of them seem relieved to be there.'

'Well, there you are. The interesting question is, Why do some of them feel relieved to be there and others feel like they're in prison? Isn't anyone doing organised research out there? You ask yourself a series of exploratory questions that enable you to

arrive at a taxonomy, from which basis you can devise differential
therapeutic approaches –'

'A what?'

'A taxonomy. You know, a system of classification.'

She pauses in her eating, her fork in mid-air, a piece of grey
duck meat suspended on the prongs. 'You think I'm not intellectual enough, don't you?'

'Kirsten, not this again.'

'You do. You're always correcting me, always telling me to be
more objective, more detached. Always looking down your nose
at me as if I'm some sort of bull in a china shop.'

'That isn't true.'

'Yes, it is. You make me feel stupid, not worth talking to. Oh,
Kirsten, she just rabbits on! You make fun of Leonie – *Professor
Leonie Marsden* – when she's not around, but at dinner parties,
every time she opens her mouth, you should see the look on
your face. You listen as if Moses were handing down the Ten
Commandments.'

'Come on, Kirsten, most of the time she bores me shitless.
What you see is just politeness, courtesy to a colleague.'

'No, it's not. It's more than that.'

'Are you suggesting that I fancy Leonie? For God's sake, she's
fifteen years older than I am.'

'Not fancy, Lindsay, *respect*.'

Two or three tears are trickling down her cheeks, trickling in that slow, mesmeric way that tears have, creating the limpid look of the victim. Kirsten sniffs, opens her handbag and grapples blindly for a tissue.

Shit. Things are going from bad to worse. In his chest he feels a terrible sinking weight, and at the same time a cold irritability. The evening is dead, a corpse all but in its coffin. When they're home and she's gone off to bed, there will be no remedy other than to walk over to High Street, get himself a couple of videos and drink his way through a cleanskin. Or two.

Look at her. God, how stymied she can make him feel! A half-hour ago just the sight of her cheered him up, and now he feels like a dead duck. Look how she's wiping her cheeks in that pained, womanly way she has, as if they're fragile and will crack open. Dumbly he watches as she blows her nose and returns the crumpled tissue to her bag. And then, as she begins to close the bag, almost as an afterthought she opens it again and takes out her notebook. Tearing off a blank page, she writes a brief message on it, just a few words, slipping the torn fragment of paper under her knife and fork which lie side by side on her plate.

'What's that?'

'What's what?'

He nods at the note on the plate. 'Is that meant for me?'

'No.'

Leaning across, he turns the plate around by its rim so that he can read the note. In her large, rounded hand she has written, 'The duck was too salty.' How like her! They're in the middle of a bitter argument and she can take time out to reprimand the chef! But he'll let that one go through to the keeper. The sooner they're out of here, the better.

Morosely they sit in silence, staring into their abandoned plates. In his large white bowl, tendrils of ink pasta curl like blackened twigs.

The waiter returns. 'Would you like to see the dessert menu?'

Lindsay looks across at her. She shakes her head.

'No, thanks, just coffee.'

Conversation is impossible now, and not once has she asked him about *his* day. He'd been looking forward to telling her about the department meeting, a prolonged bout of bickering that broke out while they were assessing recommendations for a revised first year. The old Introduction to Philosophy would be broken down into three units: Clear Thinking and Argument, Elementary Logic, and a special option on Doubt and Certainty. Klaus, who next year would be taking over Leonie's MA unit on Rationalism, had wanted to change the title to something sexier, like The Struggle for Human Nature.

'For God's sake, Klaus,' the dour Leonie had cried, 'we're teaching critical reasoning here, not mounting a soap opera.'

Lindsay thought it was funny, at the time, funny and irritating both, and he would have liked to tell her about it tonight and make her laugh with him. But they'd got into doom and gloom from the very beginning and there had been no room for his anecdotes, only for Joel and Jason and all the other lost boys, hovering like ghosts around their table.

'Coffee, madam?'

The waiter is standing beside her and Kirsten nods at him wordlessly. She takes a sip, almost absentmindedly, but then appears intent on allowing it to go cold. Normally, at this point in a spat, he'd feel angry, furious even, but maybe the headache – still there – has short-circuited his responses, because all he can think of right now is how sad he feels. Sad. It's a pathetic little word, isn't it? Here he is again, sitting in that big puddle of banality . . .

He looks up, as if coming out of a trance, and is suddenly aware of the waiter, who has returned and is standing there with the bearing of an emissary. Ignoring Lindsay, he turns to Kirsten. 'Excuse me, madam,' he begins, 'but the chef has asked me to explain something to you regarding your note.'

She gives him a weary look in which there is nevertheless a hint of impatience. 'Yes?'

'About the duck.'

'Yes.'

'I don't think you realise what a *confit* of duck is.'

Lindsay stiffens.

'It's actually a French dish cooked in salt and it's meant to be salty. It's not like your normal duck, which is often served with a sweetish sauce, like a cherry sauce . . .'

Lindsay is open-mouthed. The cheek of it! He hears her say, 'Yes, I know that, but even so, this one was a little *too* salty.'

'That's how it's prepared, madam, to have a strong finish on the palate. I think you'll find it's the same everywhere, it's just that some people aren't used to it.'

'Yes, yes.' Her voice is slow, measured, still a little thick from the tears. 'But it's like any other kind of salted meat — you can overdo it.'

'I think you'll find, madam,' he begins, and presses his point in a rambling sentence, the sense of which is lost on Lindsay because he's only half listening. He's looking instead at Kirsten, who is sitting back in her chair with her chin tilted up at a stiff angle, her bottom lip pursed in a way that he knows all too well. There is a pink flush across the ridge of her nose.

Uh-oh. Here's trouble.

Quietly but emphatically she cuts in on him. 'Will you please tell the chef that I know exactly what a *confit* of duck is, and *his* was too salty. Will you do that?'

The waiter hesitates. Then, with arch condescension: 'Very well, madam.'

45

Lindsay looks across at her and raises his eyebrows. Without comment, she passes him the small silver dish of petits fours.

Just as he is on the point of biting into a square of chocolate cake glazed with marzipan, suddenly another man, all in white, including the unmistakable hat, is standing by their table. The waiter hovers nervously behind, indicating Kirsten, and then absents himself in a way that suggests immediately to Lindsay that the chef has not come to offer his respects.

'Madam,' the chef begins, 'I believe you have a complaint about the duck.'

She smiles at him. 'It was too salty.'

'Have you had this dish before?' The baldness of this question, its abrasive presumption of her ignorance, even stupidity, is too much.

'I beg your pardon?'

'I said, Have you —?'

Before he can utter another word she has pushed back her chair and is on her feet, her white napkin fluttering to the dark parquet floor. 'Excuse *me*, but I *know* what a *confit* of duck is,' she hisses, with an apparent effort to keep her voice down, 'and I know that either *you* have rubbed too much salt into the skin or your brine is too strong!'

The chef opens his mouth to riposte but she cuts him off. 'In any decent restaurant in Europe I wouldn't be charged for this meal, never mind being harassed at my table –'

'Madam, no-one is harassing you –'

'So don't fucking come out here and fucking patronise *me!*'

Good God, she's shouting. Her shoulders are heaving, her eyes are black, her pupils dilated. One minute she's sitting there opposite him, whimpering in a pathetically female 'little me' way, the next she's on her feet and ticking off the chef! He becomes aware that the restaurant is hushed. Everyone is staring.

Rallying to her, he rises abruptly from the table, reaching into the breast pocket of his jacket and extracting some notes, which he drops contemptuously onto the cloth. Then he takes the crook of her elbow firmly in his right hand. 'Come on, darling,' he says, 'I think we've had enough bad food for tonight.'

To his relief, she makes no resistance.

Outside it's still raining, but warm, and the warmth and the wet give off a heady smell of fecund growth. For a while they walk in silence to where the car is parked. At last he says, 'I didn't know you knew about *confit* of duck.'

'I don't,' she says, 'I was bluffing.' Under the streetlight he can see that she is grim-faced, unsmiling. 'But I've eaten other kinds of salted meat, and the same principles must apply.'

Ah, so it wasn't special knowledge. Just nerve. He'll give her this, she's consistent. No-one will ever face her down. But because she is a good cook he had relied on her to be right about this, and now he can't be sure that she was. And this bothers him. She could have been making a fool of them both. Still, as they continue down the street he finds he is watching her in secret admiration. It's true that she hasn't a first-rate mind, but there is a kind of animal strength of purpose in her, a wonderful *definiteness*. And it's beginning to make him feel aroused. For all the dismal querulousness of the evening, the bad food, the overpriced wine, the condescending waiter — well, they just might make something of the night yet.

At the end of the street, they turn into a dark lane overhung with creeper and a huge bush of ghostly pink blooms. Against the fence a bespectacled young suit is on his knees, vomiting noisily under an old fig tree, his clotted mess lying in a puddle beside him. As Kirsten steps around him to reach the car door, the sound of retching comes again, a series of racking spasms, hideous and pathetic. She glances over her shoulder at the figure slumped against the fence, then climbs into the passenger seat.

'Must have had the *confit* of duck,' he says, risking a joke.

But she is impassive. In the moonlit stillness of the street he can hear the sharp metallic click of her seatbelt as it slides into its steel mouth.

'Well,' he says, reaching across and squeezing her hand, 'we won't go back there.'

Slowly, as if thinking of something else, she removes her

hand from under his. 'No,' she says, 'we won't go back.'

Though he feels the rebuff in this, the sting of it only heightens his arousal. Suddenly he can't wait to get home. No, the evening is not lost after all. Once there, he'll begin to soothe her. He'll make her a nightcap, her favourite drink of warm brandy and cardamom. Then he'll begin his atonement, will stroke her earlobes and her breasts and whisper teasing words of contrition until they lock together in reconciliation of the usual kind. It never fails. A few tears from her, a few soft words from him. Yes, it will be all right after all; it will be fine, in fact.

He looks at the dark wet road ahead of him and sees, in a momentary flash like an hallucination, the white curve of her buttocks illuminated in the flare of the headlights. And as he accelerates into the rain, he can feel himself diving down into that warm dark tunnel where he knows he will always be safe.

Home. And he has no sooner laid the car keys on top of the fridge than he begins to look along the spines of their cookbooks on a shelf beside the door.

'What are you doing?' she says.

'Have we got a recipe here for *confit* of duck?'

'For God's sake, Lindsay, don't be such a fucking idiot. Leave it alone, it doesn't matter.'

It does matter. It matters to him. The truth always matters to him. These are not mere technical details. Either she was right or . . . or she wasn't.

Kirsten is standing in the doorway and staring at him with that look – that look that says she thinks him a fool. And perhaps he is, crouched over the shelf, still in his coat, sorting through their dog-eared cookbooks with all the beaky focus of someone in a theology library searching for proof of God – only he's looking for a recipe for brine.

'I'm going for a walk,' she says.

'You can't go for a walk around these streets at night.' (Kirsten the fearless!) And it's enough to remind him of what he really wants to do. Putting aside his search – for now – he turns and holds her tenderly by the shoulders. 'I'll make you a nightcap.'

She gives him a long black look, as if she cannot decide, at this moment, what to do. And abandons all resistance. 'Okay,' she sighs. 'Okay.'

Then he can hear her soft footfall on the stairs as he pours the brandy into two tumblers and waits for the spicy milk to warm – something to soothe her, something to calm her down. But the brandy, he tells himself, is a short-term solution: ultimately he will have to think of something else. She simply cannot go on at this pitch. The job is a disaster. The baby thing is coming between them. It's time she had a distraction, some other focus for her nurturing instincts.

It's time he bought her a dog.

2

Twelve-forty a.m. on the luminous dial of her watch-face and Kirsten is peering at the bathroom floor, looking for the jar of face cream she has dislodged from the shelf. She is a little drunk, she knows that, and in the recognition of this is beginning to feel contrite. Is moments away from surrender. Soon she will lie heavily in her bed and await her husband's caress. Although her husband infuriates her – for days at a time – what he cannot negate, what words cannot undo, is the mysterious comfort of his body. If she blanks out the things about him that annoy her (his provoking pedantry), she is still able to turn to him, as one animal to another, and lose herself in the smell of his skin. Undressing, she begins to anticipate with pleasure the sensation of lying beside him.

She is brushing her teeth now, leaning unsteadily into the porcelain basin to spit, and already she can smell the salty male smell of him, is anticipating the muscular curve of his thigh, the warmth of his hip. Cupping her hand to the tap, she rinses her mouth and then, with wet fingers, opens the bathroom cabinet and begins clumsily to rummage among the tubes and jars and aspirin packs.

Where is it?

Why isn't it in its usual place?

Eventually she finds it, and squats on the floor of the bathroom, facing the lavatory bowl. Here it is then, her diaphragm. The magic circle, the white latex superdome. What a strange little blank mandala it is. Look at its white face. Blank, blank, blank. She used to be quite fond of it. She liked the fact that you could handle it and smell it and wash it and powder it; she liked its *thereness*. It wasn't some mysterious little pill that melted invisibly in your bloodstream, having who knows what kind of side effects thirty years on. It was just a dumb, honest little apparatus, a mundane piece of latex engineering. What you saw was what you got. No surprises.

She is gazing down at her diaphragm, which is lying on the floor in front of her in its white plastic case, lid off and to one side. She's beginning to sober up a bit now, and the scene in the bistro is coming back to her in unwelcome flashes. She *had* gone on about the goldfish for too long tonight, in part at least because she was determined not to talk about babies. The whole thing is getting to her, and she has begun to have strange dreams, terrible dreams that she has told to no-one. Just recently she dreamed that she had given birth to a tiny seahorse and was washing it in the kitchen sink, lovingly and with an almost aching tenderness, when with mesmerising slowness it began to disappear down the plughole. Waking at that moment, she started to sob, only it came out as a kind of groan. She saw that already the light was filtering through the blind and heard, as if through water, some gulping animal noise escape from the back of her throat, so that Lindsay woke and turned to her in bleary-eyed alarm. And when he asked what was the matter, she told him she had been dreaming of goldfish. It was the first thing that came into her head.

Why had she lied to him? She never lies to him. Well, hardly ever . . .

She yawns, and gazes at the white orb in her palm that tonight seems luminous and different, the way ordinary objects sometimes can when you stop taking them for granted. There's something about the way the rim is curled over in a perfect roll that conceals the coiled metal spring – it's a perfect cup; a soft, flexible cup. And inside her, all those eggs are waiting in reserve. All those eggs . . .

When she was nine or ten, somewhere around there, she had asked her mother where you got the eggs from for making babies, and – she can still recall the shocking thrill of this – her mother said they were all there inside you. You already had them. A million of them, maybe more. A treasure trove, an Aladdin's cave in wait-ing. Men had to make their sperm, but a woman's eggs were a given, like a dowry she brought into the world, fully formed. Think of it! A *given*. Not something you had in any way to pre-pare for. Nothing you had to save up for, or laboriously earn. No puritan grind necessary. It seemed to go against the grain of everything her mother had taught her, all the strict virtues of caution, thrift and restraint. All that Protestant moral instruc-tion, but in the end there was still this fecund gift. Her body.

Nature's bounty.

But where is the gel? She had the tube here a minute ago, the spermicide. What an ugly word — spermicide. Comically ugly, a word that belongs in a science-fiction film; little robots with antennae and ray guns hunting down sperm. She is a spermicidal maniac, killing them off in their millions . . .

Here it is, minus the cap.

Where's the cap? Woozily she scans the floor. Can't see it. Never mind, bugger the cap. She lifts the diaphragm out of its case, which isn't easy when you've drunk a gin and tonic, four glasses of red and a brandy nightcap. She crooks a fingernail under the rim of the latex cup and flips it up and out of its case. Holding it between the thumb and index finger of her left hand, she squeezes the spermicide gel around the rim — she's done this hundreds of times, she could do it in the dark — and then, transferring the sticky cup to her right hand, she grips it just below the slippery rim and squeezes until the rim on each side bends to meet its opposite in a figure eight. Then she adjusts her feet against the cold ceramic of the tiles so that her thighs are open, her knees pointing at the walls. There's a warm, subtle smell from between her thighs and she likes the rich smell of her own body. Do other women? Well, they rarely admit it, it's not a topic of polite conversation. Damn, she's losing her balance. She topples to one side, holding the gelled rubber disc out at arm's length to keep it from brushing against the wall.

Steady . . .

Taking a deep breath, she adjusts her feet to improve her balance. Then, poised on her haunches, she lowers the diaphragm to between her thighs and brings it to the opening of her vagina. She's done this hundreds of times, she could do it — oops! At the last minute her grasp slips and the rubber disc springs out of her hands and across the floor, coming to rest at the edge of the bath.

Fuck.

Still on her haunches, she waddles across, retrieves it and tries again to insert it — but again she loses her grip and it bounds away from her like a rubber sprite with a will of its own.

Jesus Christ, it's taking an age. Again she yawns, and the yawn is wide and consumes her. She shivers in the white-tiled stillness. She is squatting here naked and she is growing cold. I'll give it one more try, she thinks. But doesn't. Instead she picks the diaphragm up from the floor and wipes the gel from its rim with a tissue. I'm dizzy, I'm just a little dizzy, she tells herself. And standing unsteadily puts the device back in its white plastic container, the one that looks so like a powder compact. Then she slides it behind the king-size codeine packet in the cupboard above the basin.

All those years on the pill, she thinks, I'm probably infertile by now anyway.

And she walks, groggily, back to the bed.

Dog

3

Thursday, and overnight an autumn storm has blown in. The sky is low and grey and a fine rain patters onto the balcony outside the bedroom window. Kirsten wakes to find that she is blooming, like a sick flower, with nausea. Not the delicate kind of queasiness that creeps up on you, but a sudden, violent flooding of something bilious. Almost falling out of bed in a horizontal lurch, she staggers into the bathroom and heaves into the lavatory bowl. Between the gasps of her own retching she can hear the radio downstairs — *The markets panicked this morning after a dramatic fall in the value of the yen* — and suddenly she is fixated on this word yen. She has a yen for something — what is it? Salt. She has a yen for something salty. She wants to plunge her fingers into a big jar of Vegemite and suck off the black paste in sharp, tangy slurps.

Instead the smell of freshly ground coffee is wafting up the stairs. It makes her heave, again.

The next morning is the same, and the morning after that. But on the fourth day the nausea has abated. Maybe it's just tension, she thinks. In the past, when under stress, she has some-times lost her appetite for days and carried a persistent feeling of queasiness, though not as violently as this. In her childhood the family doctor had described her as hyper. In such a case, he pro-nounced, the metabolism is speedy and the body runs out of sugar, with the result that the stomach begins to feed off its own lining. The result: the organism experiences nausea and may even throw up.

Right now she is working alone in her office. It's a rare moment of calm, sunlight filtering through the high casement windows onto her desk where she is drafting a report. But just after ten, without warning, something shifts and surges in her abdomen, and with a soft gasp she drops her pen and leans back into her chair, suffused with a sudden flush of heat.

The second wave is accompanied by a sharp, raking pain low on the right side and she doubles up over the desk, suppressing a groan and bracing her elbows against the wood. Just then the phone rings; it's Mairéad, and the high, reedy voice goes on and on and on until Kirsten is forced to put the receiver down. Lurching to the corner near the window, in a series of quiet retches she throws up on the polished floor. Nothing much, just a little bile and what looks like phlegm, but she is shaken by the violence of it. Lightheaded and dizzy, she reaches across to the box of tissues on her desk and begins to mop up, thinking, This is absurd. I'm never sick, not in this way. A feeling of nausea, yes, but not actually vomiting. I am a woman who hitchhiked around the Javanese archipelago and didn't throw up once.

Then she remembers the phone, grasps the receiver, gasps an apology and hangs up. Squatting, she rolls the tissues into some copy paper and stuffs them in the waste-paper bin where, for the next long moment, she seems to hang over its metal edge, waiting for another tidal wave in the guts to engulf her.

When she looks up at the old cedar wall clock it's almost eleven. The taste in her mouth is foul. Hoisting herself up by the side of the desk, she waits until her breathing is steady. Then she dials Adriana in the office at the other end of the corridor to say that she is unwell. She will be going home for the rest of the day.

Walking to the car park is like stepping on eggshells, waiting for the next spasm to unsteady her. Nothing comes. Instead the air is cool and crisp. Her head is beginning to clear. Driving tentatively down the hill to the access road, she passes a small posse of boys with their tutor, spread-eagled on the grass like seals basking in the sun. She waves. A few of the boys who are looking up wave back.

Once out on the freeway, she begins to feel better. The car is her element, her second skin. She is always at home on the freeway, always in cruise control; her reflexes are excellent, her spatial sense acute. When she was a girl her father was in the army and away often, so that her mother, bored and at a loose end, had taught her to drive when she was not quite fourteen, out on an abandoned air base where only the occasional cyclist got in the way. She can still remember the rush of that first lesson, of settling into the driver's seat with goosebumps of elation, knowing that she was about to cross over some invisible line into a new realm of freedom. Somewhere she had read that driving is bad for the heart because it deceives the body into thinking it's in motion when in fact it is wholly at rest. But the brain reacts to the illusion of speed, to the outer world whizzing by in a blur, and spurs the heart into a deluded rush of adrenalin. Which is why it feels good.

She turns onto the freeway, slips a tape into the deck, and driving, as always, just a little over the limit, leans back into the seat with a sigh of release. For some time the road will simply unwind before her, until at last the city will appear on the horizon, its soft outline floating in a haze of orange smog.

It's not until she has slowed to a crawl in the congested traffic of High Street that the sickness rises in her again, not motion sickness but this other thing, so that her arms want to go limp against the steering wheel and the buildings on either side of the street blur into soft grey waves. The last hundred metres are a bilious fog, until somehow she manages to back the car into a space that is too small for it (she takes pride in her parking skills, even *in extremis*) and comes to a halt outside her own gate. Oh, no, not again — and she must jerk open the car door, shove awkwardly at the iron gate hanging from one crooked post and run up the steps to the front door. There, fumbling for the key to the security grille, suddenly she steps back to the edge of the verandah, turns in slow motion and vomits into a giant monstera bush.

Inside, the house is cool and dark, except for a slanted column of sunlight that falls through an old skylight and onto the kitchen table. Here, in the late morning sun, the poppies in the vase have burst their pale green cusps, dilating into orange and gold discs. Right now they look almost preternaturally alive, as if at any moment they might begin to vibrate.

I must lie down, she thinks, and wait for this to pass.

4

It's just after eleven and Lindsay, who has worked at home in the earlier part of the morning, is on his way now to campus. But first he must stop off at a down-at-heel café at the city end of Lygon Street. Here he has arranged to meet someone, but as it happens he is early. Settling himself at a corner table facing the door, he takes a sheaf of student papers out of his bag and begins to read. '*What can I know for certain?* Descartes asked.' It's a bald opening to an essay, but then they so often are. 'In reply, Descartes decided that he would systematically work through all of his beliefs with the aim of finding one foundational belief that he could base all other beliefs on.'

Lindsay looks up and over to the door. She had better not be late; he has a meeting at twelve.

'Descartes began by questioning his own mental states and this included trying to decipher the difference between dreaming and wakefulness. In the *Meditations* he recalls that he has had dreams that were so vivid they deceived him into believing he was awake. Thus he concluded we can never be sure whether or not we are dreaming, and therefore we can never be sure of what is real and true. This is known as the Dreaming Argument . . .'

He glances down at his watch. Eleven-twenty. She *is* late.

At that moment a woman enters. She is tall and thin and looks somehow rustic and out of place in faded jodhpurs, tan riding boots, and a white cotton shirt that hangs loosely over her bony hips. Brushing a strand of fine hair back from her forehead, she looks around as if to identify someone she has not actually met.

Lindsay waits for her to catch his eye. 'Sandra Schokmann?'

'Yes.'

She stares at him appraisingly before coming over to the table. He rises with the intention of shaking her hand but she doesn't offer it. Instead she pulls out a chair and sits opposite him with her legs sprawled wide apart.

'Lindsay Eynon,' he says, thinking all the while that she has the aura of a lion-tamer (and except for the whip she has the costume). 'Will you have a drink?'

'I suppose it would be impossible in a place like this to get a decent cup of tea.'

Her face is long and narrow with high cheek bones that give her an aloof look, but it's the way she says 'place like this' that puts him on his mettle. Up close there is something cold and unsettling about her, an outlook at once dismissive and wary.

Reaching into the top pocket of her shirt, she takes out some photos which she proceeds, without preamble, to arrange on the faux marble table. Then, leaning back in her chair, her hands resting against her thighs, she says, 'You might like to have a look at these.'

Of course, the Polaroid definition is poor. The focus seems slightly blurred and the shiny, blue-green surface has a muddy tinge. But he can see three dogs, photographed separately, each taken in full profile and then again in a frontal close-up of the head. Because of the dourness of the cheap Polaroid image, they all look serially alike: the same fluffy gold manes, the same huge pug noses, the same striking black eyes.

'This is Yellow Emperor,' she begins, pointing with a long,

slim finger stained from nicotine, 'this is his sister, Yellow Moon, and this is their brother, Golden Dragon. Their father was Victorian all-breed champion.' Her monotone delivery betrays no hint of pride.

Lindsay stares at the photos, trying in vain to find some basis for discrimination, to discern some special charm in any one of the pups. Maybe to an expert eye the signs are there, though all he can see are three balls of golden fluff with three sets of black eyes. At last he looks up and says, 'What are their, er, personalities like?'

'They're all good dogs. I breed for temperament.'

'What does that mean, exactly?'

She looks at him. 'You worried about a rogue dog?'

'Oh –' he begins, but she cuts in on him.

'It means good handling. Reliable disposition. They're not going to bite the judge.'

'I see.'

All he can do is give a tight little smile of bemusement. Was this, in the dog-breeder's universe, all there was to personality? Biting or not biting the judge? When he had looked up *The Official Guide to Registered Breeds* he was surprised to find that mostly it had attended to measurements: width at the shoulder, length of neck, size and tilt of the ears, even the preferred colour of gums (black). It was like a very specific job description in the Positions Vacant. Wanted: clerk, multiskilled, no imagination.

'I don't intend to show. This is a present for my wife.'

Sandra gives him her half-distracted stare, as if one eye is focusing on him and the other on some far point on the horizon. 'Does she know she's getting a chow chow?'

' Er, no. It's a surprise.'

'Chows aren't for everyone, you know. They're not doggy dogs.' She says this reprovingly, as if he is a small boy. Or an idiot.

'So I gather. I *have* done my homework.' He inflects this with some slight resentment, and is prepared to embark on a discussion of the breed. He wants her to know that he is both a serious buyer and a serious man; that he has done his research and is deserving of such a superior dog.

But again she pre-empts him. 'Good,' she says bluntly, as if that's all there is to it. Her tone is off-putting, to say the least.

For an awkward moment he sits gazing at the Polaroids, and then: 'I'm afraid,' shaking his head, 'I don't think I can choose from a photograph. Is there some other way?'

'You can keep the photos for a while, they may help you to make up your mind. If they don't, give me a ring in a couple of days.' She glances around the still almost empty café. 'Best be off,' she says and rises, as if nothing he might say could be of further interest.

For a moment he is stunned by her withdrawal. What an intriguing woman. Someone so individual that her rudeness seems almost impersonal. And who is she, anyway? He knows she has a small property down the coast where she breeds horses as well as chows, and that according to her assistant (to whom he has spoken on the phone) she rarely comes to town. In the brief time she was in his company (fifteen minutes?) he noticed how the skin on her hands and cheeks was dry and chafed, as if she spent all day out in the wind and sun. There was something raw and exposed about her, but at the same time lithe and queenly. Even the dirt in her fingernails looked as if it belonged there: she wore it as other women wear nailpolish. Indeed, she looked like the kind of woman who, in a past life, might have cut off her right breast. And yet she carried with her an aura of faint anxiety. Clearly she is a woman who prefers dogs to men.

Waiting at the counter to pay, he broods on the abruptness of their meeting, her cool charmlessness. He is quite attractive to women (he knows this not from vanity, but experience), but she spoke to him as if he were a minion, a lesser species. Less than dog. He thought she might at least ask why he had decided on a chow chow – such a rare breed – and given him a chance to air his research. In his experience most dog people were only too eager to discuss their preferred mutt; to gloat, even, over the finer points of the breed, as if somehow their own virtues were on display at one remove. But she had failed to evince the slightest interest.

Not that he, anyway, had intended to give all that much away. He had not planned to tell her that he had once had an affair with a woman who owned a chow, and had been impressed, above all, by how aloof the dog was – more like a cat, really. Certainly it disdained anything so vulgar as to jump up and slobber on your cuffs. Better still, it rarely barked. When Lindsay dropped in on his amour (usually late at night when her husband was away) the dog, Chun, would take one or maybe two steps forward, give a mildly congenial look of acknowledgement, wait a polite half-minute and then retreat with some dignity to his position on the verandah.

They understood one another perfectly.

And in the *Dog Encyclopaedia* he has found confirmation of that reserve: *Though intelligent, the chow is a resolute individual that seems almost to regard itself as human. It refuses to be taught tricks. On the other hand it comports itself with dignity and doesn't chew shoes and furniture.* This is just what he has had in mind. No chaos, no mess. And furthermore, he likes the historical-cultural pedigree. Bred in China, the dog dates back to the Han Dynasty when it was used to guard Buddhist monasteries in the mountains. There it was valued for its resemblance to the mythological lion-dog, so often used in Chinese decorative art as a symbol of happiness. Indeed, it could almost be said to *be* a Buddhist dog, in that its composure transcends its survival instinct, so much so that of all dogs it is the most difficult to get to breed. Perfect. For one thing, it will not be a nuisance in season. He can see it now, sitting on the verandah of their house in Northcote: majestic, equable and, above all, quiet.

On the walk to campus Lindsay thinks of his own dog, the one he had been given as a boy, a soppy mongrel that was mostly cocker spaniel with large floppy ears and patchy, black-and-white markings. No-one in the family could agree on what to call this dog. His mother had given him the ludicrously sentimental name of Pal, while his father, in an arbitrary gesture that was characteristic of him, always referred to it as Sprocket. He, Lindsay, had a secret name for the pup: when they were alone he called him Stripe. Why he called him that, he didn't know. The pup didn't have any stripe in its markings, but the name just came to him. Every afternoon after school he and Stripe would explore the low hills behind the Sydney suburb where they lived, rambling through the scrub in long, aimless walks that were a kind of reverie, some heightened state of being in which a magical bush-stillness beguiled them both. All sense of separation was dissolved, until it seemed that boy and dog were but two facets of the one mind, while light filtered through the trees with intimations of endless, dreamlike possibility. It was a feeling of communion he had not experienced since, except fleetingly in rare moments of complete sexual abandon; a feeling of living in an eternal present where there could be no consequences. He felt light-headed, disoriented almost, lighter than light. Put simply, he felt blessed. Sometimes he felt so overwhelmed by euphoria, by the feeling of an inner sap rising, that he would stop and masturbate in the bush.

Stripe was the one pet he had as a boy, and the one thing, animate or inanimate, that he had loved unconditionally. And then one night, after just eighteen months, the dog disappeared. Simply vanished. His father remarked that perhaps he had run away to escape the confusion of having three names, which, even at Lindsay's age, struck him as an unfeeling thing to say. His mother, too, was upset. Together, for days afterwards, they scoured the streets of neighbouring suburbs, knocking on doors, peering over fences into backyards, and wandering around the vacant land by the municipal rubbish tip. It was summer, the heat was stifling, and with each step he felt an invisible blanket of resistance. Some afternoons they had to struggle in the face of a hot, gusting northerly, and he recalls now his mother's dour perseverance – the way she strode ahead of him, her hair fastened with a wooden clip, her shirt flapping in the wind; recalls, too, glimpses of white skin on her lower back, the dust swirling in little eddies around her feet when she paused, winded, by the kerbside, and rubbed the grit from her eyes. It was there, in a windswept lane, that he had suddenly apprehended the paradox of the empty within the full: the streets had been full of many things but empty of the one object he hoped to find. Each night he would dream of Stripe, would see him bolt out from behind some strange iron gate, or some loose fence paling covered in creeper. Would see the dog run to him, pink tongue lolling or licking at his wrists, and with overwhelming relief he would rush to embrace the mutt. Over and over in his small-boy's mind he saw the dog clearly, but in a kind of speeded-up motion, rollicking down the slope of a cracked bitumen path, suddenly there. Only he wasn't. Everything else was there except the one thing he desired.

It was a dogless universe.

When his parents offered him a replacement pup he shocked both himself and them by shaking his head. He had made his first discovery of the heart and it was this: to love something, something alive that you were responsible for, something that might one day leave you, was too emotionally exhausting. Though only nine years old, he had had then an intimation that some things in life could never be replaced; that one moment of mind-lessness – leaving the back gate open, for example – might never be undone.

But enough of that. He detests nostalgia, preferring to savour the idea of the new dog, the present he is about to make his wife: the unexpected bounty of it, his own thoughtfulness and generosity (this is one very expensive canine). He will prepare a little citation for her: 'The Chow Chow in History'. It will amuse her, as someone with a training in psychology, to know that Freud himself kept pet chows (Yofi, Wulf and Lun) and that he regarded the chow as the dog most like humans – a kind of intermediate being, somewhere between run-of-the-mill canine and that peak of evolution, one's own self. Perhaps the attraction was a perverse one, in an intellectual sense: Freud, a disciplined thinker, might have relished the paradox of a supposedly intelligent dog like the chow being the breed least receptive to training in repetitive or 'doggy' tasks. It was more than aloof and independent, it was downright intractable. And yet, like most dogs, uncannily knowing. If Freud was midwife to the soul (secular, modern version, that is), then little golden Yofi was the guardian of the psychoanalytic inner sanctum (the modernist equivalent of the Buddhist temple?), and there was an amusing symmetry in this. In the chapter of his thesis that dealt with animal soul he, Lindsay, had incorporated a footnote citing Freud's surprise when Yofi had come into the bedroom on the morning of his eightieth birthday 'to show me her affection in her fashion, something she has never done before or after'. How, asked Professor Freud, does a little animal know when a milestone comes around?

How, indeed?

And so Lindsay is in a good mood — until he turns the corner of the corridor that leads to his office. Then he sees that the girl is there, Sonia, hovering at his door.

In an instant his mood has soured and he can hardly wait to get past her. Something about her physical presence disturbs him. It's as if the boundaries of her body are fluid, as if she is bleeding out into the corridor, exuding a kind of neediness that seeps into the surrounding ether. With irritation he recalls her letters, sitting in his desk drawer like small explosive devices, and he knows that he must deal with this now. But he sees that she is nervous — tremulous and pale. Through the thick lenses of her rimless glasses the pupils of her eyes appear monstrously enlarged and fixed, like the eyes of a doll. She opens her mouth to say something and nothing comes out, but behind the glasses her green eyes have a kind of abject, molten sensuality that is shocking in its suggestion of self-abasement. The hairs on the back of his neck prickle. My God, he thinks, I can hardly bear to look at her.

'Lindsay, I . . . I wondered if you were free for a minute.' She blushes, and that sudden tide of blood is a beacon of her shame.

Just the way she says his name makes him wince inwardly. 'Aren't I seeing you in a fortnight?'

74

'It wouldn't take long.'

What wouldn't take long? If he lets her into his room he will have to bring up the letters. Well, then, so be it. Now is the time to have it out.

'Come in, Sonia.' He's brusque, and turns away from her to open the door. Once inside he moves across to his desk to remove a fax from the machine, and studiedly takes a minute to scan it. When at last he looks up she has seated herself in a chair, with her legs crossed almost demurely, looking as if butter wouldn't melt in her mouth. He notes, with distaste, how weirdly she is dressed: a silver lurex top that bares one shoulder, a brown mini-skirt and striped bumblebee stockings.

'Well,' he says, 'how is your research going?' I *have* to mention the letters, he thinks. I will get them out of the drawer, return them to her and say that no more need be said, but that it would be best if she requested another supervisor.

At that moment there is a light knock on the open door and Leonie Marsden is peering around its edge. 'So sorry to inter-rupt,' she says, 'but could I have a word when you've finished?'

As if the presence of the older woman has precipitated a sudden loss of nerve, Sonia stands abruptly, clumsily adjusting her cloth bag against one bare shoulder. 'I must go,' she says, then falters for a moment and trips against her chair before brushing awkwardly past Leonie in the doorway.

Leonie casts a sly, amused glance down the corridor before turning to him with raised eyebrows. 'Well!' she exclaims softly. 'I think I might have frightened the horses.'

He hates the way she says this – breathlessly, and with a kind of arch familiarity. She is inviting his confidence, and for that reason alone he won't give it. 'What did you want to see me about?' he asks, pondering for a moment whether he'll tell her about the letters. He ought. He would be a fool not to. But not now, not in the present circumstances. It would be too gratifying to her prurient instincts.

Meanwhile she is giving him one of her shrewd, appraising looks. 'I haven't got your response to the new timetable,' she says.

'I haven't seen it.'

'I sent you an email.'

'So you did. I'm sorry.'

'You seem distracted lately,' she says. 'Is everything all right?'

'Everything's fine.'

At five o'clock he shuts down the computer and checks his voice-mail. His friend and colleague George Markides has rung to suggest a drink after work, and there is a message from Kirsten to say she is feeling unwell and could he do some shopping for dinner on the way home.

Unwell? Again?

Just lately she has been feeling off-colour almost every day and it's unlike her. In the eight years they have been married he can scarcely remember her having even a dose of the flu — well, there's been the odd occasion, but these were rare, in contrast to his own propensity to come down with every virus on the radar. As he contemplates their relative resistances to stress, he begins to pack his papers into his briefcase and then moves across to the open window. He will close it, since it looks like rain, but for a moment he just stands there, the better to breathe in the earthy smell of leaves decaying in the courtyard. Glancing across to the sandstone wall opposite, he sees that the faded graffiti is still there — DO ANIMALS HAVE SOULS? — but in recent days someone has spraypainted a riposte: ONLY IN THEIR DREAMS. He smiles, and would linger there, but is distracted by a slight, rasping sound behind him. He looks around.

There it is, a small pink envelope resting on the silver-grey of the carpet.

I don't believe this, he thinks. *I don't believe this.* What a nerve! He strides across to the door and jerks it open, looking along the corridor.

No-one is there.

He turns back into the room and shuts the door behind him. Lifting the envelope from the carpet, he tosses it onto a side table stacked with unmarked papers: he will not read it. Then again, perhaps he ought? It might be an apology. He retrieves the envelope and tears at the pink fold which, absurdly, is scented with a sickly musk smell. Within seconds the words on the page have brought a hot, prickling sensation to the surface of his skin, as once again he absorbs the same gush as before, the same mash of overheated sentiment and stilted pornography. How dare she do this? How dare she construct him as a manic puppet in her own fantasies? To fantasise was one thing, but to commit those fantasies to paper, to inflict them on him — the brazen presumption of it! Of course his students flirted with him, female and male, they did it all the time, and in an acceptably contained and low-key way this flirtation was the emollient of working life. But this girl was in another category altogether, a shameless emotional squatter. These fraught messages of hers were nothing less than a clumsy invasion of his being.

And there was something else, something he had failed to detect in the earlier letters: a sinister suggestion of mockery and some slight undertow of resentment. As if he, at any time, has led her on! The stupid little mouse. She wasn't even pretty. One letter he could forgive, a rash impulse, a dare even. But to persist was outrageous. If he did nothing now he'd be a fool. From this moment on he'd be threatened with complicity. He must take the letters and go to Leonie at once. He goes over to the desk, opens the top drawer, takes the two pink envelopes lying there and folds them into his pocket. Then he walks the length of the corridor to Leonie's room and knocks on the door.

The department secretary calls to him from her glass cubicle. 'Leonie just left.'

'Damn,' he mutters under his breath. And turns and heads back down the hallway.

When he enters the bar on Brunswick Street he is still agitated. George is perched on a stool, glass in hand – a short, thickset figure, dark and with a heavy beard. Seeing Lindsay, he raises his glass in a mock toast.

For a while the two men debrief, as is their habit, on departmental matters, but for once Lindsay is in no mood to talk shop: it reminds him of the girl, Sonia. To restore his equilibrium, he confides in George his plan to buy Kirsten a dog.

'Any particular breed?'

'A chow chow. It's a Chinese breed. Ever seen one?' He has forgotten the Polaroids which are still in his pocket.

'No, or if I have I didn't recognise it. No doubt this beast comes at great expense?'

'I believe so.'

'Ballpark figure?'

'Let's just say that if it serves its purpose it will be worth every cent.'

'Why don't you just go to the city pound? You'd be surprised what you can find there.'

'Speaking from experience?'

'Not recent. Ours is a cat household, as you know. The cat is a more rational emotional investment in the inner city. Needing, as it does, a minimum of space.'

'It won't deter thieves.'

'Ah, so we're after a guard dog. Family silver and all that. I suppose it makes sense, especially if you live around here. That being the case, you might as well get yourself a monster. Go for some major security. If you're going to live in an area with a high crime rate, get a real brute that'll frighten shit out of the rest of us.'

Lindsay gestures to the barman for another round. 'That could be a bonus as well,' he says.

'More than you think.' George shifts on his stool and lowers his voice, as if to offer a confidence. 'In the days when I took a philosophy class at Pentridge, I was advised by professionals. A dog is the best deterrent.'

'I didn't know you went in for good works.'

'A past life, my friend, when I was young and idealistic. I used to drive over every Wednesday evening.'

'Many takers?'

'Usually about eight, maybe ten. And in keeping with the philosophical temperament, most of my students were in for major misdemeanours. The warders used to walk me to the end of the main corridor, unlock the last set of wire gates and say, You're on your own, mate. Then they'd go off for a smoke a block away.'

'Nice.'

'The funny thing is that the one time I get mugged – this is two o'clock in the morning in Flinders Lane – these three guys jump me and king-hit me from behind. I'm lying there in the gutter, face down, with someone's foot on my head while one of them empties out my wallet. He gets to all the cards and sees my old prison-visitor's card. Sorry, mate, he says, and tosses the wallet onto the ground beside me. Then they shoot through.'

'They took the money, of course.'

'Naturally.'

'Were you injured?'

'I was concussed for two days, but there you go. Amidst the brutality of life, one small moment of civility.'

Lindsay remains sceptical. 'I thought all this stuff about dogs and thieves was urban myth.' To his mind, the whole idea of a dog as security is wishful thinking. All that an organised, professional thief needs in order to deal with a dog is a small can of capsicum spray. Then again, maybe the organic — any mutt with a set of fangs — can inspire a visceral terror that has no man-made equivalent, short of a domestic landmine. 'In any case,' he adds, 'it will be good for Kirsten to have to walk a dog. She takes the car two blocks to get a carton of milk.'

'Oh, so she's walking it, not you?'

'It will be *her* dog,' he says emphatically. 'It's a gift.'

George raises two bushy dark eyebrows above the rim of his glass. 'There's only one problem with this plan for a canine *coup d'état*,' he offers, wiping the froth from his lip after a long draught of beer. 'What if she doesn't take to the beast? What if they fail to bond?'

'Have you ever seen a chow?' Lindsay asks. 'They're irresistible.'

After the third beer, he leaves George in the dim red light of the bar and takes a tram to the supermarket on St Georges Road. It's a Thursday evening, and he and Kirsten would normally be eating out, but not tonight, and not last Thursday either. For the second week in a row, Kirsten is lying at home 'feeling liverish' and 'not in the mood'. Since the episode with the duck, he reflects, she seems to have lost her appetite — in more ways than one.

On his voicemail she had given him a list of items to buy, and that's okay because right now he is grateful for the distraction of small things, for the slight but meditative exercise of shopping alone. It's better when he's alone because then he can take his time, and in taking his time drift, perhaps, into one of those zones of mindlessness, of mundane contentment that mellows out the day. Whereas Kirsten is impatient in supermarkets, in and out like a guided missile, Lindsay likes to stroll at a leisurely pace. He likes the orderliness of these fluorescent emporia, the long aisles, the bright lights, the ambience of manufactured cheerfulness. But more than this he likes the feeling of super-abundance, of brashly cheerful plenitude. An old girlfriend of his had once claimed to feel dizzy in Woolworths. 'There's just *too* much,' she'd opined, 'too much choice.' But there wasn't, because most of it you didn't want anyway, and the underlying function of this massed variety of goods was not to feed you, but to create the satisfying illusion of surplus. Who would want to shop in a store that had only what you wanted? That would pre-empt any possibility of creating a new appetite.

Here, as in so many other spheres, he and Kirsten were at odds. He liked to choose and to plan. She liked to improvise. For a whole year she had committed to an organics scheme whereby a box of seasonal fruit and vegetables was delivered to their door once a week, sight unseen and with no input (no choice or quantity control) from them. The scheme was chaotic: one week a superfluity of apples and no green vegetables, the next week enough salad greens for an orphanage and a small cluster of green bananas that seemed never to ripen in their brown paper bag. While he had bemoaned the absence – or, at times, the predictable presence – of his favourite foods, Kirsten revelled in the anarchy of it.

'I like not knowing what to expect,' she said. 'I love it that I don't have to make decisions. I make enough decisions at work. When I come home I like to look in the box and have to make do with what's there.' And it was true she had improvised some of her better meals out of this sometimes bizarre melange.

But when it was his turn to cook he simply called in at the supermarket on his way home, consulted his list and bought exactly what the recipe specified. In good moods he would joke about how this very simple divergence of response in what was fundamentally a trivial concern was nevertheless symptomatic of their instinctive responses to life in general. His wife liked to live off her nerves, to bend the rules, as the episode with the goldfish demonstrated. The whole palaver with the goldfish was quintessential Kirsten, and this reminds him of the time he broke the news to his mother that he and Kirsten were going to marry. Looking up at him from her ledgers – she kept the books of the family business at home – she had, for a moment, frozen, and then shrugged in her characteristically grudging way. 'Oh, well,' she said tartly, 'I suppose opposites *will* attract.'

And so by the time he has peered at the eggplant and white radish and felt each for firmness, examined a new line of pasta and complained about the sell-out of his preferred blend of coffee beans, he is in good humour, has put the egregious Sonia and her letters out of his mind and drifted into his favourite mood, a relaxed state of anticipation.

Outside again, in the darkening glow of St Georges Road, he is immersed in a sensuous feeling of transition, that easy moment of passing unhurriedly between one secure destination and the next, and he turns and threads his way through the banked up vehicles on the road and across the tram tracks to the little park beside the creek. Strolling towards High Street, he passes along an avenue of leafy plane trees, where the pavement is littered with black spiky balls of seed, crushed underfoot or clustered in little piles in the gutter. This, he thinks, is the best time of the day, striding home in the dusky streetscape: neat Edwardian terraces, gardens in shadowy stillness, the cries of children calling to one another in the street.

The front door is open and as he crosses the threshold of the house the scent of jasmine wafts in from the front garden, so that he carries it with him down the hallway like an aromatic mantle. His sense of smell, always acute, is heightened now by this fragrance, a pungent sweetness that never fails to infuse him with a pagan rush of wellbeing.

Kirsten is at the back of the house, in the dim kitchen, lying on the couch with her feet up and her eyes closed. She is pale.

'Are you all right?' he says, bending to kiss her on the lips. She nods, and begins languidly to get up from the couch, so languidly he has a fleeting impulse to push her back onto it for one of those swift and slightly grubby grapplings that are, in their way, more satisfying than any elaborately choreographed seduction (certainly more interesting than the marital bed). But in his moment of hesitation she rises, with effort, and walks across to the kitchen bench where she begins, pre-emptively and with a kind of weary, mundane focus, to assemble the blender.

Dinner, then, in their cramped little kitchen.

Tonight he observes that, once again, she eats little, merely picking at her food, and also that she is unusually vague, although he finds he quite likes her in this mood. When she is vague she is less insistent, less likely to harangue him. At one point she absentmindedly picks up his wineglass and drinks from it as if it were her own, her pink tongue lingering on the rim, an almost fey gesture that affects him with a tremor of erotic impatience.

When at last, in the dark front parlour smelling of jasmine and mould, he straddles her on the couch, he is vehement in his caresses, twisting her hair around his blunt fingers, biting into her shoulder – but he cannot fail to notice that she is listless, and is startled when penetration makes her gasp, then groan as if in pain.

He stops, and says, 'What is it? What is it?' concern mingling with natural annoyance at this *interruptus*.

She just lies there, sallow and clammy in a cold sweat, waves her hand at him and says, 'Go on.' And he does, though when he comes it's a bit of a fizzer.

'What happened?' he asks, kneeling astride her on the couch and wiping between her legs with a clutch of tissues.

'I'm just a bit under the weather. I think I've got some kind of bug.'

'Still?'

'You know how these things hang around.'

Especially when you're in the wrong job, he thinks. 'Better have an early night. You go up now, and I'll clean up the kitchen.'

Before coming upstairs for the night, he takes the Polaroids from his pocket and spreads them out on the kitchen table. Perhaps the younger male of the three pups, the one called Yellow Emperor? Despite the poor quality of the images – that muddy, blue-green patina dulls the golden colouring of the dogs – he can see that there is something about the eyes of this particular pup. A gentle yearning, a soft, melancholy intelligence. Two black almonds within an aureole of reddish-gold fur.

Of course, they would have to change the name to something more interesting. He might call it Chuang-tzu, after the lesser known sage of Taoism. Chuang for short.

In the morning Kirsten is gone before he wakes, an early departure, even for her. He on the other hand is mildly lethargic and lingers over breakfast for an unusual length of time, reading *The Age* from cover to cover.

At last he stirs himself and climbs the steep staircase to the attic, where his research awaits him, spread out over three trestle tables. All morning he will work in this musty space where, despite his best efforts to maintain a clean working surface, everything seems coated with a persistent film of dust.

But before long, all this will change. Already, in his mind's eye, he can see the outcome of their soon-to-be-embarked-on renovations: an enlarged studio with twin skylights that will transform this cave of an attic into a sunny retreat, a haven of sun and light, a fitting eyrie for this philosophy bird. He likes working at home. At home he is better able to concentrate, to turn down the volume on the answering machine, put on his music and enter another world — at least on most mornings. But not, unhappily, this morning. This morning he is still distracted by the dog thing. Gazing out over the red-tiled rooftops sloping

in tiers beneath his attic window, he decides he will ring Sandra
Schokmann.

The phone has scarcely rung before she has picked up and
spoken into the other end. 'Yes?'

He decides to ignore her brusqueness. The Polaroids are not
enough, he explains. The surface is fuzzy, the definition poor;
there's no sense of animation, of personality. He would like to
see the pups in the flesh. Would it be possible to visit her and
have a look at them?

'When did you want to come?'

'Sooner rather than later. If that suits you.'

'I'm going away for a while.' She sounds guarded. 'But there's
a dog show at Kyneton in a few weeks. My assistant Melissa will
be going and she could bring the pups with her. You could have
a look at them there.'

She gives him a date and, as it happens, Kirsten will be at a
training seminar that weekend. She will need the car and he
would have to hire one. The extra expense of this nags at him for
a moment. For the first time it occurs to him that this is a project
that might easily get out of hand.

'What time should I get there?'

'Come in the afternoon. Around three.'

'How will I know Melissa?'

'Just look for the chows and there'll be a white van with

Schokmann Kennels written on the side. You realise,' she adds, 'that they're too young as yet to take home.'

'Sure. It's just that it would help to see them in the flesh.'

'Up to you,' she says.

So that's that, then.

Now he can settle to his work on Edward Craigie. Dust or no dust. In six months they will be able to afford to start the renovations and he will be dust-free, even if the mortgage is going to stretch them to the limit. Still, this year he will put in for promotion (he must get on and complete that monograph) and their combined income will just cover the new and inflated debt.

How elated they had been on that wet winter's day when they signed the contract, and even more excited on that first night in the empty house. He recalls now the giddy sensation of ownership as they gazed around the bare rooms. Without furniture those rooms looked unexpectedly small, so that he'd felt for a moment as if he were in an enlarged doll's house. The removalists were to come early the following morning, so he and Kirsten arrived around eight in the evening with a blow-up mattress, sleeping-bags, two glasses and a bottle of champagne. For a while they had wandered through the house, exuberant and silly, carrying the bottle from room to room and drinking a series of mock toasts ('To the kitchen!'), finally collapsing onto the living-room floor and making love so vigorously that Kirsten had sustained a painful carpet burn on her spine.

All that excitement for a dilapidated pile!

And now they are mortgaged to within life's breath, or will be when the loan for the renovations is approved. But at least then they can remodel the vertiginous staircase, put in a deck, transform the dark little kitchen (where the roof leaks when it rains), and, not least, renovate his attic study, which will be enclosed with its own back balcony of opaque glass so as not to alter the heritage streetscape. Then he can work at home, in peace, and without the onset of terminal claustrophobia.

Can it be only a few months since their architect had come around one early evening to look at the house? Gary Grieve had been recommended to them by a friend, and he and Lindsay had hit it off at once. Gary was a tall, loping man with a long face and long, lank hair that swung around the curve of his lantern jaw. What boyish enthusiasm he had displayed for even the simplest features, inspecting every decrepit period fitting, every sill and architrave, as if the house were a miniature gem, a domestic Taj Mahal worthy of infinite thought and attention. At one point Lindsay glanced across at Kirsten, who rolled her eyes in response, but Lindsay had warmed to the charm of the man's affectations, which, he perceived, were merely a linguistic shorthand for his absolute faith in the possibility of metamorphosis.

But inevitably some of Gary's ideas were outside the frame – the suggestion, for example, of an austere, black-marbled bathroom like a cell, with only a shower head and no other detail to mar the purity of the space.

'Where would we clean our teeth?' asked Kirsten.

'You'd have a stainless-steel cusp basin here, in a small open space outside the kitchen. To all intents and purposes it would look like a sidewall water fountain, but would in fact be multi-purpose.'

And Kirsten had rolled her eyes again.

After that they'd talked insulation (safer ground) and reverse-cycle airconditioning, and he'd left around nine, promising to bring colour charts on the next visit. Later, in bed, the two of them giggled like children at the idea that they had just been visited by the Design Police, though Lindsay confessed that he was looking forward to the next of Gary's raves. He liked the way Gary brought a utopian exuberance of focus to every small detail, as if there were no domestic limitation, however mundane, that could not be transcended, and this seemed to be most potently dramatised in the idea of the skylight. Room too dark? Simple: cut a hole in the roof. And, wittingly or unwittingly, the way architects spoke was rich in metaphor. 'The people who built these dark Edwardian houses were trying to protect themselves in all the wrong ways,' said Gary. And this – the idea of protecting yourself in all the wrong ways – was enough to set Lindsay off on a train of thought that could keep him awake half the night.

And she would jettison all this for a baby, though *she* would be the one to suffer. *She* would be the one at home in the dark, dank house with the infant, and all because she is impatient, is suffering some kind of mid-thirties panic. And as he is now tired of saying, it isn't that he is opposed to children, more that it's a question of timing. Look at his sister. She had two abortions until she could time the delivery of her son (elective Caesarean) to fit in with the reduction of her mortgage and her long service leave. Surely the whole point of modern contraception was that it allowed for rational planning? It wasn't that some things should never be left to chance, more that some things need not be left to chance. Why invite the random unnecessarily?

Of course, hearing himself say this, he knows that he sounds like a caricature of the selfish male, and he resents the fact that her panic puts him in this position – a position of unreasonableness – when it could equally be argued that the opposite was the case. There was a time when they had all but abandoned hope of a house in the inner city, close to everything they enjoy. But there is no way that the house is going to be bearable for long unless they carry out what will, in the end, amount only to modest change. It's not as if they have pretensions and are trying to reach beyond themselves.

5

Every morning now the nausea is there. Sometimes she can get to work without heaving into the plastic ice-cream container she keeps on the passenger seat beside the handbrake, but not often. Nothing ever comes up, just a desperate, stomach-rolling, chest-choking gush of saliva and phlegm, and with it a startling sensation of being about to veer over the white line. Since she has never in her adult life eaten breakfast, and leaves home early, it's not all that difficult to disguise her discomfort around Lindsay in the mornings. She talks vaguely of still feeling off-colour, of having caught some kind of bug from one of the kids. Some days she is lucky, and around ten in the morning the nausea begins to recede, like a slow outgoing tide. On other days it will drag on until early afternoon.

And she knows now why it is there.

On this particular morning she has not been at work long when there is a knock at the door. Out in the corridor is a small boy, furtive and watchful.

'Marek,' she says.

He looks at the floor, studiedly.

'Come in, Marek, how have you been?' Marek says nothing, is rooted to the spot. Kirsten gestures in the direction of the window. 'I've got a call to make. You set up.'

The boy walks over to where the chess set has been put to one side from last time. With almost comically exaggerated care he lifts it off the wide sill and carries it across the room. Just near the edge of her desk he stumbles and the board angles sharply, the heavy wooden pieces spilling noiselessly onto the carpet.

'Never mind, we'll start again.' Kirsten kneels on the floor beside him and together they gather up the crude wooden pawns – not so much carved as hacked into a likeness – and set them upright on the flimsy board. Marek has a sour, acrid smell that normally wouldn't bother her, but now that her sense of smell is heightened it makes her catch her breath. His skin is covered in dry scales from scalp to toes, and little flakes sit on the shoulders and sleeves of his navy sweatshirt. All day the prickling itch of Marek's condition makes him squirm and twitch, so that while in spirit he is silent and withdrawn, his body betrays him with its own manic life. There was a time when, nightly, his father would lace his hands into a pair of boxing gloves to prevent Marek's sleeping self from clawing his skin into bloody welts. Kirsten knows this from the file. She also knows that the gloves were a present from his father, a former industrial chemist from Bosnia who drove taxis around Melbourne for eight months, until early one Sunday morning he was murdered in his cab on the esplanade at Altona.

At that point Marek began to light fires. The last one almost burnt out the stadium at a suburban football ground and made the front page of the tabloids. She has never spoken to him of this but has read the psychiatrist's report. Meanwhile in the classroom he is withdrawn. Sent to Kirsten as his caseworker, he complained that he was bored. Everything was boring. Everything. One morning she thought to ask him this: What had he ever done that *wasn't* boring? He was silent for a time, and then he murmured, 'Chess.'

Chess? It was unusual for boys who came to Rundle House to play chess. Nintendo, yes.

'Where did you learn to play chess?'

'My father taught me.'

At which point Kirsten had sent him to the games room where there was a chess set, rarely used. When he returned she asked him to set up the board on her desk.

For the next half-hour they played in silence. 'I have to do some work now,' she said at last, 'but whenever you want, you can come to my room and play. I'll speak to your teacher and it will be okay.' In the next staff meeting she had argued for this to become policy on no other grounds than intuition, and to her surprise the staff psychiatrist had agreed. They had devised a protocol whereby Marek must always ask for a note from his teacher and go straight to Kirsten's room in the company of another student, with no detours along the way. Mairéad had expressed her doubts and had them noted in the minutes. But it was a win to Kirsten, though one she felt uncharacteristically uneasy about. In her heart she knew that intuition was no basis for policy, and that sooner or later she must come up with acceptable rationalisations.

In the meantime Marek has come to her room every day.

This morning, however, queasy and unsettled, she is too distracted to play, and after only ten minutes or so leans back into her chair and says, 'Marek, I'm afraid I'm not feeling very well. I might even have to go home soon.'

He nods, but doesn't move.

'I'm sorry, but we'll have to put our game off for another time.'

Marek just stares at her, looking glum, but at last gets up out of his chair and carries the board back across to the windowsill, his silver-blond hair sticking up in thin, dry wisps so that he has the look of a blighted troll.

'I'm sure I'll be feeling better tomorrow.'

When he has gone she rests her head against the cool surface of the desk and takes a few deep breaths. Then she looks up at the clock.

Four hours to go.

At that moment the father of her child is in the middle of a seminar.

'When an animal looks in the mirror, does it recognise itself?' James, a shy nineteen-year-old, is mumbling his way through a paper on the emotional life of animals, beginning with the work of Lesley J. Rogers.

'When most animals first see their images in mirrors they behave as though the image was another member of their own species. Unable to recognise their own likeness, they may attack the reflected image, display fear, or engage in social behaviours towards it. They may even go behind the mirror to see where the rest of the body is. The remarkable thing is that even after prolonged exposure, most species do not perceive that the image is of themselves.'

Outside it's a perfect autumn day, bright with sun and a mellow haze. Through the open window, Lindsay can see the faint golden aureole of smog that hovers above the city, softening the blunt verticals of high-rise. For most of the time, however, his eyes are closed. It's an affectation of his to sit and listen to student papers with his chin resting on his palm and his eyelids lowered. This is his listening position. Undistracted by anything visual, he can tell a lot from their voices: are they merely parroting, or is there conviction of tone? From time to time he looks up, and jots an occasional note on a loose sheet of paper. James is really quite bright and the paper is going well.

'An important figure in the opposition to Descartes was the

Dutch experimentalist, Nicholas Hartsoeker, a biologist of the vitalist school. An observation he made in his early youth created a deep and lasting impression on him when, looking through his microscope, he was startled to see "animalcules" or living bodies in the semen. To explain the progression of life and how it provides for all its needs, Hartsoeker developed the theory of plastic soul, a version of the old idea of *anima mundi* or world soul –'

Someone in the room gives a low groan. There are titters. James falters. Lindsay opens his eyes and can see nothing amiss. Opposite him a leggy girl called Samantha is sitting with lips compressed, staring down at her knees with a quality of concentration (not to mention the small tell-tale movements of the shoulders) that suggests to him she is doing something on her mobile phone.

'Continue,' he says loudly.

James shuffles in his seat and casts a sideways glance at Samantha, as if waiting for her permission to resume. Samantha places the mobile phone on the table alongside her purse and composes herself with the fixed stare, that slightly startled look, of the shop-window mannequin.

'Animal soul is a part of this, a kind of inferior or secondary intelligence, a subset of the *anima mundi* which it merges back into after the death of the body. This vegetative soul has a direct effect on the body to create involuntary movements. To create voluntary movements in the human organism, the rational soul gives orders to the vegetative. According to Hartsoeker, the superiority of humans lies in their having a rational soul. Nevertheless, in beasts the vegetative soul is intelligent, not mechanical.'

Suddenly there is a series of refined beeps from Samantha's phone.

'The ghost in the machine,' says Lindsay drily. And then, 'Turn that thing off.'

6

'Congratulations.' The doctor is looking at her gravely. 'You've had a good result.' He says this as if she has won a prize in a raffle, or done well in a maths test.

Kirsten has gone to some trouble to find this man, has asked around about doctors. The choice of an obstetrician is second only to the choice of the father, her GP had joked, but the juxtaposition of the words 'choice' and 'father' made Kirsten wince. She had hoped to return to a gynaecologist she saw three years ago, when she had been mysteriously plagued by a sharp pain at the moment of orgasm. The doctor, Ian Brodie, was funny and smart (she had flirted with him), with bright rooms full of hi-tech equipment and reassuringly glossy surfaces, not to mention a wonderfully witty fertility pipe from the New Guinea highlands – all bamboo, ochre paint and feathers – which hung over the door of the waiting room. But when she had asked her cool young GP, Trinh, for a referral, Trinh had blinked several times and announced that Brodie had died just under a year ago, from a rare form of leukaemia.

Gone? Brodie? How was this possible? Doctors weren't supposed to die young. They were supposed to grow old, develop gravitas and invest in vineyards.

'How old was he?' Kirsten gasped.

'Forty-one.'

A tremor of delayed shock hung in the air between them.

'Who else, then?' she asked bluntly. The nausea was making her single-minded.

Dr Lloyd is an older man, in his early sixties she would guess, small and slim and dapper in his dark pinstripe suit with a red carnation in the buttonhole. He is not how she imagined he would be, though how to imagine an obstetrician? She had thought somehow (perhaps it was the idea of forceps) that he would be more robust, like a surgeon carpenter. She feels she is about to enter into a peculiar relationship, not unlike a brief marriage in which two parties make a wholesale commitment, knowing all the while the exact date at which it will end.

She stares at him across his dark wooden desk, at the neat white blotter, the gold fountain pen, the old-fashioned desk calendar made of paper and brass, the black ceramic paperweight in the shape of a scarab beetle. The carnation is the only thing of warmth, the beetle the only thing of mystery.

Yet the studied impersonality of his room is calming; it suggests focus, order, discipline and control, not to mention a paring away of the extraneous.

'I thought, after all those years on the pill . . .'

'Yes?'

'It wouldn't happen so quickly. If at all, because . . .' Again she falters.

He waits with impeccable courtesy to see if she will finish her sentence. At last he says, 'How long were you on the pill?'

'Since I was fifteen. Except for the last twelve months when I've been using a diaphragm.'

'What led you to make the change?'

'I don't know really.' She sounds like a dopey female. How to tell him that she had begun to stare each night at that small rectangle of foil with its tiny tabs and to hate the sight of it? The tabs themselves looked like eggs in follicles. They mocked her.

'A woman's fertility is a very mysterious thing,' he says. 'I've been over thirty years in practice and it still surprises me.'

'Oh.'

All day she has waited for this moment, and yet she is finding it difficult to listen, to respond to anything he says. It's the dragging hum of nausea that rises up into her brain like a miasma, clouding the synapses in a furry whiteout. Each day it gets harder to pay attention. To anyone. In the past weeks, some senses have become dulled, others abnormally heightened, so that, for example, she is alert in an almost tactile way to the austere dullness of this room. A plainness that had at first been calming now begins to feel almost painful in its absences. She wonders why the room has to be so dour, so full of a kind of brownness, like the doctors' surgeries she remembers as a child. The only thing that could be interpreted as ornament is a large photograph of a rowing eight, posed in front of a boatshed — a group of awkward, raw-boned youths, like soldiers in shorts only they carry oars instead of guns. There is a plaque at the bottom that reads: HEAD OF THE RIVER. Was this, she wonders, the highlight of his youth?

Lloyd is standing now by the door, which he opens (his every gesture, no matter how simple, suggests some special delicacy of concern), and barely altering the inflection of his voice, he says, 'Just pop the bottom things off and hop up on the table, would you.' And leaves the room.

When she is undressed and settled with her legs in the stirrups (it's as if Lloyd has materialised in the room rather than re-entered it) he continues their earlier conversation with no regard to the break, and with the practised ease of the true bed-side manner. 'Just because we can produce a baby in a test tube doesn't mean we know everything,' he says, palpating her womb and looking into the distance with that slightly abstracted gaze of concentration doctors wear. 'Science does its best, but it doesn't have all the answers.'

She can feel her thigh muscles begin to strain — she must do more exercise — and hopes he isn't about to launch into some discourse on enigmatic and unfathomable Woman, or worse, God's unknowable Will. Trinh had recommended him as a deeply conservative but highly respected obstetrician. 'A lot of nurses go to him,' she said, 'and *they* know.' Asking around, Kirsten had heard he was a Catholic with five children of his own, and that his wife had never had a job. This did not inspire confidence. She does not plan to be that kind of mother.

What kind of mother does she plan to be? Looking up into the fine, clustered knot of crimson petals in Lloyd's buttonhole, it still seems unreal to her that she is to be a mother at all. Her only reality seems to lie in her guts, where, at this moment, the nausea is blooming in a yellow mandala, oozing out from around her navel — a jaundiced sphere enlarging to encompass the known world.

'You're a social worker,' he says, still probing.

The mandala breathes, viscous and supple.

'Yes.'

'And in what area?'

'Child support. Rundle House. It's out near Warrandyte.'

'Then you would have seen the recent government report on children in care,' he says, and eases into a polite commentary on the findings, as if this is the most natural thing in the world to be discussing with a half-naked woman with her legs in stirrups and your latex-gloved hand up her vagina. But she is sensible of what is a careful courtesy in him: he knows that young women are educated, are professionals; he will not patronise them by speaking to them as if they are just a womb on legs. She appreciates this worldly tact and so is obliged to answer in like terms, though she feels strangely dissociated as she does.

And then they are back in their chairs and seated in face-to-face position. 'Do you have any questions?' he asks.

She smiles weakly. 'I'm sure I'll think of a dozen once I leave here.' She doesn't like to say that her mind is blank. In fact her mind *is* blank.

When she gets up to walk she can feel a wetness between her thighs, thin cotton clinging to pubic hair. Lloyd's mellow, physician's voice is wafting her to the door. 'Please don't hesitate, Kirsten,' he is saying, 'to bring your husband with you to these consultations — that is, if he would like to come and if you, of course, would like to have him here.'

'My husband?'

'Yes. It's very much the done thing now for couples to come together, whenever they can. Often I find the husband has more questions than the wife, and sometimes even,' he smiles, 'firmer views.'

'Views?' Still in her sick trance.

'About things such as, say, natural childbirth.' He gives her what is really a very tender smile. 'I do sometimes wonder if they truly desire it so passionately, or whether they feel they have to be up with the latest.' By this time they are at the door, to which, with old-fashioned courtesy, he has walked her.

She thanks him, and turns to the receptionist with the intention of paying the bill. She does not want anything posted home, not at this stage. As for Lindsay having firm views on natural childbirth – he who has firm views on so many things – the idea is so comically inapposite she finds herself smiling inanely into the vase of spotted mauve orchids on the reception desk. Looking up over winged reading glasses, the smartly coiffed receptionist says, 'Are you all right, dear?'

She means to answer but somehow doesn't, the strong rolling nausea, like a wave of surrender, carrying her down the stairs and out onto the street in a cold sweat.

Ah, but the minute she turns the key in the lock of her front door, she enters into a painful lie. It's not in her nature to keep anything from her husband, so how will she bear it? How will she bear to be with him in the house tonight while she considers her options? In the past she has told him everything — often, as he has made clear on at least one recent occasion, the night of the duck, more than he wanted to know. Tonight, if they sit together in the same room for any length of time, she will have to tell him. And it would be too soon. First she must make her own decision about what it is that *she* wants.

An abortion would not be out of the question. It would not be her first. She has been pregnant before, but not to a man she loved. It has been so hard these past two weeks not to collapse into Lindsay's arms and allow him to look after her. Because the irony of her situation — one of many — is that Lindsay is always so good to her when she is ill; at his best, in fact. Perhaps it's because he likes having her dependent, enjoys the idea of being in charge, but it's one of the things she warmed to in him from the very beginning. Like the time they had gone away to Hepburn Springs for what was supposed to be an erotic weekend and she had come down with a hideous head cold, snuffling and gasping and breathing through her mouth like a beached seal. Lindsay rubbed her back (those strong, warm hands), and topped up her water and made her fresh orange juice and even, one evening, read to her. So quaint, and yet so endearing.

To make it all the more difficult, tonight he is in a good mood, teasing and affectionate. It would be too easy to sit beside him on the couch, lean her head against his shoulder and make a sentimental declaration.

Instead, preparing dinner, she bangs and clatters the pots around in misplaced frustration. Her hands tremble and she almost overturns the wok. And then, ladling the burnt stir-fry into bowls, to her immense relief she remembers something that in her anxiety she had completely forgotten. Tonight she has promised to drive over to her friend Alison's and return some videos. She can escape the house.

And so after dinner, when Lindsay is settled on the couch in the front parlour watching the news, she puts her head around the door and says, 'I've just remembered I have to take some videos over to Alison. I'll be back in an hour.' Grabbing her bag and bolting out the door.

Once in the car she wonders if she will in fact drive to Alison's. Maybe she should just go and sit in a coffee shop. But no, the thought of that makes her shudder, the sheer inactivity of it. By this time of the day the nausea is gone, and in any case she is agitated, too anxious to sit still. Besides, it has occurred to her that she might confide in her friend, although this thought is undermined by a sense that it would not, *could* not, be right for someone else to know of the existence of a child before its father.

It's only a short drive over to Brunswick, where Alison lives in a stucco-fronted bungalow with her daughter, Tara. Theirs is a busy street and she is relieved to find a parking space right outside. In the reserve opposite she can see shadowy figures walking their dogs.

She knocks on Alison's door and waits. No-one answers, though she can hear voices inside giving what sound like hurried and urgent instructions. She knocks again, louder this time, and the door is opened by seven-year-old Tara, a delicate child with black corkscrew curls who is dressed in shorts, a T-shirt, thongs and oversized gardening gloves that dwarf her small hands. The child is breathless and excited, almost dancing on the spot. 'We're trying to catch a spider,' she says, 'it's a big, crawly huntsman.'

'Who is it?' Alison's voice echoes down the hall.

'It's Kirsten.'

In the big, glassed-in family room at the rear of the house, Alison is standing on a chair, haplessly brandishing a broom. Her hair is awry and she is flushed. 'There's a huntsman in the bookcase,' she says, 'and we're trying to dislodge it.'

Kirsten looks up but is unable to see the source of all this alarm. 'Why don't you just spray it? Have you got some flyspray?'

'I never use it, it's toxic. In any case, I can't kill it, you know that.' Alison is a Buddhist and won't kill anything if she can avoid it, not even a cockroach.

'We're just trying to capture it,' says Tara, 'and put it outside.'

Kirsten smiles and brushes a lock of hair from the child's forehead. There's something about the way she says 'capture', so ingenuous, so naïvely self-important, that is touching. 'Why are you wearing gloves, Tara?'

'Because I hate spiders, especially huntsmen, they scare me and I'm frightened that when we try and catch it, it might accidentally get on my hands or something.'

'But your feet are bare, what about your feet?'

'Go and put your sneakers on,' says her mother, still aloft on the rickety old bentwood. She looks down at her friend. 'I'm trying to get in and reach it so I can flick it onto the floor, and then Tara will put a jar over it and we can take it outside. I just can't reach the damned thing.'

'Do you want me to have a go? I'm taller.'

'Would you?'

This is ridiculous, she thinks. She has no liking for these large, hairy creatures but nor is she afraid of them. When they appear in her own house she simply takes a fireside brush and pan and flicks the huntsman out the door into the leafy protection of the garden.

Her friend's peculiar blend of fear and respect, hysterical revulsion on the one hand and spiritual scruple on the other, is absurd.

Tara has reappeared meanwhile in her pink sneakers, laces trailing untied. Alison gets down from the chair and Kirsten climbs up. The chair wobbles. 'You need to tighten the screws on this thing,' she says. 'Here, give me the broom.' It's a stiff, straw garden broom and she lifts it high up towards one end of the dark-stained bookcase that is bolted to the wall and reaches almost to the ceiling. The huntsman is splayed across the wood, its long legs angled as if for sudden take-off, ready for a rapid retreat.

'I'm surprised you spotted it against such a dark background.'

'We were bathing our feet before meditation and I saw these hairy legs emerging from between two books.' Bathing their feet before candles and incense is a part of Alison and Tara's night-time ritual. The television is switched off, the phone is taken from the hook, and mother and daughter sit straight-backed alongside one another with their feet in red plastic washing bowls of warm water scented with aromatic oils. (How inopportune of the monster to appear at this precise moment.)

'You'd better stand clear,' says Kirsten. 'I'll try and flick it onto that patch of rug there by the door, and then you pounce. Have you got the jar ready?'

'Get the jar, Tara,' says her mother.

The child picks up the jam jar standing on the lid of the

wood box. 'This jar's not very big,' she says, looking at it askance. 'What if we miss?'

'Look for a bigger one. There's some in the cupboard in the laundry.'

'Just get a large bowl if you're squeamish,' says Kirsten, 'and then slide some cardboard under it. Or better still, get a bucket.' The preposterousness of their measures is such that she is beginning to enjoy herself. Tara's delight in being both scared and repulsed, and at the same time part of an important adult drama, is beguiling to behold. She has stepped back to the far side of the room now, with her grotesquely gloved hands held up to her chest, alert, apprehensive, excited. I must be careful not to flick the huntsman onto her head, thinks Kirsten, and gestures to Alison to stand back as well.

'Ready?'

With a short, delicate jab of the broom's straw bristles the beast is dislodged and drops to the beige carpet. To all appearances unhurt, it scurries sideways with great rapidity, its long brown legs frantically scaling the skirting board. Alison pounces, and using a long plastic ruler to flick it back onto the flat of the carpet, traps it beneath a white enamel bowl. 'Eeuuukkk!' she exclaims. 'I'll never be able to make salad in this bowl again.'

Kirsten steps down from the chair. 'Have a ritual cleansing of the bowl later,' she says wryly. 'Have you got the cardboard?'

Alison rummages in the bottom drawer of her desk for a manila folder and watches nervously as Kirsten slides the custard-coloured cardboard under the rim of the bowl. Then, lifting cardboard and bowl carefully from the carpet, she walks towards the back door. Tara, who has been standing well back, runs ahead to push open the screen door, standing almost to attention beside the wire mesh as Kirsten walks through into the large, leafy garden.

Outside, the night air is mild, the garden petrified in a shadowy stillness. At the back is a high red-brick wall overgrown by creeper, at the base of which is a cluster of low bushes, and these, thinks Kirsten, will do. She walks over to the wall and, holding the bowl on its edge against a jutting ledge of brick, raps firmly on the base of the enamel. But the splayed arachnid seems stunned and makes no move. She raps again and then, grasping the bowl in both hands, shakes it over the bushes, suspecting all the while that the spider is injured, possibly even dead.

'Is it all right?' asks Alison, tiptoeing barefoot down the path.

'I think so,' she says, fudging it. 'It's difficult to see.'

'Where did you put it?'

'In the bushes?'

'Which one?'

'Al, does it matter?'

Alison giggles. 'I suppose not.'

The two women pause for a moment and look up at the sky, smudged with blotches of inky cloud that here and there are backlit by a full moon. In this unseasonably warm autumn they are reluctant to go inside, content for now to linger in the garden, to absorb in silence the sap and stillness of the evening. The woody cedar scent of the bushes rises up to meet those pungent night smells that waft across from adjacent lanes and alleyways in a heady commingling of rotting food, dog shit and incense. But more potent than any of these is the sharp, acrid scent of the creeper, its showy trusses of white, trumpet-like flowers sprouting from a thick knotted canopy above the trellis gate. The sound of a car horn blares from across the street in a long, syncopated riff that dies away in a melancholy swoop, and they look up knowingly and smile at one another with a kind of wry, feminine complicity. A large moth flutters above their heads, drawn by the coach light beside the gate. Kirsten brushes at the air, and in moving, turns away from the garden and back towards the house. There, barefoot on the slate verandah, as if arrested on the garden's threshold, Tara is standing in a rectangle of light that flares through the open doorway behind her so that the child is lit like an apparition.

'What are you two doing out there?' she calls. 'Is it safe to come out?'

Back in the kitchen a feast is called for, or at least a boisterous supper, and they sit around the polished wooden table, with its vase of flowers set down on an embroidered Tibetan placemat, and sip at their hot chocolate. Tara has spilled the bag of white marshmallows, which lie scattered across the table like seed.

'What would you do if it was a redback or a white-tail?' asks Kirsten.

'I've never seen either of those around here.'

'It's a hypothetical question, Alison. What would you do if you were confronted with one, say, on your bathmat? Lindsay's mother found a funnel-web in her laundry once. You would know that in trying to remove it you'd run the risk of being bitten. Surely that's not a risk worth taking? No-one could reproach you for whacking it with a slipper.'

She expects her friend to defend her reverence-for-life stance with categorical firmness, but instead Alison looks troubled, and fingers a marshmallow distractedly, rolling it back and forth between thumb and forefinger. 'I don't know,' she says. 'I don't know what I'd do. You can't say what you'd do in any situation until you're in it, I suppose. You can only have goodwill and hope for the best.'

Kirsten stares into her cup. She hates it when Alison says things like 'you can only have goodwill', hates the sanctimoniousness of it. Sometimes her old schoolfriend can seem a little, well, precious.

Tara yawns. 'Can I sleep in your bed tonight, Mum?' she asks. 'I'm freaked out.'

'Okay. Go and clean your teeth.'

'I want some more hot chocolate.'

'No, you won't sleep.'

'Well, can't I wait up until Kirsten goes?'

Alison sighs, and smiles the smile of maternal indulgence. 'Get your project out to put by the front door so we don't forget it tomorrow like we did this morning.' And then, turning back to Kirsten, 'Tara has done the most hysterical project on our family tree.' When Tara returns she says, 'Show Kirsten your project.'

While Kirsten dutifully surveys the pasted-on contents of the white cardboard square decorated at the edges with rainbow stripes, Alison becomes distracted again, dropping into that fey realm of thought that can suddenly take her over.

At last Kirsten gets up from her chair. 'I brought your videos back. They're in a bag on the couch.' She nods in the direction of the living-room.

'You look tired,' says her friend, emerging suddenly from her preoccupation.

This is the moment to say what's on her mind, but she hesitates. Friends who have children are never quite wholly with you. In the presence of a child it's impossible to get a parent's full attention, and nothing less, at the moment, will do.

Driving home, it occurs to her that it is only ever Lindsay that she is truly able to confide in. At least, that used to be true. When she first met him she had been struck by his faculty for giving someone his complete attention. He was one of the few people she knew who could create the impression that they were actually listening to you. It was a rare thing, and at first she put it down to the quality of his intellect, his ability to concentrate with an intense, single focus. But then she began to see that it was more than that; it was a physical thing, a fine, animal watchfulness and receptivity. There was a certain way he had of sitting still, not stiff or wooden, but relaxed and receptive, exuding a calm that was reassuring. He would cross his legs and lean back in his chair, and his hands would rest on his thighs like flags of erotic sympathy. His hands are large and well formed, graceful but strong. It used to be that whenever she felt at her worst she would lift his hands to her face and feel a current of warm, electric energy course through her cheekbones.

By the time she climbs the staircase to the bedroom it's after eleven and her husband is asleep, his body sprawled naked across the bed. The ceiling light is still on, and for a moment she just stands there, captive beneath its lambent glow. And then, looking down at him, feels a wash of tenderness, but a remote tenderness, like she is peering at him through glass. How well made he is, how perfectly proportioned. No man has ever held her in such physical thrall. It's the glow of his skin, the contours of his head, the careless charm of his body; that relaxed and engaging way he has of leaning his head on his hands when he's tired, his elbows resting on his thighs. And the graceful way he sleeps, his smooth brown shoulders angled away from her, his back tapering to the waist like a shield.

At last she undresses and sits on the side of the bed, waiting for him to stir, which he does, turning towards her in his sleep. At that moment she is filled with a dumb ache of possession, followed by a sudden lurch of panic, a dizzying sensation of free-fall.

For a long time she lies on her back in the dark, unable to sleep, listening to her husband's light snore. All she can think of is this: what will she do? Of all the feelings in her life that cause her pain, the thing she is least able to bear is moral confusion. She can fight the case on behalf of the goldfish because she knows she is right, but her underhanded means, her covert path to conceiving a child – its reckless unilateralism – is something else. All right, there were extenuating circumstances: she was drunk, she was angry, she did not expect to be fertile at that moment. She was not, as they would say in a court of law, in full possession of her rational faculties.

The goldfish was a different matter – in essence its intrinsic value was low, its death a mere blip on the screen of the cosmos (even if Alison might argue otherwise). The whole point of that campaign had been the boy, not the goldfish. Although Mairéad accused her of being sentimental and allowing emotion – 'misplaced empathy' – to cloud her professional judgement, she, Kirsten, did not in the end care about the goldfish itself. It was the boy, and his relationship to his pet – his need to love something and to have that something as his own, unbeholden to the institution – that was the point.

And of course there were limitations, even here. Marek, for example, had wanted to bring his dog with him, but Kirsten had no interest in mounting a campaign for a mutt to take up residence at one of the cottages of Rundle House. Dogs were dirty, greedy and anarchic – in her view, the least desirable of pets, although she has known people of either sex who appeared to love their dogs more than their spouse or offspring. She remembers going on a school excursion and visiting a famous children's author, an old woman who lived in the bush in a stone cottage with her husband. On the hearth before a roaring fire sat two enormous Great Danes, insolent, proprietorial, and luxuriating on a grubby Persian rug in which coals had burnt a galaxy of black holes. Over in a corner by the window the author's husband, a small man, sat meekly in a moth-eaten armchair. The dogs had all the presence in the room, the husband none. It was almost as if they had drained it out of him, and she recalls thinking, I would not want to marry a man who could be overshadowed by a dog, not even a Great Dane.

This was the thing about Lindsay that had bowled her over at first sight: his animal presence. And what made that presence irresistible was that he himself seemed scarcely aware of it. He was so in his head, so full of intellectual certainty, even arrogance, that it seemed to have the effect of making him blind to his own physical charm.

But what of this other thing, this thing in her womb — some animal in transition between fish and human? This being she has come to think of as a seahorse, serenely afloat in its amniotic bubble. How blissfully unaware of the limits of that bubble it must be, as if it were in some infinite cosmic ocean rather than a human goldfish bowl, a vulnerable and highly permeable sac. What is its status? What are its rights? In what is the single most important moral contract two people can enter into, she has recklessly disregarded not only her husband's wishes, but also his rights, behaving like a loose cannon on the quarterdeck of marriage. She has behaved *unreasonably*. While he has always held himself to be the virile rationalist in their coupledom — and she the earthy, impetuous one, the gut-feeling maverick of the moment – this is in fact a myth. Behind a sometimes tempestuous façade, her actions are more often than not extremely calculated. The goldfish business is a good example. Far from being a sentimental subversion of rational bureaucratic regulation, the emotional and therapeutic logic of her argument – its inner and outer consistency – was impeccable. The worst outcome was that one small fish – a replaceable fish – might die. Any number of fish might die in the interests of Joel's wellbeing.

But a baby – a baby was a primeval force that changed everything in its field. No such emphatic, lifelong commitment could be undertaken without weighing up all the options, not to mention an acute feel for timing. And she had subverted all this in an instant – of what? Was it drunken carelessness, or a secret, liverish defiance? Not for one minute had she believed that her body would rise so promptly to the occasion, that she would fall, as her mother's generation used to say. (Fall into what?) Who could believe that, after twenty years on the pill, the foundation of her life as a free woman, her body would rebound with such atavistic opportunism? *Who would have thought?* All those women queuing in waiting rooms in fertility clinics, nursing their urine samples in plastic bottles disguised by brown paper bags, and here is she, a one-ticket winner of the big-egg jackpot. And, yes, she feels a perverse pride in this result. But that pride is misplaced. *Unearned.*

Meanwhile, in her mind's eye, she can see this thing in her womb, this seahorse, this tiny, translucent bubble of tissue and membrane. At seventeen she had an abortion, and another at twenty-five, and the feeling both times was one of overwhelming relief. But now she is thirty-six, and haunted by a conviction that she has played with – gambled on – her body for too long. That's one thing. The other is that she has, in essence, undermined and betrayed her husband. Shut him out, subverted his wishes. By her impatience, she tells herself, she has shown contempt for his needs, his all too reasonable sense of timing. After all, a man has as much right as a woman to choose the moment of conception of his own child. With this she would not, and never has, sought to argue. She has sought to persuade him, but not to subvert him.

If she were seventeen again and a student it would be simple, she would have an abortion. If she were thirty and involved with a married man, ditto. But this situation is intolerable. This is something she wants, but something she has gone about getting in the wrong way. She should confess all and share the burden with him, but would this be to dump on him a moral dilemma he has done nothing to deserve? She got herself into this, she should get herself out of it.

The clock ticks on. One-ten ... one-forty ... two-ten, and still she is wide awake. Every now and then her husband stirs in his sleep, his great, solid body shifting its weight like a dark mass anchored in a seabed. Occasionally he mutters something, the coded conversation of his dreams, and sometimes he'll frown and gasp, as if roused from drowning on some other plane. At these moments she is almost in awe of him, of the secret, slumbering mystery of another's body, programmed, in its deepest regions, to be unknowable.

Tonight she is agonisingly separate from him. And that pain is all the more difficult to rationalise away because it is nobody's fault. If Lindsay had said that he never wanted children, that he did not *ever* want them, then it would be within her woman's right to assert her biological destiny. But all he has ever argued for is deferment.

Ah, but here was another thought. What if she were not subverting him, but saving him? What if she were rescuing him from himself? From his own neurosis, his inability to make a decision? It was just too easy for men these days to put things off, to postpone paternity into their mellow middle-age, until they too heard the subtle drumbeat of their own mortality. One of her psychology lecturers had talked often of the burden of decision-making, itself anchored in a set of broader questions arising out of the dilemma of free will. Certain decisions, like having a baby, had greater magnitude and finality than others. It wasn't like going out and buying a dog and dumping it at the pound when you tired of it. Her lecturer quoted extensively from a philosopher called

Kaufmann, who argued that the freedom of modern life could result in a syndrome he had dubbed decidophobia. Decidophobia was a condition of modernity whereby some people simply had too much choice, and while certain stresses had been removed by this phenomenon, the plethora of choice resulted in a new form of stress. Too many options, too much freedom from necessity, could engender a chronic state of living in moral and emotional paralysis. 'Any confrontation with fateful alternatives engenders dread,' he had written, and the greater the freedom of choice, the greater the degree of decidophobia. One way out of the fear and guilt inspired by fateful decisions was to avoid making them, and this accounted for the well-known phenomenon of the young couple who give up birth control not because they want to have a child, but 'just to see what happens'. Hence the syndrome of the so-called planned accident.

What contempt she had felt in the past for such self-delusional woolliness! At least on the evening of the incident with the duck, she had been drunk . . . but then again, not all that drunk. So was it an exercise of her free will, or had it just happened? Was she culpable? Or the occasion of a random event? How had she, a practical woman, become trapped in such a philosophical conundrum?

Hearing Lindsay sigh again, instinctively she moves to touch him, and then, at the last minute, withdraws her hand.

7

Days pass. His sense of unease, of something looming just beyond the edge of his vision, returns. Kirsten, it seems, is never quite with him, never quite herself.

One evening, over dinner, she asks him if he has ever heard of a philosopher called Kaufmann.

'Yes,' he says, 'why?'

'Just someone I saw quoted in a paper.'

'What does he say?'

'Nothing. Just something to do with work.'

Nothing. Something. This is her new strangeness. Lindsay sighs. With some deliberation he puts his fork down on the kitchen table and stares at her. Luckily, at that moment the phone rings. It's his mother, calling from Sydney, and they are both distracted.

All week it has been wet, and when the rain comes it brings with it the smell of mould to every corner of the house. The sky can darken in a minute, so that he is soaked to the skin by the time he gets home. But he refuses to carry an umbrella, hates the sense of being encumbered. On more than one occasion he arrives home drenched and strips off to stand for a long time under a hot shower. Turning the jet on full, so that it's like an abrasive hosing, he gazes, steamy and unsighted, at the way the soap bubbles sit in the clotted hair on his chest, or run in rivulets down his abdomen and into the crevices of his genitals.

One night after dinner, when he has gone out for a drink with George, who should come into the bar but Sonia, in the company of an older man. He ignores them, but her presence unsettles him. He has considered before now whether he should confide in George, but some inhibition prevents him. It may be that he can succeed in having her passed on to George for supervision, in which case the less said about the letters, the better.

Kirsten has announced that she no longer wants to eat out on a Thursday, so they stay home with takeaway and a video. More often than not it goes like this: he comes home with a stack of plastic containers full of Japanese delicacies and she turns up her nose and munches her way noisily through a packet of salty crackers spread thickly with Vegemite.

On a Sunday morning he returns from a swim at the local pool to find her at the kitchen table with a guilty air, eating a meat pie spread with tomato sauce and slices of cheap, vinegary gherkin.

'I had a sudden craving for a pie,' she says shamefacedly.

'You hate pies.'

'I know. It's weird.'

The smell of the pie turns his stomach.

8

Any day now, she thinks, he will become suspicious, notwith-
standing the fact that modern viruses are known to hang around
for weeks, and sometimes, even, to trigger long-term malaises
such as chronic fatigue — insidious termites of the nervous and
immune system that eat away at the alpha state of wellbeing com-
monly supposed to be the base metabolic state of the healthy
adult animal (if only).

And then she is given a reprieve of a few days in the form of
an unexpected smokescreen. Lindsay's sister Anna rings from
Bendigo to ask if her son can stay for the weekend. 'I know it's
short notice,' she says, 'but Rowan has to travel down for the
national final of the Tournament of Minds. The school organ-
ises a billet, but the boy whose family was to billet Row is sick
and his mother is worried it might be contagious. Would you
mind . . .?'

No, of course they wouldn't mind. Lindsay is fond of Rowan
and announces he'd be happy to ferry him around, and indeed

would be interested to sit in on the tournament itself, with its combative feats of extemporisation and quick-wittedness.

Good. Then she will have Saturday to herself.

Late on Friday afternoon, Lindsay collects Rowan from the station and Kirsten buys a large tray of lasagne from the Greek deli in High Street. Sometimes the smell of parmesan can be enough to send her reeling, but today has been one of her better days. From a late-night trawl of the Internet she has discovered that grated ginger in hot water can ease the symptoms of nausea, and so far it seems to be working.

Just after seven she hears them at the gate, and Rowan lanks up the hallway to give her an awkward hug. There is now almost six foot of him, pale-eyed and fair-skinned like his mother, and with some fleeting resemblance to Lindsay in the coarse, dark hair. And perhaps in time the boy will fill out into his uncle's robust, muscular frame. Rowan seems too wound up to want to eat much but is full of nervous energy and keen to talk, and she is grateful that he is not one of those sullen teenagers who have nothing much to say. After dinner, while Lindsay makes coffee, she asks Rowan about his plans for next year, and is he still interested in computer studies? Yes, he says, he wants one day to work as an analyst programmer.

'Is that the same as a computer programmer?'

'No.' He corrects her with a slight, knowing smirk. And waits, with adolescent condescension, for her inevitable question.

'What's the difference?'

'It's on another level from ordinary programming. The programmers are like builders and the analyst programmer is, like, the architect. They come up with the overall structure and the programmers plot out the various bits of it.'

'Sounds quite godlike,' she observes.

'Well, it is.' He gives a schoolboy laugh, and blushes slightly. 'There's a guy, Martin, in Dad's office, and he describes himself as a virtual sculptor.'

'A virtual sculptor? Now, that's poetic.'

'Well, you're sculpting something you can't see and that's why it's virtual. The sculptures exist in the mind's eye of the analyst programmer, who constructs them out of pathways of Boolean logic.'

'Boolean logic?'

'Yeah, it's what computer programs are constructed out of. It's a simple pathway logic – if this, then this, and so on. You build up a network of pathways and these enable the materialisation of the endpoint, which is the image on the screen, but this is just a thin layer that sits on top of the core.' His speech comes out in a rush.

Lindsay carries the coffee pot to the table. 'What do you mean by the core?'

'It's like this,' says Rowan, and with his finger he inscribes an imaginary circle on the table. 'If you draw it as a circle, the user interface is like a crust around the outside, and there's the bit in the middle that supports that. Analyst programmers construct the bit in the middle.'

'Presumably you aim to specialise in some particular area?' says Lindsay.

'Yeah. There are these guys who make compositing systems for film and TV. What you do is build libraries of code that . . . well, there's a whole area of working with special effects for people who make movies where you create user interfaces for film and video compositing systems. You might write a program, say, that will enable people in Hollywood, or wherever, to super-impose images on one another in a layering effect. You superimpose a foreground on a background, say, and, um, perhaps put some other elements in.'

Lindsay is clearly charmed by the boy's eager pedantry. 'Give me an example.'

'Well, Luke Skywalker's light sabre, for instance. You create a program which enables the technician to put the light in the sabre which may not actually be there. The actor's probably just holding a flashlight with no batteries in it.'

'I see.'

'That's why they call them virtual sculptors. You're sculpting something. You've got something which has well-defined behaviour but you can't see it, you just know it exists and you know its behaviour.'

'Will you have some coffee, Rowan?'

The boy, arrested mid-rave, recalls his mother's warning. 'No, thanks. I'd better ring Mum and tell her I got here.'

'Phone's by the stairs.'

Kirsten waits until she can hear his disembodied voice floating down the hallway. 'All that,' she says, raising one suggestive eyebrow at Lindsay, 'so that Luke Skywalker can have light in his sabre.'

Lindsay grins. It's the first time in weeks that they've shared a joke.

When Rowan returns she gets up from the table. 'It's been a long day, and I need an early night. I'll leave you guys to it.'

It's true she is tired, and growing more so each day. From someone who always had a restless mind and took at least an hour to get to sleep at night she has turned into a torpid slug and falls into a snore minutes after hitting the pillow.

But tonight is different. After dozing for a time she wakes, and sees that although it is late, Lindsay is still downstairs. Needing to pee, she gets up and walks past the open door of the spare bedroom, where she sees her husband standing by Rowan's bed. The boy is asleep, but somehow his long, restless frame has entangled itself in the covers and is half exposed. At first, in the gloom, she can't make out what Lindsay is doing, and then she sees that he is adjusting the bedclothes, stooping to rearrange the smooth fall of the cloth. And she feels a pang. Yes, of course he would make a good father. Hasn't she always, instinctively, known it? The only person who can't see it is him.

His tenderness towards Rowan has a perverse effect, and for the first time in weeks she feels a surge of sexual arousal. For what seems a long time she lies in the dark, waiting for Lindsay to come to bed so that she can embrace him. But the house is uncannily quiet. Suddenly she is no longer tired at all, and in a lightning instant it occurs to her that now, yes, *now*, might be the moment to tell him; now, while they are closer than they have been in months. And she pushes the bedcover aside and swings her legs onto the floor, reaching across to the bedside chair for her old cotton kimono.

At the bottom of the stairs she can see the light flaring up from the front parlour overlooking the street. He'll be in there reading, and drinking his way through a cleanskin most likely, and she will sit on the soft velour couch beside him and take his hand . . . But as she arrives at the open door, her nerve falls away. What if he reacts badly? What if there is a scene and Rowan is woken? Tomorrow is his big day at the Tournament of Minds, and how could they do anything that might upset him?

'Kirsten?'

She puts her head around the door. 'I was just getting up for some water. Everything okay with Rowan?'

'He's fine. A bit wired. I put some brandy in his cocoa.'

'Oh.' An open bottle of red is sitting on the polished floorboards beside him, and glancing down over his shoulder she sees that he is reading a book about dogs.

'What's that?'

For a moment he stares at her blankly. 'What? Oh, this? Just looking up something. Something that came up in a seminar on animal soul.'

'Will you be long?'

'Another half-hour.'

She nods, and heads back down the hallway.

9

Kyneton is just over an hour's drive, straight up the Calder Freeway. It's been a while since he's driven out this way, and the number of cars on the road seems to have grown exponentially. Still, it's not enough to kill his mood, and by the time he reaches the outskirts of the town, green from the recent rains, he is in a groove of high anticipation. Following directions from Sandra, he branches off to the showground and all the way in he trails behind a white Camry hooked up to a rectangular steel box on wheels that bumps and sways and rattles around the corners. The box has grille windows and he assumes it to be some kind of dog-mobile. How comical it looks, like a miniature mobile gaol.

Once through the gates of the showground he is surprised by the size of the event. The oval is completely ringed with cars and vans of all descriptions, and as he heads towards them he can see that many of the vans are travelling pet shops, specially designed to open out on one side to display their goods, a garish melange of dog paraphernalia. Up close, everything looks peculiarly rubbery and synthetic, even the food, which is coloured with crude dyes that bear no resemblance whatsoever to anything in nature. And then there is the unimaginable range of dog toys, spilling out of cardboard display units, or hanging like so many rubber sausages in a butcher's shop, festooning the sides of vans. Large chipboards display collars in all sizes, and there's a carnivalesque profusion of leads, dog blankets, dog baskets, dog sweaters, books, medicines, and mugs, caps, pens and barbecue aprons imprinted with the image of your favourite breed. Each van a department store for dogs, the whole oval a dog fête. Or would be if most of the dogs weren't in cages.

These cages stand in a long line around half the perimeter of the oval, just inside the white-chalk boundary line. Strolling along, he finds it impossible not to stare, which is okay because staring is the point. Here is a Great Dane, next to it a poodle, next to that a borzoi, then a beagle and then some dog he can't identify, and so it goes on, with breeds he's never seen before. The variety is astonishing. But even more intriguing is the relationship of the owners to their dogs. Take this one, in the outsize cage – an Afghan hound, slim and regal behind its curtain of tawny hair. This dog is in superb trim, elegant and aloof with liquid black eyes that look not so much at you as through you. As patrician a dog as could be imagined, and yet how squalid its surrounds. The cage itself is ugly, but worse, on one side is a litter of food wrappers and empty drink bottles and on the other a brown plastic water tray and spilled packet of dog biscuits, fluoro-orange and shaped like miniature bones. And behind these, a mound of crumpled clothes: cardigans, an anorak, an unzipped tracksuit top, a pair of grimy thongs.

It's been a piece of folklore ever since he can remember that owners grow to resemble their dogs, but strolling around the ground it seems to him that the relationship is more complex than this suggests. In the section for toy breeds, for example, he has seen a massive truck-driver type unloading a cage of three Maltese terriers, each with a pert black bow between its ears, and it was clear from the man's proprietorial handling that he was their owner. Resemblance? Nil. And here opposite him is a Russian borzoi, a tall, sleek wolfhound of impossibly aristocratic mien being brushed by a small, shapeless man of melancholy demeanour whose grey tracksuit is shabby and stained. The dog's muzzle is long and shiny, its eye sardonic; its master's eyes, sunken within doughy flesh, are dull and resentful. Then there's the boxer, gold with white markings, clean-limbed, with a muzzle that is broad, deep and powerful. Such high-tensile litheness, such intimations of springy ferocity, yet here it is being groomed by a woman of about thirty-five whose straggly hair, bleached and badly permed, hangs over a low, pitted forehead; whose pale blue ugh boots are caked with mud.

The dogs are magnificent. They have a perfection of line and feature, a gloss and finish that is otherwise found only in images of women in fashion or sex magazines. And whereas those are touched up, airbrushed into an illusory ideal, the dogs are living perfection. It's as if the owners have abandoned the futile hope of achieving beauty for themselves and put heart and soul – all higher yearning – into a creature they know, through breeding, to be perfectible.

But where are the chows?

At last he finds them, four dogs, each in a separate cage – three golden-red and one enormously large black one with a glare of uncharacteristic ferocity. The minute he sets eyes on these animals he experiences a curious feeling of affinity; his body becomes more relaxed, the pores of his skin breathe deeper and his mouth widens into an involuntary smile. Ah, yes, they are quite as handsome as he remembers. More so! The burnished feet, the bushy tail, the black tongue, the leonine face rimmed by a ruff of reddish-gold fur. This is *his* dog.

But where is Melissa? Are these the Schokmann chows or are there others?

A young man is leaning against one of the cages, smoking, and when approached directs him to the opposite side of the ground. 'See that white van? Over there.'

And indeed in front of the van he can see two golden chows being attended to by a slim young woman in jodhpurs whose dark hair is tied back in a ponytail. From a distance she could be mistaken for a youthful clone of Sandra.

Within minutes he has introduced himself and explained his mission. He of course is affable and courteous, but Melissa, and another young woman who accompanies her, scarcely make eye contact, except to give him an occasional glancing look of cloudy appraisal. It's as if he is somehow an interloper and a nuisance. Melissa opens up the back of the van and inside is a cage with three puppies, just over six weeks old.

My God, here he is smiling again, because they're almost comically engaging, like live teddy bears, and he gives a short, half-suppressed snort of delight.

'Do you want me to get them out?' says Melissa.

'Perhaps one at a time. Will they run off?'

She shakes her head. 'Not these dogs.'

Between them, the two women manage to scruff hold of the three pups and set them down on the grass beside the van. In keeping with the temperament of the breed, they are relatively calm. All are golden-red chows. Melissa identifies the sex of each and he takes an instant dislike to the female, who is clearly the strongest of the three and would make the best watchdog. She has a sinewy alertness and a keen eye, but with it a sharp, foxy expression that he finds off-putting. The most beautiful of the dogs, and he is a very beautiful dog indeed, is the one Sandra identified as Yellow Emperor. This boy is even more beautiful than in the Polaroid. Here is the perfect leonine head, without the suggestion of squatness and chubbiness he has seen in many of the photographs in books. Here is a refinement in the gait, a softness in the eyes (unlike his foxy sister), a dignity of bearing that you would not expect to find in such an immature pup. He bends to stroke the golden fur on his head.

'Why isn't the boss here?' he asks jocularly (it is, after all, supposed to be one of the highlights of the dog calendar). And the second girl, who is not so much aloof as shy, offers, 'Sandra doesn't like shows. She hardly ever comes.'

Driving home, he finds he is already thinking possessively of this dog, Yellow Emperor. Here is a dog deserving of some ceremony, and the idea comes to him that he might devise some kind of ritual for its presentation to Kirsten. He could surprise her with the pup one Sunday morning over a champagne breakfast. If all goes according to plan, he could collect the dog the day before and leave it overnight with George, stepping out for a few minutes the following morning to walk it back up the street.

Meanwhile, even though he knew Sandra wouldn't be there, he is feeling a little miffed by her absence. For some peculiar reason he had wanted to see her again. Perhaps she is a recluse? Very likely she is, and he thinks of how in other circumstances it might seem odd to him that the leading breeder in the country doesn't like to attend dog shows. But since meeting her that day in the café in Lygon Street, nothing about Sandra would surprise him.

After dinner he strolls to the bottom of the street to see George. He has a favour to ask.

As usual George is seated at the kitchen table, the living-room being the permanent preserve of his thirteen-year-old daughter Imelda, and the television. The kitchen is a mess, the table obscured by books, papers and opened mail, and a bunch of dried flowers has dropped its leaves onto the floor where they crackle underfoot. The small patch of the table that remains bare is smeared with grease and crumbs and there is a coffee cup sprouting mould on a low shelf near the door, alongside a motley collection of ceramic urns coated in dust. The urns belonged to George's wife, Miriam, who died of breast cancer three years ago.

Imelda, a stocky, muscular girl with a dry wit and spiky black hair (the image of George), is rinsing something in the sink, though she is clearly not about to wash up. Someone must do it occasionally, and Lindsay wonders if they toss a coin once a week. He guesses that they eat well, for George is a good cook. One night he had invited them to dinner and Kirsten complimented him on the osso bucco, though the conditions in which they ate it were pretty much as they are now and Imelda had bickered with her father all the way through the meal, coming in and out of the kitchen in a sullen rage arising from some obscure but intimate dispute that had been underway before the arrival of their guests. The symbiotic testiness of father and daughter was unexpectedly touching, perhaps because it conjured up the absent woman whose photograph still hangs above the fridge.

He remembers the period of Miriam's illness, and how the day before she came home from hospital for the last time, one of her friends had dug up the overgrown patch of front garden and filled it with flowering plants in reds and yellows and white, so that the little patch sang its colour into the grey street. Kirsten had been particularly moved by this. Did she or Lindsay have a friend, she wondered aloud, who would do such a thing for them?

When her mother died, Imelda cut those of the blooms she liked best and pressed them between the pages of her father's heaviest books. Lindsay remembers two elephantine antique volumes of the work of Fichte (George liked to rummage in antiquarian bookshops) that had been especially favoured.

George looks up. 'What are you doing here, Herr Professor?'

'I have a favour to ask.'

'Uh-oh. I think we'd better have a drink.' He gets up to open a bottle of red, but is fazed for a while by his inability to find a corkscrew amidst the mess. For a moment he stands in the middle of the squalid kitchen with a look of complete bewilderment, and then it occurs to him that he might have left the missing implement by his bed.

While he is absent Lindsay tries not to notice the sticky food stains on the floor, or the dust and stray crumbs in every corner. The disorder of the room makes him feel ill at ease, almost physically uncomfortable.

George returns flourishing the corkscrew and over the next hour they drink their way through a cleanskin of red, in the course of which Lindsay finds himself drifting into a confidence.

'Something funny is happening with Kirsten,' he begins. 'She's stopped talking about having a baby.' Thinking, How like her to work herself up to fever pitch over an issue and then suddenly make a right-hand turn without signalling.

'She's being strategic, giving you a rest.'

'How did you and Miriam decide to have Imelda?'

'I can't remember. I think I might have wanted to more than Mim. I don't really remember. Some things you don't think about, some things you just do.'

'You think so?'

'I think spontaneity is the key to being sane.'

'You must be joking.'

George cackles into his glass. 'I think I detect a note of world-weariness,' he says. 'We need another bottle.'

For a time, in the ebb and flow of their conversation, Lindsay forgets why he came, and then it returns to him. 'You remember I told you I'm buying Kirsten a dog?'

'I do recall some such plan.'

'Well, in a few weeks I'm going to hire a car on a Saturday and drive down the coast to collect the little beast, and I was wondering if I could park it here overnight.'

'The dog?'

'Yes, the dog. I want to give it to Kirsten on the Sunday morning over a champagne breakfast.'

George stares at him.

'Of course, I'd provide everything. Dogfood, a box to sleep in, I suppose. Whatever.'

'I sincerely hope I'm not expected to walk it.'

Lindsay grins. 'I'm confident it can survive twenty-four hours without exercise, though I'm not so sure about you.' And he tells George about the dog show, expounding on his theory of the canine as an ideal form that humans can never hope to attain. At which point Imelda comes into the room, breathing smoke.

'You took my disc out of the computer again.'

'I've told you not to leave it in there all night.'

'So where did you put it this time, George?'

'It's on the fucking desk. Why don't you just look, for Christ's sake?'

Suddenly George is morose, and begins to yell at Imelda above the smash-and-grab level of volume from the TV that blares down the hallway.

Time to go.

His own house when he reaches it is dark, which can only mean that Kirsten has gone to bed early. He turns on the light in the kitchen and sees that, uncharacteristically, she has not bothered to clear away. The newspaper is strewn across the middle of the table, abandoned half read, and a bag of vegetables has been dumped carelessly, the eggplant spilling out onto the floor.

10

Each day now is like a long inhalation, the mental and emotional equivalent of holding her breath. And yet, within her body, something is beginning to give, like a slow tide receding from a warm, deep lagoon.

And then, to her relief, she is granted an amnesty (or so she thinks of it) when Lindsay departs for Sydney to attend a conference, and at the same time visit his mother.

Five days alone. Five days to marshal her thoughts. Five days in which to make a decision. This is it, Kirsten, she tells herself. You can procrastinate no longer.

The first night, then. It's just after six when she gets home to an empty house, and what she feels is a small rush of panic, imagining for an instant her life alone here as a single mother, she and her child braided into some sweet, dark cocoon. But alone and unprotected.

Unprotected? What is she thinking of? It's not like her to think in this way. When has she ever needed anyone to protect her?

Later that evening Lindsay rings and they have a desultory conversation. Can he hear the deception, the fake cheerfulness in her voice?

When at last he rings off, she is unnerved. I need a drink, she thinks, a long cold vodka and lime, but when she opens the cupboard where she keeps the vodka, a pile of old cookbooks spills out onto the floor. What disarray! No wonder they collapsed. For a long time she has been neglecting them, large books stacked askew on top of small ones, with recipes that have been ripped from newspapers and magazines tufting out at every angle, squashed between the pages of expensive picture books or crumpled into a corner of the cupboard, creased and torn and yellowing with age. Something that has been yanked on impulse from the garish gloss of a cheap lift-out now looks like an archival document; something carelessly handwritten on a scrap of office paper has the appearance of ancient parchment. And it occurs to her as she bends to gather the spillage that everything she looks at seems now to have two realities, the one she has taken for granted for years and the one that is latent.

She reaches into the cupboard to extract a thick black exercise book with stiff covers that lies on the bottom of the shelf, and as she attempts to slide it out from under the bigger books on top, the entire collection collapses. Swearing softly, she kneels to tidy up the mess, but there are too many bits and pieces scattered across the worn brown linoleum for her to collect in one go, so she clears a space on the mat and sits cross-legged, thinking, in an absentminded way, that she will sort them, and she will do it right now. She cannot go on living with this mess.

She glances down, and beside her knee is a recipe for chocolate cake that her mother sent her when she first left home. It's part of a letter, typed in an ink that is crude and uneven, thick on some lines, pale almost to the point of unreadability on others. It must have been an old typewriter ribbon. 'My dearest girl,' she reads, 'I have been working all day on making up curtains for the new sunroom. You wouldn't believe how it has transformed the house. Now at least the light comes in and we have a place in the sun to sit . . .'

At this she begins to cry, a few tears dropping with surprising suddenness onto the crumpled letter. Her mother is dead these five years and never more missed than now. 'Have children when you're ready,' Freda advised, 'my generation had no choice.' Or, in speaking of her youth, 'I enjoyed my job and I might never have had kids if I'd had the freedom of young people today.' And yet she had doted on her only daughter. When Kirsten was living in London her mother had sent her a box packed full with

Christmas food, as if she were a refugee in a camp, or in gaol; as if she were in some remote outpost of civilisation and not at the centre of European affluence; as if there could be only one true source of nourishment, and that the maternal breast. The thought of the Christmas hamper makes her smile, and she reaches up and puts the letter on the bench above her. She will read the rest later. Now she must do something about this mess on the floor. She will get out the scissors and some glue, and paste all the desserts into one notebook, all the soups into another, and so on. For once in her life she'll be methodical.

She works at the kitchen table. The books she stacks neatly on the cupboard shelf in ascending order of height and weight and then she sorts through the litter of torn-out magazine recipes, screwing into a ball those she knows she will never use again (if ever she did): time-consuming confections, preposterous combinations of ingredients, recipes for chicken soup that take all day, anything with gorgonzola, anything that assumes a Tuscan garden, or indeed any garden at all.

An hour later she has finished the task and by now, though still faintly nauseous, she is hungry. In the fridge there are some noodles with ginger, and after she has microwaved them she grasps a half-full bottle of wine left on the bench and carries the bowl upstairs with the intention of eating out on the balcony at the rear. About the wine she is ambivalent: if she is going to have

the baby she should not be drinking. If on the other hand...
In any case, it's only one glass.

In the bedroom she pauses to look for a shawl, and then she
unlocks the french doors that open onto the balcony. Here she
can sit and gaze out across the terraced rooftops to the horizon
line beyond, a fine blue haze above a rim of pink, breathtaking in
its delicacy. At this moment she is alive to an almost mundane
beauty, and if she could deliver herself from time she might be
content – that is, if her body were not locked into a sick and disorienting momentum that every day takes her further and further
from her old self. And a question, an odd question, spins into her
head. Whose body is this? This is not *my* body, not any more.
Her old body was easy; it never failed her. Though she endured
painful lapses in morale from time to time, though her mind was
feeble or thoughtlessly impulsive, her body was a fine-tuned
engine that could stride out ahead of the pack, any time, any
place. 'You're built for child-bearing,' her mother used to say,
'you'll have no trouble.' But she was wrong. In the past few weeks
she has turned into a sickly thing, a limp dish-rag; a reaching,
heaving, gagging lump with not enough wherewithal to wash her
greasy hair. And for the first time in her life she has lost the appetite for sex; she can't bear the thought of it, or the smell or touch
of her husband. Though she still loves the look of him, it's only
from a distance, and when he rears above her, with his big-boned

hips and wide buttocks, or encloses her with his sweaty, hulking chest, it's . . .

It's impossible.

Some inner part of her is being annihilated, but slowly, painfully, by attrition. Perhaps for good. And who or what will come out the other side? It's not just a question of how Lindsay will react – how will she, Kirsten, deal with this? How will this body, this once reliable body, deal with it? Supposing she has the baby – what will be left of her after the momentous release of birth? For the past few days she has experienced intermittent terror at the thought that she might soon cease to be the person she once was. And what would this mean? It would be so simple to short-circuit all her fears by having an abortion, but just lately the very vibration of that word brings on one of two reactions, depending on her mood. Either she begins to burn with a defensive hatred, or she falls into silent and hysterical sadness.

If she does not make up her mind soon, her willed self, the sane one, will fall away and she will be exposed, a two-headed madwoman lashed to the prow of a ship, a human figurehead sailing into the storm.

Where did that image come from? Even the way she thinks has changed. She can sit now, as she has been sitting here for the past forty minutes, and daydream . . .

And how soothing it is here in the evening dusk, the leafy

boughs of the old plane tree fluttering at the edge of her vision. How rare to sit becalmed alone in the ripening dark. When in the evening the nausea goes she is left with something else, a lethargy she's never felt before, a not unpleasant sense of drift, of hovering in the moment . . .

But now she must go inside. Possessed by a strange sense of some other self, she rises, and glancing back over her shoulder at the night skyline she gathers up her shawl. Inside, she stands for a moment, alert and still, enlarged by a peculiar feeling of readiness.

Within the house, every gesture of her evening ritual seems to come to her now in slow motion: the bolting of the back door downstairs, the rinsing of her bowl in the sink, the climb back upstairs to the bathroom, the thick spread of cream to remove her makeup, the warm towel across her skin, the languid brushing of her teeth, the lifting of the lavatory lid, the methodical folding of her clothes, and, at last, the drawing back of the bedcovers and the turning out of the light. Mercifully, since Lindsay called, the phone hasn't rung all evening. Though tired, she is at first unable to sleep. Lying there in a state of alert relaxation, from downstairs she can hear the exhalations of the old fridge, an ancient Whirlpool that lets out a long, slow, rumbling whirr as if it were breathing. At last she dozes, drifting in and out of some state on the edge of sleep, until, glancing at the luminous alarm clock, she sees that already it is almost two a m. Enough, she says to herself, and turning onto her right side, falls into a deep sleep.

And dreams that she is on a train, travelling across a desert plain. The train is an old-fashioned one, with wood panelling, red velvet seats and windows of engraved glass. The journey is long, monotonous and surreal, until, when the train is some distance across the plain, a black man, tall and thin, comes into her compartment and sits facing her. A meal appears on the fold-up table between them — a large, live duck on a silver platter. But they do not eat. Instead they embrace, locking together in an effortless union, entirely without agitation or lust.

And then she is somewhere else, no longer on the train but alone and buffeted by a raucous mob on the streets of a small walled city that stands high on the edge of an escarpment. The mob is panicking, surging along the flagstone streets because floodwaters are rising behind it. She hears someone call her name, and sees her black friend from the train standing on a low rooftop nearby. He is holding out his hand, and grasping him by the wrist, she climbs up onto the roof beside him. 'Up there,' he says, pointing, and he leads her up a wooden stairway to a rampart that runs along the top of a high wall. This wall is built of dark red brick and drops from the edge of the escarpment down to the desert plain below. Once up on the rampart she becomes aware that all the while she has been carrying a baby, a plump little cherub like something out of a painting, with only a wisp of fine gauze around its waist. Scarcely has she time to react to this, however, when her black guide beckons her to the edge. 'Within an hour, the flood waters will rise to the height of the rampart,' he says, 'but the wall is strong enough to contain them. All you have to do is climb down to the plain and you will be safe.'

But all she can see is the sheer face of the wall, and her mind dissolves in a panic.

'I'll go first,' he says, 'and show you how it's done.'

That's all very well, she thinks, but you don't have the baby.

But already he is braced against the edge, his head pointing to the earth. Arms and legs splayed outwards in a cruciform, he seems to find invisible finger- and toe-holds, and she sees that he is like a giant insect, labouring against the surface of the wall. And oh, the agony of his descent. All the way down he screams with the torment of it, and his pain is a vibration that drums against her skin so that she closes her eyes and cannot bear to look. But at last she must look, and peering over the edge she sees that, despite everything, slowly, inexorably, he is making his way towards the base, and that gravity does not destroy him. And she knows then that she too can do this, but only at a cost, and the cost is her excruciating pain and terror. *My God, I am going to have to do this, I am going to have to endure this torment.* But in that instant, she knows that she will do it; there is only the pain and the pain is finite, and when the pain is over she and the baby will be safe. Hoisting the infant onto her back, she clasps its hands around her neck. Then, lying prostrate, with her chin jutting out over the edge of the rampart, she splays her fingers taut against the wall.

'Hold on,' she calls to the baby.

Headlong they begin their descent.

When she opens her eyes, she can hear the birds outside her window. Light is beginning to show at the edges of the blind. In a state of half-wakefulness she looks up at the ceiling and sees a mirage of the wall looming above her. She has done it; she has got to the bottom. She is safe.

On the long drive to work she is in a kind of relieved trance, which lingers for most of the morning. In her lunch break she goes for a stroll down the grassy bank of the hill, past the cottages, each with its vegetable garden, past the recreation centre, the basketball courts and the school block. At the creek she turns and walks back along a wide avenue of Cootamundra wattles. Beside the raked gravel, fat black crows peck in the grass while the feathery blue foliage of the trees dances at the edge of her vision.

All day the dream stays with her, the residue of some other world, some unexpected and baffling transfiguration of desire.

Driving home along the freeway in the late afternoon sunlight, she realises that something is changing, something is slipping away. You go along in a certain groove in your life – one reality that you think is *the* reality – and then one morning you see that, imperceptibly, the field has changed, the energy has shifted. Some slippage has occurred in the tectonic plates of the psyche and what had seemed firm and fixed and literal and plain – and reassuringly dull, even – is shot through with a new electrical charge, so that all your atoms seem to vibrate on a different frequency and the landscape is flooded with new potential.

Is this how it will be from now on?

The next morning, in the middle of a meeting, she gets up and goes to the lavatory and there, on her pants, is a cluster of small brown bloodstains. Oh no, *oh no*. It's been so little time since her pregnancy was confirmed and now this.

Perhaps, then, she will miscarry, and the decision will be made for her. She won't have to tell him anything.

Back in her office, dialling Lloyd's surgery, her heart is in free fall and she feels sick, only this time it's a different kind of nausea, a vertigo of loss. Something is about to slip away from her, to leak from the ocean of her dreams. And here is his receptionist whose plausible, singsong voice at this moment is as irritating as sandpaper against the ear, and she's saying that no, doctor isn't in, he's been called away to a delivery, and she should ring again later in the afternoon, around four.

Around four!

That afternoon at four on the dot she rings, and when she is put through to Lloyd – when she hears his low, soothing voice on the other end of the phone – she is afraid to open her mouth for fear of bursting into tears. Lloyd enquires carefully after her symptoms. Then he says, 'This isn't something we should panic about just now. Come in tomorrow and we'll do an ultrasound.'

That night, Lindsay phones. His mother is fine. She had a slight fall the day after he arrived and her face was bruised, but no real harm was done and she is recovering. His paper went well, and Hartley from Michigan came up to him afterwards and expressed interest in the monograph.

'How's work?' he asks her (a sure sign that he is in a good mood).

'Fine. Marek didn't come for chess today, or yesterday either. Hasn't come for nearly a week. I thought he might be sick and rang his teacher, but she said he seems to be more with it in the classroom lately. She thinks he might have struck up a friendship with a new boy.'

'So he doesn't need you any more?'

'It would be good to think so.' How normal her voice sounds, when what she wants to do is slam down the phone, collapse onto the floor and wail. All day she has been a walking bloodstain. All day she has been unable to think of anything else. Her entire consciousness has dissolved into this mundane blot. The bloodstain looks out from her eyes, the bloodstain nestles in the crevices of her ears. There is only the bloodstain and there is nothing else. Tonight she will be a bloodstain asleep on the sheets.

The following day is Lloyd's teaching day at the hospital. At 9.10 she calls in sick and in a state of heightened apprehension drives up the long, autumnal avenue of Royal Parade where the plane trees are turning towards winter. The hospital is a vast complex, a jumble of buildings from many eras set down over four city blocks and dominated by a grand Victorian façade, but the obstetrics clinic is easily accessed from the lower ground floor of the maternity wing, though the view is unkind, looking out onto a loading zone and car park.

The anteroom is stuffy, fluorescent-lit and hung with a tall screen of pale green curtains. It's just after eleven, she has been here an hour and forty minutes and is awaiting her results.

Only minutes before, Lloyd had examined her in the adjoining consulting room, she in her usual 'consulting' position on the narrow surgical table, he in the immaculate pinstripe with the red carnation. First he had smeared her abdomen with a cold jelly and then he had run a scanning device called a transducer across and around the surface. To one side of the bed, on a stand, the screen of the ultrasound machine, like a portable television, showed a greyish white blur of smudges that made no sense to her at all. Then, abruptly, he had been called to a consultation in an adjoining room, had excused himself and asked her to dress.

Now here she is, waiting for the results, contemplating that word *transducer*, and its weirdly apposite connotations of traduce and transgression.

'What exactly is a transducer?' she had asked him.

'A device for converting the energy of one transmission system into the energy of another transmission system,' he replied, as if he were reading from a manual; as if, absorbed in the process, he had forgotten his customary bedside manner and was merely a technician, thinking aloud.

A minute ago she had attempted to pick up a magazine but she's too nervous to read. Instead she makes an inventory of the room. Opposite her is a box of children's toys and two enormous picture books, *The Children's Giant World Atlas* and *Big Book of Wild Australia*. Above them is a notice printed in bold type asking for mobile phones to be switched off. (Has she? Yes.) The chairs have blue mock-suede upholstery and on the side table is a stack of out-of-date magazines and a book entitled *Dad, Best Friend in the*

World. There is a small glass vase with yellow and white roses and in the far corner a tall plant in a tub, over eight feet high, with waxy, oval leaves of such unnatural gloss, such uniform perfection they might just as well be plastic.

Behind the partition of thin curtains she can see Lloyd's shadowy outline as he moves across the room from one side to the other, followed by a huddle of medical students. She can hear his voice and, through a gap in the curtains, see him talking now to a young woman and three young men in white coats, and they are all of them staring up at a series of images illuminated from behind on a special screen, and Lloyd is saying—she can hear him quite distinctly—'See the cyst there, quite large, but we know it to be benign. It makes no sense to remove it now, in the middle of a delicate pregnancy. It makes no sense to touch anything, or make any alteration that isn't absolutely and categorically essential to the preservation of life. The less we interfere in any pregnancy, the better. We take a conservative approach. We're here to conserve whatever is there.'

One of the students asks a question in a low, deferential voice that she can't make out. There is some more muffled discussion and then, suddenly, the curtains part and he is beside her, looking very solemn.

Instinctively she stands. Her eyes are level with the red carnation.

'Well,' he begins formally. 'The situation is this. You are bleeding because a small layer of cells is coming away from the lining of the womb in one place. But this is not significant.'

She opens her mouth, meaning to say something, but no sound comes out.

'You can think of it as a room, a perfectly sound room in which the wallpaper is peeling away just a little up in one corner. It may go on a bit longer but eventually it will stop. There's nothing to worry about.'

'What about the cyst?'

He frowns. 'Cyst?'

'I'm sorry, I could hear through the partition...'

'Oh,' he says, and smiles, 'that was someone else. Nothing to do with you at all. I'm sorry if we alarmed you.' Then he assumes his customary grave expression. 'As I said, there is really nothing to worry about. You are a pregnant woman, you are carrying a child,' and with this he puts his hand on her shoulder, 'and you are to go away now and do perfectly normal things.'

For a moment there it was almost okay, and might have remained so if he hadn't touched her, but this hand on the shoulder, this unprofessional touch, is her undoing.

'Thank you,' she rasps, and is breathless with onrushing tears.

On the way to the car park she takes a wrong turn and finds herself in a clinical green tunnel, long and narrow. Here she dissolves into heaving, silent sobs, the tunnel blurring into green fog so that she is unsighted, and scarcely knows the direction she is walking in. This is too much, this is all too much and she will have to tell him, she will tell him this minute. She can no longer carry the burden alone. When in her blur of tears she finds her way to the car park, she is at first unable to locate her car, but slumped at last in the driver's seat, she fumbles in her bag for her mobile. She will ring him, she will tell him now. She will ask him to walk down from his office and drive her home.

The phone rings and rings, and doesn't answer.

Ah, but of course. He's in Sydney. She lays her head against the steering wheel and sobs uncontrollably.

By evening she is calmer, though still resolved, rehearsing in her mind the phrases she will deploy to break the news. She sees herself drive into the great, grey car park at the airport, layered like a concrete torte. She sees herself waiting patiently in the arrival lounge (or is she pacing up and down?), greeting him as he emerges from the crowd, taking his arm warmly and smiling up into his dark brown eyes. Once they are home (of course, she will have to wait until then) she will make some tea and they will sit at the kitchen table, as they so often do, and she will say, 'Darling...'

But when on the following afternoon she collects him from

the airport, he is moody and hung-over. Down by the baggage carousel they wait and wait and still his suitcase fails to appear. 'They must have sent it on somewhere else by mistake,' she says, but Lindsay just glares into the distance and swears. Without another word, he breaks away and strides across to the baggage counter to complain, leaving her stranded.

Then, on the drive home, there is a bottleneck on the free-way from an accident – a bad one, two ambulances – and he is still irritable, grunting almost, and to himself, as if in some silent dialogue with another presence. Now and then he sighs and swears brutally, and she knows that once again his mother has upset him.

By the time they turn into their street there is a separation between them that can't be bridged.

'I'm whacked,' he says, climbing out of the car. 'I need a shower.'

Some vortex in her chest opens up and her heart falls through the floor of the car. She steadies herself against the handle of the door and takes in a long, deep breath. This isn't the right time, she thinks, I'll tell him tomorrow.

But in the morning he is unusually sluggish and stays in bed while she gets ready for work. Just before she leaves, she hesitates at the foot of the stairs and wonders if she should rouse him, but nothing about the moment feels right.

And so another day passes.

11

On the tram to work Lindsay reflects on his trip to Sydney, or more especially, the visit to his mother. He had been looking forward to seeing her, and yet once in her presence everything about their reunion put him on edge, perhaps because on the very first evening he had asked if she remembered the time they went looking for Stripe. 'Of course, I remember,' she had said. 'How could I forget *that*?' And he felt a pang of childish gratification that the occasion still held its charge for her.

But it was downhill from there. 'You made *such* a fuss,' she said, when his own recollection is of how stoical he had been. Nor could they agree on anything else about that day. He said it had been hot and windy; she said it was cool and rained. He recalled having traipsed over hills; she claimed, on the contrary, they had walked on the flat near the river. He said they had searched for two days, at which point she corrected him tersely and said, 'Three.' They could agree on nothing.

And all the rest of the time she was full of her gloomy stories. The boy up the road, with whom he had played as a child, who became an accountant and father of four, had been eating out with friends only last month and choked to death on a fishbone, there in a family restaurant overlooking the esplanade at Coogee Beach, his wife alongside him. Then there was his old schoolfriend, Michael, who had just had open-heart surgery at the age of thirty-eight. Unbeknown to him, he had been born with a minor malformation of the heart, and while having his teeth filled, some bacteria had found their way into his bloodstream and eaten away at a valve.

Every time he came home she did the same thing. Summoned up his imminent death.

It's just after two in the afternoon when he takes his only class for the day, and when he opens the door to the small lecture theatre, he enters, as if through an invisible curtain, into the distinctive sound of the day folding in on itself — a kind of lazy hum; a living, breathing torpor. This is the most difficult hour of the day to teach, the time when bodies are slumped in a slow metabolic daydreaming. The students who have had lunch are sleepy and the ones who have skipped it are irritable and restless. All through the lecture they will fidget and rustle unseen items in their bags, as if feeling blindly for a stray apple or chocolate bar. Every now and then one of them will surreptitiously slip something into their mouth, chewing quietly, self-consciously, with feigned indifference.

He steps up to the lectern, adjusts the microphone, and embarks on a brief recapitulation of where they had left off last time. Then he turns to the first page of his notes. 'The seventeenth century saw a remarkable spread of interest in scientific studies and an expansion of experimental method across a broad range of fields. This resulted in the appearance of learned societies, some independent, some supported by national and local governments, for the purpose of promoting research and providing a forum from which new discoveries could be promulgated. The members of these academies – the so-called experimental philosophers, or *virtuosi* – concerned themselves with every aspect of knowledge, most often with useful and "improving" ideas, but also with trivia and the exotic. Collections of various kinds were soon started, and every society had to have its own cabinet of curiosities – a calf with two heads, a lamb with two hearts – thus creating a demand for better methods of preservation.'

At the mention of a calf with two heads the students begin to settle. He has their attention.

'In the medical schools, too, a premium was put on permanent anatomical preparations, which contributed immeasurably to, among other things, the ability of anatomists to study the circulation of the blood.' He pauses, and picks at the top of the media console. Someone has shoved a Mars Bar wrapper into the headphone connection.

'A number of men, for the most part in Holland, became remarkably skilled in the arts of preservation. Perhaps the best known in his time was Frederik Ruysch, born 1638, Professor of Anatomy at the University of Amsterdam. Ruysch became famous for his cabinet of curiosities. One could open the doors of this huge cabinet and find almost anything that had once been alive now dead, but impeccably preserved and as near to lifelike as could be imagined. According to one biographer, writing in 1825, Ruysch brought the art of injection to such a pitch of perfection that no-one has ever been able to equal it. He succeeded in making beautiful anatomical preparations, preserving them in the most perfect state of integrity, the injected parts maintaining their consistency, plasticity and flexibility, even improving with time because the colour of the injected material rendered them more lifelike. News of such proficiency spread, and each day a small crowd of the curious would assemble in Ruysch's rooms.'

He looks up, and there in the back row is the girl, Sonia, gazing at him.

'These included eminences from all over Europe who travelled great distances to see the famed cabinet of curiosities: a torso with hermaphroditic genitals, a hand with webbed fingers, and so on. But it was the ordinary, the everyday, that evoked the strongest sentiments, and when Peter the Great was shown the embalmed body of a baby, so lifelike it seemed to smile at him, he insisted on giving it a kiss. So enchanted was the czar with this morbid infant that he expressed a desire to own it. After some haggling between Ruysch and one of the czar's courtiers, a price was settled on and the baby packed in a trunk to be transported back to St Petersburg, along with the czar's many other souvenirs.'

Already he has decided that he will confront her at the end of the lecture. Some visceral distaste has prevented him from doing so before this, but her presence here today is a spur to his commonsense.

'Now,' he continues, 'we have, in a sense, our own cabinet of curiosities, only ours are in cyberspace. Take for example the male cadaver known as Adam. In origin Adam is the convicted murderer, Joseph Paul Jernigan, who donated his body to science before being executed by barbiturate poisoning in Texas in 1993. Eighteen hundred and seventy-one wafer-thin slices were cut from the frozen body and are beamed digitally through the Internet – a microscopic surgical map of the subject's insides. In this way, from the opposite side of the world, we can have access to curiosities unimaginable to Peter the Great, although,' and here he pauses and stares directly across at Sonia, 'not being kings, we do not, as it were, get to kiss the baby.'

At the end of the lecture, when he looks for her in the corridor, like a ghost she is gone.

But the minute he opens the door to his office, there it is. Another pink envelope resting on the grey carpet. Really, this is the limit, and he will go at once to Leonie and present the evidence of this harassment. But first he will open the damn thing, since God knows what he might be accused of.

'Dear Lindsay,' he reads, 'when I look back on the past few weeks I can't tell you how mortified I am that I have allowed my stupid fantasies to inflict themselves on you, and I write now to most unreservedly apologise. Can I please ask that you return my letters and I will apply to Professor Marsden for another supervisor . . .'

Immediately he breaks into a cold sweat and slumps onto his chair. Thank God. This thing has really gotten under his skin, has niggled at him more than he realised, until now. But look how suddenly it has resolved itself, with no effort from him. In the long run this bizarre little aggravation has proved to be a demonstration of the truth of one of his gut instincts: in nine cases out of ten, if you do nothing, a situation will resolve itself.

He is so relieved that he rings George and suggests a drink.

12

Saturday morning, two days now since he returned, and still she hasn't told him. This is partly because he has scarcely been in the house, except to sleep, with a late seminar on the first evening back and then a drinking jag with George that saw him fall woozily into bed. And in that brief but critical interlude she has had a new thought. There is one more move to make. One more hurdle to jump, one more test to put herself through, and then she will know what to do.

But now she is even more withdrawn from him, and has taken to compensating for her indecision with a series of ruthless fantasies. She will deliver him an ultimatum and if he reacts badly she will leave him. She will live somewhere in a small, light-filled apartment and it will just be the two of them, mother and child. The sperm has flown to the mark: the father has served his purpose and he can be dispensed with.

These fantasies come to her like little jabs of false cognition, and then fade.

In the early afternoon, when he has gone out, she takes a tram to the largest bookstore in the city. Unfortunately it's next door to a busy arcade where the smells of fast food and frying lard catch in her nostrils and stir up that queasiness that is now mostly confined to the mornings. Still, best to come here where there is most likely the biggest selection of books in the category she is seeking and the most up-to-date publications on the new technology. Under other circumstances, she would make an appointment to discuss her options with Trinh, but Trinh is away on leave and she cannot bring herself to open up her anguish with a locum. The last locum she saw was a fresh-faced young thing of blond good looks who was roaming around suburban medical practices at odd intervals so that he could write a novel. Though he stared at her very intently, she had the idea that his mind was on other things.

The bookstore is on two levels, with nooks and crannies in which she might easily hide herself. There is a rule against taking unpurchased books into the coffee shop on the mezzanine, but she has no intention of throwing money away on a book she may have no further use for, at least not in the short-term. After browsing the shelves and finding three pregnancy guides that impress as substantial, she tucks them under her arm and jogs confidently up the stairs to the mezzanine. Here she can read in comfort and return the books to their shelves on the way out. Who will notice? Lindsay would be scandalised at this mild breach of book protocol but he is a pedant. She on the other hand can see no harm in it; if she spills her drink on the book, she will of course pay for it.

For just over an hour she sits and sips at ginger tea, for her nausea, and reads her way through the clinical prose of the guides. Here are the facts set out plainly. She is thirty-six, an ageing mother-to-be, and there is a higher than average risk that the foetus she is carrying will not be normal; it may have an extra chromosome, or spina bifida. What if she were to go through the agonies of confessing to Lindsay her unilateral action on that night of the duck – along with all its possible consequences, not least the possibility of permanent damage to their relationship – when she might, anyway, have to abort a defective child?

She opens the first of the books at the index and scans to C, looking for chorionic villus sampling, or CVS, a delicate procedure wherein a five-centimetre needle is inserted through the lining of the womb to withdraw a sample of placental tissue. She knows about this test because one of her colleagues had one only the year before, and now, approaching ten weeks into her pregnancy, is the moment to have it. Within days she would know the result. Of course, if the results were in any way positive, she would abort. But there was also a risk: the same degree of risk to a healthy baby as there is of her carrying an unhealthy one.

There is also an amniocentesis test, which is not as risky to the foetus but which can only be carried out later in the pregnancy. This would mean that, if the test were positive and she wanted to end the pregnancy, by then it would be too late to abort and she would have to be induced and give birth to a dead baby. More to the point, right now, is the fact that she would have to delay having the test for another five weeks.

Too long to wait.

'The chorionic villi,' she reads, 'finger-like outgrowths on the edge of the chorion, are genetically identical to the foetus. They develop earlier than the amniotic fluid, so examining a sample of the chorionic villi will provide valuable information in regard to your baby's genes and chromosomes before amniocentesis is possible.'

Good. The sooner the better.

The primary group in need of CVS, she learns, are those deemed to be at risk of Downs Syndrome. Other defects that can be detected through CVS include abnormalities of haemoglobin, such as sickle-cell disease or thalassaemia. Here the underlying problem is an enzyme deficiency. A direct enzyme analysis is carried out on the chorionic tissue, and this can yield a diagnosis within two days. The use of CVS can also detect a number of single-gene disorders, such as cystic fibrosis, muscular dystrophy, Huntington's chorea and haemophilia.

Oh yes, and the baby's sex.

It's all so detached and rigorous and logical that she feels like an account executive who has just received a briefing on a small regional economy. The irony is that she is about to acquire a whole lot of knowledge about a child that her husband doesn't even know exists.

She reads on. The CVS test is carried out under ultrasound control, usually between ten and twelve weeks of pregnancy and before the amniotic sac has completely filled the uterine cavity.

There are two approaches that can be utilised, the trans-cervical method and the trans-abdominal. The latter procedure is carried out after an ultrasound scan has determined the position of the foetus and the placenta. The doctor uses ultrasound to pass a long needle through the abdominal wall, which has been numbed with anaesthetic, and then into the uterus. A small amount of placental tissue is withdrawn.

Kirsten scans down the page for a reference to the risk factor. 'The risk of miscarriage for CVS is approximately two per cent higher than for spontaneous miscarriage.' Two per cent? That sounds reasonable. She'd be prepared to settle for that. She sits back and pours herself another cup of tea.

The last of her books is by Sheila Kitzinger. Kitzinger is famous. Kitzinger issues a warning. Although the CVS test has been hailed as a breakthrough because it can be performed earlier, there is a greater risk of losing the baby. According to Kitzinger, there is a relatively high incidence of infection, bleeding and miscarriage following CVS. In her view, the risks outweigh the benefits. Some women, it seems, have 'nervous' wombs and this can create problems. It has been known for a baby to be born with a nick on its cheeks where the needle has scratched the surface of the foetal skin. And there is another problem — apart, that is, from the insult of the method. Unlike the amniocentesis test, CVS cannot detect spina bifida.

But she would have to wait up to five weeks longer to have the amnio! *Impossible.*

In Kitzinger's text there is a diagram showing a foetus on its knees, face down in a position of supplication, with a giant needle poised above its head. Kirsten makes a wry face. Really, she thinks, the illustration is ill chosen. Are they trying to scare me? She will ignore this. She has heard that Kitzinger is a zealot, a fanatic about natural childbirth (and all that this implies). As an afterthought she looks up morning sickness in the index.

'Morning sickness may start to lessen from eleven weeks. Women who experience this are less likely than others to have miscarriages. This can be a cheering thought.'

This can be an ironic thought, given what she is about to embark on, the miscarriage she may be about to precipitate.

'Kirsten?'

Shit, it's George Markides. He plonks his heavy frame on the chair next to her as, with feigned languor, she leans across the open page so that her elbow obscures the diagram. But the books beside her teacup, spines facing towards him and hence eminently readable, have already given her away.

George is dipping his chin and staring over the rim of his glasses in an expression of comic abashment. 'Jesus, Kirsten,' he mutters.

She looks away.

And then, 'You haven't told him, have you?'

'It's none of your business, George.' And she stands abruptly, leaving the books open on the table behind her.

Later that afternoon, after some initial nervousness, she feels both physically and mentally brighter. George will say nothing to Lindsay and meanwhile she has a plan. It's always a relief to have a plan. She has a handle on her destiny and soon all will be resolved, one way or the other. All she has to do is get through the next few days. She considers suggesting to Lindsay that they stroll up to their favourite Thai restaurant for a meal, but thinks better of it. They would have to talk and she is not up to face-to-face chitchat. Instead she will suggest a walk. If he doesn't agree to this, she will go alone.

As it happens, he likes the idea.

Once outside on the pavement she takes his arm, as if to close the gap that for weeks has lain between them, and he looks at her sardonically, with raised eyebrows.

'What?' she says.

'Nothing.'

For several blocks they stroll on, past the small front gardens with their climbing tea roses, their giant Chinese lantern bushes, their dark-leaf camellia trees and wispy seraglio ferns.

At last they turn the corner into a street lined with old plane trees, and suddenly they are on the fringe of a small crowd that is clustered along the footpath, and spilling out untidily onto the road. A passing car swerves, blaring its horn aggrievedly.

'Oh, look,' says Kirsten, rather too brightly, 'an auction. Isn't it a bit late in the day?'

'Any hour of daylight will do,' says Lindsay drily. 'We're in the middle of a real-estate boom.'

The house is a small Federation bungalow with a big red AUCTION board posted on its white picket fence. It's almost dusk now and the lights of the house have been switched on for effect: there are lace curtains at the windows, and in the tiny front garden a shiny black coach lamp on a column with a bright electric bulb. Up and down the street neighbours have come out into their gardens to stare from a distance.

The front door is open and they make their way up the path. Lindsay is always interested to look at other people's renovations but Kirsten hangs back. 'I'll wait for you here,' she says.

In front of the genteel fleur-de-lis spikes of the cast-iron fence, the estate agent is directing his lieutenants, younger men in navy blazers and red ties with the agency's logo fashioned into a tie pin. On the top step by the gate the auctioneer surveys the scene and waits for the nod. This is not a top-end-of-the-market agency, and the auctioneer has a slightly seedy look. His cheeks are pockmarked, his hair hangs below his collar, and he tugs at the jacket of his dark, double-breasted pinstripe suit, the trousers of which are too long and hang down over the built-up heels of his scuffed black boots. In his hand is a document, a long list of regulations which he begins to read in a hoarse, hectoring voice.

As if in competition, a cool southerly springs up; it swirls the leaves along the gutter and around the feet of the onlookers, flapping the pages of the auctioneer's document so that he loses his place and has to joke awhile with the crowd until he regains it.

The atmosphere at house auctions is always the same, tense and expectant. But this twilight auction is weirdly festive, though with a melancholy undertow, the sense of an ending rather than a beginning. It's like being in the train of a funeral crowd, towards the rear, where those people who knew the deceased only slightly whisper to one another in asides as they half listen to the cleric's ritual phrases wafting on the wind. 'Property Act of 1900 . . . historic Ramsay estate . . . capital gain in the last five years . . . tastefully renovated . . . period charm . . . state-of-the-art kitchen . . . European laundry . . . ducted heating and alarm . . . private courtyard for contemporary alfresco dining . . . lifestyle facilities nearby . . .' Until at last the preliminaries are done with and a burly man in track pants and thongs opens the bidding with a curt nod. Just in front of him and to one side is a young couple, taut with nerves, who offer a counter-bid. The husband, expensively dressed in a casual way, has the air of a man both anxious and arrogant; beside him his diminutive wife stares up at the auctioneer with a strained smile, like a child awaiting the bestowal of an uncertain gift. The fat man in thongs, old enough to be their father, gives another curt nod of the head and so it goes, one pair of wills against another, and all the while the onlookers are in thrall to the contest. There are moments when the crowd emits a collective gasp, and then, after a prolonged hesitation during which it appears as if the young husband may be about to throw in the towel, the crowd becomes uncannily still, like a large beast holding its breath. When at last the husband nods his head to further up the ante, the crowd breaks into relieved applause (for he is clearly their favourite).

The wife just grows more and more tense, her face furrowed and grim. She has a light cardigan around her shoulders which she adjusts nervously as she stands on her toes and cranes her neck to follow the auctioneer. And all the while a bullish young agent is moving among the crowd — his hair slicked down, his cheeks flushed — back and forth, back and forth between the warring parties, like an official urger, until the moment when at last the auctioneer cries out with a hoarse, half-strangled cry, 'Are you all done, are you all done? Are you silent now?'

And indeed, for a moment, they are all silent. The street is still. Even the traffic seems to have vanished.

'Sold!' The auctioneer extends his pinstriped arm in salute to the man in thongs, who nods again and adjusts the sagging waistband of his pants.

Lindsay looks over at the young wife, who is braced, her mouth open as if in shock, and then there is a shuffle at his elbow and a soft thump. The woman beside him has fallen to the ground in a faint. Kirsten kneels quickly beside her and lifts her head with one hand, while with the other she tugs at the woman's skirt which has risen indecorously above her knees. At that moment, Lindsay feels an uncanny presence. Instinctively he turns and looks behind him. And sees Sonia on the nature strip just a few metres away. She is standing at the edge of a shadowy plane tree, staring at him. How waif-like she looks in the dark, poignant almost, and when she meets his gaze with a startled stare he finds that his body is flushed with a kind of erotic sympathy that takes him by surprise, even as she starts and steps backwards into the shadows, leaving behind her a whiff of some musky animal scent.

On the walk home Kirsten is unusually quiet, which is fine with him. They eat an omelette in front of the television and say little. After a while, Kirsten dozes off on the couch.

Later, upstairs in the bedroom, they undress in silence, and when he offers her a nightcap she demurs. He returns to the kitchen to make himself one, and pads heavily around the scuffed lino, barefoot, almost stepping on a big black beetle that waddles away from his tread and under the fridge. When he has poured himself a slug of Scotch he wanders into the front parlour to slouch in front of the late news, absorbing as panacea the bizarre facticity of the SBS weather forecasts: ... *a warm front continuing across Zimbabwe and thunderstorms easing in the Congo basin* ...

By now he is in a state of irritable arousal, and the longer he sits there, the more restless he becomes. The house seems unbearably stale and stuffy, pervaded by a rank but airless humidity, a kind of invisible weight that hangs in the air. Another drink and then another, and he is sitting in a fug of his own discontent. What he needs is a shower, a long, hot torrent of water, but it's late and Kirsten by now will be sleeping. Well, then, he will shower downstairs where he is unlikely to wake her, and he pads out to the squalid alcove beside the laundry, the one they so rarely use and which will be torn down in the renovations. But here the water pressure is even more feeble than upstairs, so that after much minute adjustment of the tap the best he can manage is a scalding drizzle. Steam fogs up the seedy plastic surround of the shower bay, creased with grime, and he begins to feel as if not only his body but his brain is sodden. He is tumid and heavy, his vision involuted. The blood pounds through his body to every pore, every extremity — a hot flush of unseeing, of sightlessness, like one of those marine creatures in a rockpool, all blind gelatinous head and an infinite number of fine, wavering feelers.

Still half damp he lumbers upstairs and slumps into bed. How is it possible to feel so heavy and yet so wide awake? He puts an arm out to embrace his sleeping wife but she sighs and pushes him away. He tries again, slipping his hand in under her loose top and rubbing her nipple, but she flinches and shrugs her body out from under his cusping arm, squirming away to the edge of the bed. Is she asleep, or only pretending to be? The build-up of energy at the base of his spine is unbearable.

At last, around two in the morning, he falls into sleep, only to dream that he is wandering alone through a strange house as it is being auctioned, and he can hear the auctioneer ranting in the front garden, tramping up and down, up and down among the tall weeds and shouting hoarsely into a high wind. Down a low hallway and passing by many rooms he comes at last to a dim, old-fashioned parlour at the rear of the house. And there in the middle of the room is a wooden cradle, and inside the cradle is a baby, only it's Sonia, lying naked on a white sheet and looking up at him with her arms extended, like the infant in the nativity. What are *you* doing here? he thinks, but before he can receive an answer he wakes with a painful erection.

For most of Sunday he is at Monash, running a workshop for teachers on a proposed new scheme to teach philosophy in high schools. He returns in the late afternoon to find Kirsten asleep upstairs. When she gets up she seems vague, and slouches around the kitchen barefoot, assembling dinner in a sullen and distracted manner. They eat in front of the television, and say little.

The next morning, watching his wife drive off, half resentful, half anxious for her, Lindsay experiences a jittery apprehension that they both, individually and alone, have been caught up in some micro-dust of malign particles, some eddy of negative charge.

Striding along the trash-strewn street, he has the feeling that this could be a difficult day. He wishes it were a day crammed with meetings and classes, but in fact he has nothing scheduled, nothing but his research, and he can scarcely conceive of sitting still for even an hour.

As he unlocks the door of his room, the phone begins to ring. He almost snatches at the receiver. 'Yes.'

'It's Sandra Schokmann here.'

Ah, the dog.

'You can come and get him whenever you like.'

He hesitates. 'I haven't a car.'

'That's all right. Most cab companies have a dog taxi. If you give them half an hour's notice, they can usually manage it.'

A dog taxi? She can't be serious. And then the phone rings a second time, and it's Kirsten. She's hesitant, and seems to have no particular reason for calling.

'What's up?' he asks.

'I don't know, I'm tired, I'm behind on everything...' Her voice trails away. He waits patiently for her to finish her sentence, but at the end of the phone there is only silence.

'Take a few days off,' he says. It occurs to him that then he could have the car. But she'd want to know what it was for, and that would spoil the surprise. And the surprise, he reminds himself ruefully, is the point of it all.

'Take it easy,' he tells her.

13

When Kirsten puts the case for a CVS test to Lloyd it is no surprise to her that he is reluctant to agree to the procedure. He is the conservator. It goes against the grain.

'It isn't necessary. The odds are overwhelmingly in your favour.'

She knew he would say that. Hadn't she overheard his lecture on conserving and non-interference?

'First of all, you're not very old. You're only thirty-six, and at that age there is still only an infinitesimal chance of abnormality. The higher risk begins at around thirty-eight, but statistically, the figures for above forty are the most significant.'

She glares at him. He is splitting hairs.

'Secondly, there is a risk to the child you are carrying. Having come this far, would you want to take such a risk?'

Is it that he sits there so dour and impassive? That touch of compassion when he put his hand on her shoulder in the green-curtained anteroom has all but faded from her mind. He is giving her a line, like a stern Jesuit reacting to heresy. He is precise, patriarchal and certain. Yes, he is very certain. And isn't certainty exactly what you want in a doctor? So why isn't she reassured?

'It's a risk either way, isn't it?'

'Yes, that's true, but one of these risks is a natural one. We are often happier in ourselves if we relax and let Nature take its course.'

'Then we wouldn't do vaccinations.' She does not like his tone; he's beginning to patronise her.

'Ah, now, there we are dealing with a different set of statistics. Much higher risk factors.'

She sits there nodding to herself. Why should she trust nature? Look what nature does to others. Nature creates these deformities in the first place. Nature fails; nature goes haywire; nature is not predictable, is capricious and unjust.

'I'm willing to take that risk. It's my decision, surely.'

He sighs. 'Have you discussed it with your husband?'

'As far as he's concerned, it's my decision.'

'I must tell you it is my professional view that this test is not necessary.'

At that moment it is on the tip of her tongue to say she will go elsewhere if she has to, when suddenly he capitulates. With one sharp nod of the head he picks up the phone and puts in train the necessary steps. The procedure is so dangerous that only specialist operators are able to perform it.

'Would you like to see a genetic counsellor before making a final decision?' he asks.

'No.' The emphatic way she says this displeases him, she can tell.

The appointment is made.

That night she lies awake in her bed, cocooned in an invisible blanket of anguish. In Lloyd's rooms it had all been so simple. His very disapproval had made the test seem imperative. Tonight she's not so sure. Tonight she feels as if she is the captive of some strange, hurtling logic.

14

So now the moment has arrived.

The room is painted a warm, grey colour and this is reassuring. Still, she is extremely tense, is on high alert. She is telling herself the same things, over and over. The room is clinical but not in an unpleasant way. It is stripped bare of the superfluous but the grey of the walls is warm and stylish. A minute ago she had changed in the anteroom into a pale green surgical wrap, and on the wall there was a framed print of brightly coloured fluorescent tubes arranged in a symmetrical pattern—a faux skyscraper that glowed. Even the flower arrangement in the foyer had spare, ikebana lines: grey wood, orange flower, purple leaf. She is alert to these details; she is always alert to rooms, to what might confine her at any particular moment.

The doctor who is to perform the procedure is young, not much older than she. He introduces himself as Michael Franks.

Now she is being directed up onto the surgical bed by the doctor's assistant, Merrill. Merrill is in her early thirties (she would guess) and has her chestnut-brown hair pulled back in a bun. Her face is thin and fine-boned, and the very fineness of the bones suggests intense concentration. Merrill, Franks, the surgical bed, the machine—the whole room vibrates at a low level with waves of precision.

Franks, casually dressed in an open-necked shirt with the sleeves rolled neatly to the elbows, is reading from a clipboard. He looks up. 'Dr Lloyd has explained all this to you?'

'Yes.' Sitting up on the high surgical bed, she feels preternaturally calm. Her palms are not damp, her pulse is not racing, she has entered some zone of necessary composure, and she has done this by shutting down all other systems but the one that observes.

Franks begins to talk her through it. First the cold gel on the abdomen and then the metal transducer. Merrill is at action stations in front of the machine, is looking up at the blank grey screen, waiting for the first images to appear – and suddenly there they are, the same surging black and white masses of fuzzy resolution she had seen previously with Lloyd, the same amorphousness and lack of clarity. How on earth will they be able to pinpoint the exact spot by looking at this?

The exact spot to insert a supersize syringe!

The screen is ghosted by a white webbed measuring graph and bordered with luminous green numbers. Within this modest frame she is being calibrated; she is being framed and graphed and sonically mapped.

Franks administers a local anaesthetic through an ordinary syringe and then turns away to consult with Merrill for the short time that it takes for the drug to work. For two, maybe three minutes they confer in a terse commentary over the image on the screen. Here is the placenta, here the (she doesn't catch the word – anterior?) wall of the uterus. They speak quietly, though not so quietly she can't hear them; they would not want her to think they are concealing anything. It's just that they are wholly focused on the screen, absorbed and – and something else. Now she recognises it. *They* are tense. They are specialists, they would have done this countless times, but they are tense. They must get this right to within a fraction of a millimetre, because if they get it wrong and the foetus is damaged, all blame is on them.

Franks moves a few paces towards her on the bed. He looks at her and smiles (it's a professional smile, but nice), then glances back to the image on the screen, looks down at her abdomen, back at the screen, down again, then mutters something to Merrill, who writes it down. His eyes move in a measured way, almost in a rhythm; she can feel all the atoms in his body coming together, closer and closer. Or is it the atoms in her own body she can feel? At this moment their atoms feel interconnected, hers, Franks' and Merrill's, looped and threaded together by the machine, all in a tight mass of concentration. But *she* is not tight. Oh no, she is light, so light it's as if she is floating a centimetre above the bed.

Now Franks has an ordinary marker pen in his hand and he places a small black cross on one side of her abdomen. 'We're going to go in here,' he says, and with a studied lack of ceremony turns away from her and then back, only this time with the monstrous needle in his left hand.

This is her first thought: He's left-handed.

'It's a beauty, isn't it?' he says, and then, almost to himself, 'It's made more than one expectant father pass out, I can tell you.' He glances across to Merrill with a half-smile. Merrill the grim doesn't smile back. Her naturally stern expression is set now in a mask.

'I'm going to need you to stay very still,' he continues. 'If for some reason you feel you have to move, signal to me immediately by raising your right hand. Okay?'

She nods. Will she look? No, she will not look, she will stare at the wall beyond his head – the room in a subdued light, and all around her the walls are that nice warm grey, and yes, she really does like this colour and perhaps when they do the renovations she'll paint the walls of the kitchen in this shade. The machine to the right of her bed is also grey, gunmetal grey, except for the shimmering screen with its rhythmic, surging image criss-crossed with lines of precise measurement, reliable to within a micropulse, and through the window, into the courtyard, she can see some kind of climbing vine with a deep pink flower –

Ah! It's then that she feels it, a violent contraction of her abdomen. Her head jerks back, away from the window and towards Franks, who is poised beside her, the needle in his hand only centimetres from the numbed surface of her skin.

But he is not looking at Kirsten, he is turned away from her towards Merrill.

'What happened?' he asks. His voice is low and terse.

Now he's afraid. She can feel it.

Merrill is staring at the bright screen. 'It looked like the uterus contracted.'

It's Kirsten's turn. 'What happened?'

'It looks like your uterus contracted. I could actually see the surface of your abdomen pitch.' He's frowning and looking back again to that bright screen, and for this one moment, prolonged, everything in the room is in frozen space, everything except the screen, where life is a surging mass of microdot points.

'Okay,' he says to Merrill, and Kirsten can almost feel him taking a deep breath, 'we'll check the alignments and try again.'

She hears her own voice. Cool. Disembodied. 'How many tries does it normally take?'

'One. It always goes in the first time.' He does not look up.

He is like a pilot, she thinks, checking and rechecking his calculations. She recalls those stories of black boxes recovered from the wrecks of planes in which the last words of the crew are a measured reading of instruments with no note of panic, scarcely a raised voice or rising inflection.

And still she feels calm.

'Okay,' he says again, 'lie very still.'

This time she cannot look away. She must look, must stare at the long needle, guiding it down to the small black cross by her navel. She knows that something is going wrong and she must be a reliable witness to her fate. The needle is descending purpose-fully and then — *whoomp!* — it happens again. This contraction is even more violent. She feels the jolt at the same moment as she sees it, a lightning quiver of her midsection, a shudder of the uterine wall that ripples across the surface of her skin.

Now, for the first time, she is sick with fear. Her mind has lost its grip. The body has asserted itself and anything could hap-pen. Open-mouthed, she stares at Franks, who is gazing at her navel. He turns away and sets the needle down on the trolley behind him. There it lies innocuously, on its surgical-steel tray.

She watches as Franks moves, with some deliberation, across to the machine. There he exchanges a quick, anxious glance of bafflement with Merrill, and they stand and stare at the surging black and white image on the screen. When, after a minute, he turns back to Kirsten she raises herself up on one elbow, and now her heart *is* pounding and her palms *are* sweaty and she hears her voice say with quiet authority, 'We're not going to try this again, are we?'

'No,' he replies with grim emphasis, 'we are not.'

When she is dressed and seated in the anteroom Franks opens the door of the ultrasound room. Behind him she can see the machine. It is shut down now, the dark grey of its screen null and void, a no-thing, no longer illuminated by her fuzzy uterine map. Franks is visibly upset, awkward and apologetic; he wears the bemused and disappointed expression of a frustrated boy.

'This has never happened to me before,' he says. 'I don't understand it.'

What can she say to console him? She is too elated to speak.

'This is the first time ever that I haven't been able to complete this procedure. I've been doing this for years and I've never once failed to finish the test.' He shakes his head. 'I've never seen a uterus react so violently.'

She wants to help him out but she can't. She knows why he was unable to complete the procedure, and in a week or so, when she is not on the edge of euphoric laughter, she will phone and tell him.

'I know this must be very disappointing for you. We could of course try again on another day. You should discuss it with Dr Lloyd, see what he thinks.'

'Okay,' she says with soft reasonableness, knowing that she won't be back.

It's over, she thinks, it's all over. They have tried, they have done their best, and the seahorse has defeated them.

A taxi is called, and within twenty minutes she is home, scrambling up the stairs in a state of manic elation, grateful that Lindsay is not there to see it, that she need conceal nothing. This thing in her womb, her child, has spoken to her for the first time. From within its amniotic bubble it has sent the strongest of messages, a tidal wave of rebuff', a violent morse code of self-defence.

For a long time she sits there, upright in her bed, like a small continent, cupping with her hands the smooth contour of her belly, lost in a silent, secret gloating. Every now and then she talks to this being inside her. Stay put, she says, just stay there and don't move. Just go on breathing. This is your mother speaking, who was a fool but is no longer.

From this moment on, the pressure is unbearable. She must share the experience with someone. She picks up the phone.

'Ah,' says Trinh. 'Nature asserted itself.'

'How come nature doesn't assert itself with all the other women who have the test?'

'All the other women are not you.'

'What does that mean?'

Trinh just laughs.

'You think I'm bloody-minded?'

'Just a bit.'

They both laugh.

'When are you going to tell Lindsay?'

'Saturday. I'm going to prepare a special dinner, all of his favourite dishes. A feast.' She laughs. 'And then I'll break the news.'

15

Saturday, then, and once again, for the second time in a month, he is out on the open road; has rented a small car and is headed, this time, for the Great Ocean Road. As distracted as he is now, as volatile his mood, he can't be bothered with the ritual of the champagne breakfast and stowing the dog with George. He will take the mutt straight home and present it to his wife forthwith.

After the rains it's a perfect late-autumn day and he is grateful for the cloudless sky and good weather. What a relief it is to be out of the city, to be en route, to be going in the opposite direction to his restlessness, away from civilisation and its discontents; to be going somewhere he has never been before, even if it is to see the remote and enigmatic mistress of the leash. How good it is to let his mind drift, to surf on a wave of freeway momentum, and in the free association of his thoughts he recalls a fragment of conversation he'd had with his nephew about the boy's ambition to become an analyst programmer. Row, in his enthusiasm, had extolled as the 'ultimate project' the attempt to build a computer that could mimic the human brain. The problem, as Row explained it, was that for the computer to function with the high pattern recognition of the brain, and at the same speed, programmers would have to find a way to factor in the quality of randomness.

'This is one of the challenges of this kind of deal,' declared Row, with all the flip know-how of the prodigy. 'The functioning of the human brain is not linear. The brain makes leaps and the problem is how to replicate that facility. That's the key to coming up with a sophisticated system. It's kind of like the computer needs random fluctuations in order to jump out of one hole and into another.'

When Lindsay had asked Row how this was currently being achieved the boy shrugged and said, 'Well, just by sort of playing.'

'Playing?'

'You just sort of jiggle the system around enough until it becomes optimal –'

'What do you mean by jiggling?'

'A random fluctuation.'

'And wait for it to throw up a solution?'

'Yeah.'

'What if this takes years?'

'That's the problem. We don't know enough about it to figure out how you'd do that in an optimal way.'

Which sets Lindsay to thinking how, a week ago, he had planned to spend this Saturday cleaning up the garden, and then he'd received the call from Sandra and now is on his way down the coast, and at any moment he might collide with a semitrailer and die, and that, he guesses, would be a random fluctuation. Except that nothing is ever completely random.

The journey is around two hours' drive. Over the Westgate Bridge, down the Geelong Road, and forty minutes of transit through flat, denuded country relieved only by the smoky outline of the You Yangs. Approaching Torquay, he catches his first glimpse of the coastline and the effect is stunning. On through Anglesea, past Aireys Inlet and then, coming around a bend in the road, he has to brake sharply because some kind of procession has emerged from the scrub. People are spilling onto the road off a rough track that winds down the hill. A festive crowd is gathered behind a group of dark-skinned young men who are dressed in white and bear on their shoulders an enormous wooden tray, above which a silk awning is suspended over a light frame. On this rough palanquin, precariously balanced, sits a pale, blue-grey statue over a metre high, a clay idol of Ganesha, the Hindu elephant god, garlanded in flowers and sitting cross-legged, his long trunk curled around onto his chest in an expressive curlicue of sly mischief.

The procession is a long one, much bigger than it at first appeared, and Lindsay has to wait some minutes while it crosses the road. The buoyant, pear-shaped figure of the idol bobs its way above the heads of the crowd as the bearers cross to an outcrop by the edge of the road. Far below them the surf is roaring in, with a strong westerly whipping up a salty spume, so high he can almost taste it through the open window.

But how slow the procession is, it's taking an age...He drums the heel of his palm against the rim of the steering-wheel, waiting for the stragglers in the rear to reach the grass on the other side of the road.

At last! He slips the car into gear and accelerates down the hill.

The Schokmann property is not difficult to find. It lies only a few kilometres past the town and is, according to Sandra's clipped directions, set on the brow of a grassy rise at the foot of a steep escarpment. At the turnoff there is no sign, but he is confident he has the right place and follows the dirt road up a winding ascent into thick bushland, through which he can occasionally glimpse small patches of cleared land.

The road ends abruptly at a gate that blocks off a muddy drive. Beside the gate is a sign saying SCHOKMANN KENNELS, and he wonders if he should leave the car at the gate and walk up the hill to avoid getting bogged. Deciding on caution, he unlatches the gate and heads on foot for the drier edges of the crusted mud. Further up the hill is a big open shed built of iron, and as he approaches he can see that each inner wall is lined with cages of black wire. All the cages are empty, except for one at the front in which, standing on full alert, is a huge black chow, full-size and fearsome — an unusually large dog for the breed, it seems to Lindsay, and with a ferocious bark. Quite the worst bark he has ever heard on a dog.

At least she will know he is coming.

By the time he reaches the top of the muddy track he is puffing a little, and pauses to survey the scene. Just ahead of him sits a two-storey timber house of vertical board stained dark brown, with a small conical tower rising from one corner in the whimsical style of the seventies. He cannot imagine Sandra commissioning such a turret and surmises that she must have bought the house off someone else, some urban hippie who had second thoughts. The house is surrounded by stock fences built of rough, unprocessed logs. There is no garden, not a single flower or ornamental shrub, only grass and mud and empty cages. And no-one in sight.

Has she forgotten?

The front door is ajar and he knocks loudly, hoping some black, tufted beast is not about to spring at him from the hallway.

'Just a minute.' It's a light, female voice.

A slim girl comes to the doorway and he recognises her from the dog show.

'Yes?' she says. She is holding a baby's bottle and there are what appear to be milk stains on her shirt.

'I'm Lindsay Eynon. I had an arrangement to see Sandra about a dog.'

The girl looks at him blankly. 'Oh,' she says, 'I remember you. Sandra is down at the beach at the moment, exercising some of the dogs. I've just been feeding the pups.'

'I did tell her I was coming.'

'Oh? She didn't mention it.'

He looks around, and back down the driveway. In the distance he can see the far rim of the beach, but no Sandra. He grimaces his displeasure and says coldly, 'Would it be possible for me to have a look at the pups?'

'Well, I suppose so. You could have a quick look, but I'll have to lock them up in a minute and go.'

'Do you know when Sandra will be back?'

'I'm not sure. You could go down to the beach. She'll probably be there, she hasn't been gone long.'

On the drive back towards the township he keeps an eye out for a woman with dogs walking up the road, but no-one appears. He can see that to one side of the main stretch of ocean beach is a sheltered lagoon. Although Sandra is more likely to be on the ocean beach, he is drawn on impulse to the lagoon. It bears an uncanny resemblance to a place where his family used to camp when he was a boy.

Above the lagoon is a gravel turning circle and he parks on the grass beside it. When he gets out and looks around he can see no-one, but is content to just stand for a while, inhaling the sharp, brackenish smell of weed and water that drifts up from the lagoon.

How still it is. He could be miles from anywhere.

Behind the lagoon is a patch of light-green scrub, and behind that a line of spindly casuarinas. Further back he can see she-oaks, bleached to silver in the white light. The lagoon is sheltered from the wind and the still surface of its water has a delicate pink tinge, reflected off a bank of lavender-grey cloud. To his left is a clump of granite boulders stained with red lichen that spill from the edge of the promontory and into the water.

He looks at his watch: two-thirty. Some drowsy effect has come over him and he is beginning to vague out. He should go back to the car, back to the turning circle.

Up the track then, and once more he is on the road. To his right he can see the great white sweep of ocean beach, and he swings the car around and down onto the gravel road that leads to a line of low sandhills covered in boobialla. She must be on the other side.

Leaving the car by the road, he follows a narrow track that winds down to the beach. The track leads him through another dense tangle of boobialla that rises above his head, so that he feels as if he is in a maze, a natural labyrinth of glossy green thicket. Soon he can see through to a clearing only a few metres below and, to his relief, there she is, a distant stick figure on the beach accompanied by three large dogs. It has to be her. Stumbling onto the rocky sand he raises an arm and waves, feeling slightly foolish, but the figure turns and continues to walk on, away from him and towards the far end of the beach. All he can do is stand and watch as the dogs, each of them a reddish-golden colour, run in spurts along the wet sand at low-tide mark, sniffing at dead birds and driftwood lodged in clumps of seaweed. Now and then they charge at one another, feinting and snorting and bounding before suddenly stopping dead, then trotting off, with their superbly insouciant gait, in the opposite direction, their magnificent heads turning from side to side.

My God, they are impressive! And for the first time he begins to have doubts. Whatever made him think he could keep one of these rare creatures incarcerated in a small garden in the city?

Still she hasn't seen him. Or maybe she has? Even if she has, he wouldn't register with her, since she is too far away to recognise him and clearly she has forgotten his coming.

What is he to do?

Though almost three in the afternoon it's still pleasantly warm. Behind him the dark green hedge of boobialla creates an illusion of isolation, of wilderness. Finding a sheltered spot, he sits and lies with his back against a warm rock. Here he can wait, protected from the wind, and lift his face to the sun.

The wind is rising now and the glare off the water is intense. With half-hooded eyes he gazes out at the white arc of beach and its rolling ocean swell. Unlike the lagoon, the beach is exposed to the westerlies and the wind is beginning to blow in off the water, sending a milky spume of foam into the air and ruffling the fur of the dogs as they canter along the sand, or veer off suddenly into low-lying sandhills. All along the sandhills the wispy spears of grass sway in the wind like ears of wild wheat and the scene before him is mesmerising. The smoky-green trees with their yellow tips, the dun-coloured grass undulating in waves, the dogs trotting in and out of windswept banks of reed, their fur the same colour as the grass. And both fur and grass, grass and fur rippling in the wind, so that from where he sits they are virtually indistinguishable, as if merged, one and the same element of nature and all one rippling, energetic field.

Warmed by the sun, he is beyond impatience now, lulled into a soothing mindlessness, a sense of numinous presence akin to that state of grace he knew at the beach as a child, as if he has passed through some invisible barrier into another zone. He finds himself drifting into reverie, back in time to a moment of transcendental clarity that came to him once around the age of ten. It was early one afternoon when the family was on holiday in Tasmania and he was swimming alone off a remote beach known as the Bay of Fires. It was a hot, hazy day and his parents were dozing on their towels after lunch. Leaving his sister to clamber over the rockpools, he had paddled out on his board through a sea of glinting calm. On either side of the bay were huge boulders of such plasticity, such alluring curves and warmth, that they seemed to hum with a subtle vibration. The whole coastline was alive.

Suddenly he was filled with a new and startling knowledge. It was as if all the other knowledge he had acquired in his ten years had been preparing him for this one thought: *the rocks breathe.* And in a flare of foresight he saw how he would race up the sand and bring this news to his parents when he returned to shore. But later, when he waded into the beach and sought them out in their tent, already the mundane world had closed in on him again and he could not find the words. And the knowledge itself, the truth of his experience, was already dissolving into a white fade. Still, for that quiet hour on the water, he felt himself buoyed by fullness, some fathomless bounty that lapped at the edges of his surfboard until he floated in a trance, mindless but alert, floating on the wave of an eternal present as if he were a benign automaton, or an animal moved purely by instinct.

And he knows through his senses, through the feel of the sun on his hair and his skin pressed against the warm rock, that it's not that he wants to have a dog, but that he wants to *be* that dog; a bundle of instincts, moving freely without the suffocating blanket of personality, a perfectly programmed organism without the blight of free will. He wants to merge. He is tired of his separateness, tired of that fine, discerning intelligence that he has spent a lifetime thinking is his greatest asset, tired of the capacity to judge and discriminate in which he once took such pride, tired of the burden of self-consciousness – here, on the beach, where everything seems possible and nothing seems possible, and where, if anything, the no-thing is more desirable than the every-thing.

His reverie is broken by a short, sharp whistle. And then another. It's her, summoning the dogs from their camouflaged predation in and behind the sandhills. He sits up and sees her turn in his direction and begin her long, striding walk back along the beach.

When she is ten or so metres away he stands and brushes the sand from his clothes. He walks towards her, across the thick sloping carpet of shells that crunch awkwardly beneath his feet so that he is inclined to lose his balance, while she stands with her hand raised to her eyes, squinting at him in half-recognition. The dogs are ranged alertly beside her, and the closer he gets to them, the more impressive they look. Yes, they are aloof, making no sound as he approaches, neither barking nor growling. They simply look at him, not so much with indifference as a majestic impersonality that is generous but contained. So beautiful are they that for a moment he cannot speak.

'Lindsay Eynon,' he says at last. And, without resentment, 'I thought we had an appointment.'

She stabs her stick into the sand. 'We did. We do. Had to get the dogs walked before four. Didn't Melissa look after you?'

'She had to go.'

'Well, come up to the house then.'

Really, this is all too casual, is rudeness itself. But what does he care? What is the point of resisting? He has hired the car, he is here now, he has no intention of coming back another day. He will buy a dog and go.

Up the dun-coloured road they drive, in mini-convoy. When they get to the gate she stops, and leaning out the window of her white Pajero, says, 'I'll take you up.'

Halfway up the hill they park by the big open barn and she gets out, releases the dogs from the back of the car and locks them into their black cages. All the while he is watching, observing her lithe, elegant boniness, her flat-chested swagger as she tops up their water from a hose.

'What about the black one?' he asks.

'Victorian All Breed Champion. The father of the puppies won in the same category three years ago.'

'The black one seems fiercer than the others.'

'An illusion of colour. Just because they look devilish doesn't mean they are.'

'Well, he barked at me as if he meant business.'

'Some of them are more highly strung than others.'

'I thought you bred for temperament.' He says this, he hopes, jocularly.

'I breed for a lot of things.'

Does she have to be so relentlessly charmless? Or is it something else? Impersonal, that's what she is. Like her breed.

As before, the door to the house is open. Sandra strides ahead of him into the hallway and on through a door on the left, and the minute she opens this the smell hits him: a stomach-churning stench of wet fur and dog piss, and something else, worse than either.

When he follows her into what is clearly the main living area he can hardly believe his eyes. At one end of a large, open space is the kitchen, which appears to have almost nothing in it except a big aluminium pot on the stove, simmering with the reek of unseasoned meat. On the other side of the white formica kitchen divide, the living space is stripped bare. The floor is grey concrete and there is only one item of furniture in the entire room, an old tweed sofa pressed against the wall at the far end. The front wall is mostly glass, a picture window from floor to ceiling that looks out onto the downward slope of the hill, but the true focal point of the room, and its only ornamentation, is the internal wall. Here, four widely spaced wooden shelves have been bolted into the brick, and each shelf is crammed with metal trophies of all shapes and sizes. There are so many that they nudge one another and overlap, a haphazard arrangement of gold- and silver-plated cups, some of them monstrous, some shoved irreverently to the back. Those at the front are bedecked with ribbons – big red and blue rosettes stamped at the centre in gold lettering with the words Ist and CHAMPION.

Altar of dog.

Another young woman (not Melissa) emerges from behind the kitchen counter; she's dark-skinned with blonde hair pulled back in a tight knot. She is carrying a bucket of hot soapy water and a mop, and Sandra says bluntly, 'Leave that until we've sorted the pups. Bring them out.' She does not bother to introduce him.

The girl puts the bucket down and opens a door into what he guesses is a bedroom, and indeed it is – a bedroom for dogs. Within is a yapping, scuttling chaos of puppies – he hasn't time to count but there has to be at least seven or eight of them. Sandra must be reading his mind because she says, 'We've had an unseasonal cold snap on the coast and it's too cold for them to sleep outside.'

Something about the house tells him that they sleep inside anyway.

Between them, Sandra and the girl manage to grasp hold of three of the puppies – they know the ones they want – and set them down on the concrete floor so that he can, at last, make his choice. Once again he takes a dislike to the female, who is clearly the strongest of the three and, yes, would make the best watchdog. In the intervening weeks she has grown even foxier in her conformation, even more sinewy and alert. Still the most beautiful of the dogs is Yellow Emperor, the one he warmed to from the very first. Here he is, his own little Chuang, grown larger and sturdier, though still possessed of that refined virility that characterised him from the start. Gesturing in the pup's direction, he looks up at Sandra, who is leaning against the kitchen bench, arms folded.

'This one's perfect,' he says. Perfect. The very word is a heart-felt sigh of recognition. 'When can I take him home?'

'You can take him now.'

'Good.' He says this softly, almost absentmindedly. And again. 'Good.' Then he squats on his haunches so that he can look into the pup's eyes and fondle him behind the ears. It's then that he feels it, something round and hard. His fingers are caressing a large lump.

Ah, but the animal is *not* perfect! There is a growth on his left ear, some kind of tumour. And he remembers Sandra speaking of this in the café, and it had meant nothing to him then, it was academic. But now the growth *would* prove to be on his dog.

'This dog has a flaw,' he says. 'Look, there's a lump.'

'I mentioned that,' says Sandra flatly. 'It's a benign tumour.'

'What does that mean?'

She shrugs. 'It's just a kind of cyst, probably mostly fluid.'

The reek of dog meat assails his senses. It's everywhere. He could heave. 'What causes it?'

She shrugs again, saying nothing, leaving him in a kind of limbo.

The pups are frisky now, and have begun to sniff their way around the room. The girl walks over and claps her hands to summon them back towards the centre of the bare floor. She looks upset. Perhaps she senses a stalemate.

Lindsay waits until the puppies are collected together and then he bends again to study the blighted animal. 'But this is the dog I want,' he says, almost to himself. And looking up: 'How much?'

'If you want this one you can have him for two hundred less and no papers.'

'So that's how much?'

'Seven hundred.'

Seven hundred? Only two hundred dollars discount on a dog whose breeding is queered? He frowns. He should get it for less, but he is not inclined to bargain. He's never been any good at it and besides, he's not interested in the other dogs and he can tell that she has already sensed this. But he's damned if he'll pay veterinarian fees for the surgery.

'I'd like the ear taken care of. Can you arrange that?'

She nods impassively.

'For no extra cost.'

'You won't be able to take him now.'

Damn her. He's come all this way and still the deal isn't done. Trust him to want the flawed dog! There are eight pups in the house and he has to bond with the one with the tumour. Why do apparently simple things always turn out to be complicated? Nothing in his life is ever quite as he plans it.

By now the smell of the dog meat is beginning to get to him. He is steeped in it, nauseated. How do these women live with it, day in, day out? He glances again at the wily sister. From all practical points of view, she is the pup to buy.

Sandra watches him intently.

'What will be the effect when the tumour is removed? Will the ear be permanently affected?'

'Could be,' she says bluntly. 'Hard to say. It may be that when they cut the cartilage, the ear won't stand up straight again.'

'So ... what? It would sort of flop over?'

'Could do.'

For a moment he gazes down at the floor, frozen in indecision. This is — was — an impeccably bred dog. A strong, perfectly proportioned body. A handsome head with the most benignly intelligent expression, neither the vixenish slyness of his sister nor the doleful gruffness of his brother. A prince of dogs, now blighted by a tumorous ear that will at the very least be permanently scarred and perhaps bent. Lindsay knows that every time he looks at that ear it will annoy him; it will be like looking at a stained-glassed window with a smudge of paint on it.

And yet he's come all this way.

'I'm sorry,' he says at last, and purses his lips. 'Perhaps you could let me know when you have the next litter.'

Her eyes do not flicker. She gives the faintest of nods. 'Suit yourself.'

The final pleasantries are strained as the girl accompanies him to the door. It's late afternoon now and the sky is beginning to darken. A dense bank of charcoal cloud has blown in from the west, hovering out to sea, and he can feel a nip in the air, a sense of oncoming winter. The character of the day has become melancholy, or is it an after-effect of the austerity of the house, and his own departure empty-handed?

Skirting the muddy ridges along the track, he makes his way

down the hill. When he gets to the big shed he stops, and looks into the eyes of the big black chow in the cage. Then he turns and retraces his steps. At the open door of the bungalow he can hear the two women talking, their voices blending in a low murmur. He doesn't knock.

Sandra is in the kitchen, ladling the steaming meat into plastic bowls.

'I've changed my mind.'

She puts down the ladle. Waits.

Lindsay reaches into the inside pocket of his jacket and takes out his cheque book. Resting the book against his thigh, he writes out a cheque. When he hands it to Sandra, she nods in the direction of the girl.

'Give it to Nerida,' she says.

Nerida takes the cheque and without hesitation drops it unceremoniously into the nearest gold cup on the shelf beside her.

'Well,' he says, and offers his hand to Sandra. They shake, and her hand is dry and cool, and as absent as a hand that is present could be.

'When would you like to pick him up?' she asks. 'We're driving up to the city in a few weeks and you could collect him there.' It's the most she's ever said to him in one breath.

He hesitates, though not for long. 'I'll take him now.' And

with the sudden confidence of ownership, he bends and lifts the bundle of golden fur into his arms.

'I'll give him a sedative,' she says, 'so he'll sleep for you on the drive back.' She opens a cupboard and removes a small vial of white pills. With expert dexterity, she forces the jaws of the pup open and pushes a tiny white pill down his throat.

Lindsay, taken by surprise, has hardly had time to consider this. 'I'd better get him home,' he says.

She nods. Turning away from him, she says to the girl, 'You can do the floor now.'

Nerida hesitates, her eyes tracking him until he reaches the doorway, at which point she picks up the bucket and, tilting it away from her, begins with rhythmic motions to sluice the foamy water across the grey concrete floor.

'Tide's in,' says Sandra laconically, and she almost smiles.

By the time he reaches the cavernous shed with its cages (she does not accompany him, she did not farewell him, she has not once smiled or offered a single pleasantry since he arrived) it is almost five. He stops to look in again at the ferocious black chow in the cage, so unlike the pup he has chosen for himself, little Chuang, who is nestled quietly under one arm. Gazing into the adult dog's imperious black eyes, he wonders for an instant if he has made the right choice. He thinks of what George will say. No point in having a dog in the city that is not a strident watchdog, that does not suggest a gleeful inclination to rip the flesh from your leg for the sheer delight of grinding its incisors against your shinbone. The black dog exudes a clear message, and the message is this: the only thing that would prevent it from killing you is the contempt it would feel at having to expend the effort.

He would not want to live with such a dog. Such a dog was for Sandra. They were soulmates. The thought of this makes him laugh out loud, and as he sets off down the hill he gazes at the bundle of golden fur with the bung ear that he has just paid a small fortune for – almost enough for a week in Bali! – and with hapless irony congratulates himself on a triumph of sensibility. George had advised him to go for ruthlessness, while he himself had intended to go for beauty. Instead he has just purchased a dog that can guarantee neither. It's as if, somewhere on the beach, he has lost his bearings.

In the boot of the car is an old blanket he has brought with him in anticipation, and still with the pup under one arm he drops it on the floor of the back seat and smooths it into place. 'There you are, mate,' he says. The dog is subdued now, woozy from the effects of the sedative.

On the drive back, Lindsay's feeling of disorientation stays with him, and the odd thing is this: that feeling is not unpleasant.

Shadows lie across the bush in a smoky blue mantle; the sea below him flickers with silver light. Somehow the restlessness, the peevishness that has afflicted him for the past few months, has fallen away. He thinks of the soft pink waters of the lagoon, the spume-swept beach, the wind ruffling the yellow grass, ruffling too the yellow fur of the dogs; of seeing how the dogs became the grass and the grass the dogs, without distinction. And then the mud-encrusted driveway and her house – that strange tabernacle stuck out in the bush. It ought to have had curtains and carpet and a television set in the corner and a coffee table with a pot plant and coffee mugs – but it had nothing, nothing but a concrete floor and a shelf of gold cups bedecked with triumphal ribbons.

That house was ugly, that house had made him gag, but here he is recalling it already with a kind of rueful nostalgia. What was it about the interior of that house that had so affected him? The austerity of those rooms? The smell, the squalor? Was it squalor? No, he thought it too controlled, too managed to be squalor. It was just different. In that house everything extraneous, every bauble of comfort and domesticity, had been stripped away, leaving only the relationship between the women and their dogs. In that house the dog had equal status; there seemed scarcely any distinction between dog and human, and with this thought he has a vivid flash of the three women romping naked together with the puppies in some giant double bed in one of those closed bedrooms, sheets in disarray, white flesh and golden red fur tumbling together in a raucous, yapping delirium.

Yet she treated them brusquely, without affection. And when they matured they were expelled from the inner sanctum, out into the cages in the shed. She was a breeder, and the dogs existed to win prizes. What did those prizes mean to her? he wonders. Was it the perfection of the dog for its own sake, or the achievement of the goal? He has never in his life met so unsentimental a woman. She was like a goddess, but an unforgiving one. The dogs might be one with nature on the beach and sleep in the bedroom as pups, but in their magnificent maturity they were in cages, a valuable commodity that could not be allowed off the leash. And the money from the sale of the dog had meant something to her, of this he was certain; he had sensed it in the tension of Nerida when he walked away the first time, and in Sandra's look when he wrote out the cheque. Perhaps they had minimal cashflow and lived on very little, and the price of Chuang was enough to feed women and dogs for another few weeks at least.

He liked to think so. He liked to think that, if only for a brief time, he might have been essential to them.

By the time he gets to the bluff he is in a weird state, something akin to euphoria. On impulse he stops and pulls the car over to a grassy knoll. Casting a backward glance at Chuang, who is curled up and asleep, he opens the car door and steps out into the sharp tang of the sea breeze.

Looking down to the beach below he can see that it is thronged with people, and he recognises the religious procession with the elephant god. It appears now to be arriving at some point of climax, with the train of worshippers watching from the shore as the young men in white – still bearing the idol aloft on its tray – rush headlong into the breaking waves. The crowd looks on as the men stumble about in the surf, struggling with exuberant joy to push their god out to sea. With an almighty shove they at last manage to release the idol from its palanquin and into the water. Several times they combine to thrust the clay mass ahead of them, waiting as it bobs jovially on the surface of the water, only to have the next incoming wave wash it back into their unwilling grasp. Lindsay is fascinated, and watches as the young men press on, wading further and further out in an attempt to reach a position where they can hoist the god over the rise of the next breaking wave. And all the while they are hampered by their own laughter, their shouted directions to one another, broken by loud whooping and breathlessness until they are chest-deep, their thin garments drenched, their slender arms upstretched and still holding the clay god aloft.

The crowd on the beach is applauding now, cheering and laughing; mocking the young men. Then, in an instant, success! The idol has sailed past the first line of breaking swell and on out into the choppy ocean. There, within seconds, it disintegrates, broken against the incoming swell. At that moment, with a muted roar, a huge wave breaks into the shallows, surging up over the beach and submerging the feet of the crowd, so that they laugh ecstatically and scamper about in the shallow foam. From where Lindsay is standing it looks as if they are dancing.

Far out, beyond the breaking waves, fragments of blue-grey idol float on out to sea.

16

In the kitchen of their Northcote house, Kirsten is preparing her feast. The duck is spread-eagled on a baking tray on the table. At the bench she is making the stuffing, a mix of her own devising with dried sour cherries, green peppercorns and – and what? She thought this through all last night and now has forgotten the other ingredient. She is not feeling well. There is a dragging sensation in her lower abdomen and moments of dizziness when she sways above the kitchen bench.

When did this start? Earlier in the afternoon, when she was setting the dining table – with the silver candlesticks her parents had given them as a wedding present, the white linen (Lindsay is a traditionalist in all these fine points), and a vase of hothouse freesias whose strong perfume has wafted through the ground floor of the house. Perhaps it was just that she'd been too long on her feet today, shopping and vacuuming, and her haste and exertion had combined with an exhausting cocktail of elation, anxiety, and a sense of defiant urgency that felt almost like vertigo. And then a falling away of energy, a dull creep of pain, and now suddenly the heat, a rising flush, as if she is running a temperature. Something surges in her guts and she drops the knife with a clatter into the sink and braces herself against the benchtop. Damn, not now. Can't she orchestrate even this?

Perhaps if she just lay down for twenty minutes. But first the duck, she must finish the duck, stuff and truss it and put it in the oven. Then she can put her feet up while it roasts. The timer is a shrill one that can be heard in the front parlour, where she will rest on the long couch, or maybe she will go upstairs. Yes, the bed, she can lie more comfortably there . . .

When Lindsay arrives home it is almost seven. He turns the key in the lock and at that moment, perversely, he is thinking of Sonia. While driving home he had been ambushed by the memory of that dream of her in a cradle, in that dark little room at the end of the hallway. But that was just a phantom, whereas here, in his arms now, is the real; the coarse-coated, barrel-shaped body of little Chuang. Even through the thickness of his jacket he can feel the warmth of that pliant but muscular body, can feel the heart beating with a rapid pulse. He looks down, and the pup gazes up at him from a pair of depthless brown eyes.

'Kirsten?' he calls, and walks down the hallway to present his gift.

Dildo

17

A soft moisture hangs in the air like balm and the streets are wet from the warm drizzle of summer. Up and down High Street the cars move slowly and the air is heavy with invisible grit. I stand on the corner and try to remember where their house is. It's so long since I've been here.

I walk on for a few blocks, scanning the side streets, and then I remember how I used to take this route to the movie theatre, the old Valhalla. Suddenly I've got my bearings.

Just two weeks ago, Eva called and asked me to work on a new project with her, a documentary on the iconography of the heart. I had worked for Eva before, in the early days, as a researcher on short films, and she remembered that I once planned to write a dissertation on the cultural rhetorics of the heart.

'What about it, Sonia?' she asked. 'You must have some ideas. You must know a few people who would be good on camera.'

I thought of Lindsay.

The next day I rang and asked if I could see him. I had not expected to find him quite so easily but there he was, still on campus, still on the old extension. As I dialled his number my hand began to tremble so that I misdialled twice, and had to stop and take a deep breath. But when he answered, when I heard his voice, then it was all right.

At first he was guarded, but I held my nerve and waded my way slowly through an account of the project. He relaxed, and was friendly in the old way, though with no trace of intimacy. I listened for some tension or tremor in his voice, some residue of the past, but there was none. Not a quaver.

People say the past is like a movie, as if the events we look back on belong to someone else, but as I walk along High Street the past is alive to me now and I am back in that dreamy, hypnotic space of desire that connected me to them: Lindsay and Kirsten. They were everything to me then. They were the golden couple, and I was a mad girl living in a fugue.

I say 'I', but at that age I had no idea who 'I' was. I lived in a squalid cottage in Northcote, I worked hard and I fancied myself a thinker. I spent hours in a private-study room in the research library, working my way through countless books while the muted roar of the airconditioning rumbled overhead. Every night before I went to bed, I looked in the mirror to see if I was still there. I could not sleep until I checked on my reflection.

This was a superstition I had carried with me since child-hood — that unless my own face was the last thing I saw at night before I went to sleep, I might never wake up. And what I saw in the mirror was an ordinary-looking girl, of medium height, with light brown hair and large myopic green eyes shielded by granny glasses. But there was something opaque about this image, and something contingent, as if, were I to blink, I would disappear.

It was my own fault. I was quiet. I faked a passive demeanour. I kept my head down and complied with what was asked of me. In time I had so fortified that 'I' with deceiving behaviour that when I looked in the mirror all I saw was the ghost of my own construction.

It had been that way since the day they took my mother away to a clinic. In that year some animal sense of who I was left me; I became a question mark in my own mind. When she came back she just sat, and smoked, and it was as if she weren't there anyway. After that it was just us — my brother Carl, much older, and me.

Carl rigged up a treehouse for me in the backyard. It was old fence planks and hessian bags and some canvas he carried home from the tip. In so far as I had a home it was there, my space of retreat. Sometimes I slept there overnight, high up on my pre-carious platform, though Carl warned me against it, saying I should always sleep at home. But what was home? I had no sense of it. It sounded like a golden realm that belonged to another country. When I returned to the house in the afternoon, after school, I would look in through the window at my mother who would be sitting at the kitchen table smoking and working her way through a book of crossword puzzles. The crossword puzzles were always a good sign. Sometimes, if she was in a good mood, she would let me crawl in under the table and paint her toenails, and I would string the process out for as long as possible, layer after layer after layer. So many coats.

'An eleven-letter word for baggage,' she would say.

'Portmanteau,' I'd reply, from under the table, and I'd feel then the slight adjustment of her body as she pencilled in the word.

On bad days I would look in and she would just be sitting and staring out at the garden, but smoking, always smoking, like her fingers were smouldering and the thin smoke rising into the air was her only vital sign. Three times she set fire to her bedroom, but after the first time Carl slept in the hallway outside her door and was roused by the smoke. He said he could smell it in his dreams. He had the instincts of a hound.

Carl was my mainstay. Carl was clever. In time, he got a job as a software engineer with a firm in Richmond, and when our mother died he moved into a tiny apartment close to work. For a while he lived there with a woman called Carole, and everything in his life seemed to be charmed, until he had his experience with the voices. This was something he couldn't, or wouldn't, explain.

'If I tried to explain it to you it would sound trivial,' he said. 'You had to be there.'

'Had to be where?'

'In my head.'

At first it was thought that Carl had had a schizophrenic episode, but the voices never returned. Every now and then I would check on him. 'Do you ever hear from the voices?' I would ask. And each time he would say the same thing. 'No, Son. No need.'

After that he became a kind of urban feral — well, a vagrant, really. Someone who prayed a lot and lived in a van. By this time I was at university and living in a shared house in Northcote: four dark rooms, a rotting sink, a colony of ants, and three medical students who drank heavily and had wrestling bouts on the kitchen floor. These would begin as a game but could turn in an instant into brawling dogfights.

Every now and then, out of the blue, Carl would pull up in his van. I would hear its lumbering chassis come to a halt in the gutter, then the distinctive clunk of the handbrake. Without even a phone call he would turn up out of nowhere and drive me across the city to some park or other where we could walk. Carl didn't like to be in houses. 'I can smell all the bad karma,' he would say, and smell seemed to be his primary sense. He would raise his chin, jut out his lower lip and sniff at the air like some divine bloodhound.

The van was an old airport bus, a 1978 Toyota Coaster with folding doors in the middle. There were two bucket seats in the front and behind these a narrow bed, a fold-away sink and a gas ring. For a while there was a gas fridge, but one year he drove it to the tip and dumped it, saying it was too much of a problem. The van was white and had white curtains at every window. I thought of it as a great white womb.

Sometimes, when he ran out of cash, Carl would go back to his old firm of software engineers and they would put him on for two or three days a week. Then he would give me money. Most nights he parked the van in the company's parking lot, which was good because you couldn't see it from the street. But sometimes he just drove to a park and slept on the edge. I worried that one night someone would break into the van and kill him.

Whenever he turned up outside my place he would beep the horn loudly and I'd stroll out to the gate and get in. And always he would look distracted, his skin greyish and his sandy hair tied back in a ponytail. We went often to Albert Park, one of his favourite places, and he'd stride off across the grass in the direction of the lake. On the way he would ask me about the progress of my studies and I would fake a lucid account of my intentions, until, halfway across the lawns, we would come to one of those small silver drinking fountains. There we'd stop, and I'd wait while he produced a toothbrush from his pocket and began to brush his teeth. I'd watch him cup the silvery water in his strong brown hand and think, Is he is mad? Because he seemed so entirely at ease with his life, whereas I was at ease with nothing.

One late afternoon, when he'd appeared suddenly, he drove me back to my street and I could hear, even from the van, that my housemates were in the middle of a violent argument. The front door was open and it was as if the bellow of their voices sucked all the air from the narrow street.

'I'm not in the mood for this,' I said.

'You can spend the night in the van.'

'Where?'

'In the bed. I'll sleep on the floor. Doesn't bother me. I just have to do a load of laundry first.'

Carl liked to wear mostly white clothes, though in winter it wasn't always practical, and he had a favourite laundromat where he went as a matter of routine. While he washed all of his whites, I sat and read my way through a dozen dog-eared magazines. The laundromat was warm and permeated with a not unpleasant smell of detergent and rubber.

The van, on the other hand, smelled of a cloying musk incense. We pulled into the empty lot behind his sometime office and I was grateful that he hadn't wanted to spend the night beside a park. Carl lit a candle, and I made a warm milk drink with spices on the gas ring.

'You might as well get into bed,' he said. 'I'm going to sit here and pray.'

I stripped off to my pants and T-shirt and climbed into the narrow bed. From there I watched as he settled, cross-legged, on the floor. On the fold-out table stood a small plaster statue of Jesus in blue and white robes, and next to it a white votary candle glowed in the dark. Somewhere in the distance a dog barked, and there was singing coming from the pub on the corner. Feeling comforted, I drifted off to sleep with the sound of my brother muttering under his breath.

Between me and the rest of the world there was an invisible membrane. On the one side there was the ordinary and the normal, and on the other side there was me. The membrane, I knew, was permeable and there was a knack to getting through it. But the more I pushed against it, the more I seemed to rebound from its invisible surface. Somehow, I reasoned, if I could rearrange myself, I could fool its sensors and slip unnoticed to the other side.

There were days when I spent hours in front of the mirror just wondering how to dress. How should 'I' look (this 'I' that was so contingent)? Shirts hung from me half buttoned, skirts sat around my hips unzipped. Trousers, scarves and T-shirts would be scattered across the floor. My bed was an island in a sea of crumpled clothes. I could never escape the perception that clothes were an absurdity, arbitrary objects that invited mockery. On some days they could appear dull and ordinary enough, but on others they looked like the sloughed-off skins of domesticated reptiles, waiting to be collected and disposed of. In any shop I entered, each item of clothing confronted me with its more or less preposterous contours: a headless tracery. Somehow I had never acquired the knack of taking all this for granted. To me, nothing seemed natural; everything was artifice. The maps that others seemed to read effortlessly made no sense to me at all, or only fragmentary sense, and then with great effort. This was my problem, that I could take nothing for granted, not even my own body. I had to start at the beginning and invent everything. I was a self-assemblage kit that had lost its instructions.

The strain was immense. I could conceive of only one release. Annihilation. 'Sonia' would have to be erased so that 'I' could start again.

Love was the solution. I could be annihilated by love. But of all things, this seemed the most difficult. I knew very little of love and what I did know seemed threatening. My father had disappeared; my mother too had left me, in her way. I had grown up with a kind of mad freedom and it was all I knew. To maintain that space of freedom I had had to guard my perimeter. But it meant I was trapped. I was my own gaoler. It seemed there was no solution to being an 'I'. It was either one prison or the other. Perhaps that was why Carl lived in a van. In the space between.

Meanwhile I was twenty-two and still a virgin. Hard to believe, but true. I could scarcely believe it myself, but I was sick of it, bored with myself and with my condition, which I thought of as a kind of disablement. For whole days I glided through the world in a trance, anaesthetised, unable to experience desire in the moment. I could experience it in anticipation, in daydreams, but when the moment came I froze, perhaps because I had a deep fear of penetration. I saw what became of women who were penetrated. They were abandoned and became mad. They sat in the kitchen smoking and doing crosswords. Every time a man touched me, I contracted. I was strongly attracted to men, I had been with men a number of times, but at the crucial moment I flinched. The truth is I couldn't bear the idea of possession, that someone could turn a key in me as if I were a box. That they could open me up and empty me out, just like that.

There was one relationship, especially painful, where I grappled with my lover as if we were both manic toys. I was fond of him, I was not afraid of him, I even at times felt sorry for him, but I would not let him enter me.

One day I went to a doctor, an old man in his sixties who had treated my mother. He was very kind, in a matter-of-fact way. I lied and said I had a boyfriend and we wanted to marry but I had this problem with . . . I hesitated. I wanted to say 'with being possessed', but instead I said 'with penetration'.

'Vaginismus,' he said. 'Muscle spasm.'

Such a simple cause.

'Just nerves,' he went on. 'Just a matter of getting used to it. You young girls sometimes think about things too much.' And he got up out of his seat and moved across to a glass-fronted cabinet full of all kinds of strange objects and weird apparatus with steel tubes and rubber bulbs. He opened the door and extracted a cone-shaped object made of stainless steel, which turned out to be three cone-shaped objects, in graded sizes, one inside the other, like a set of Chinese boxes.

'Here, take these home,' he said, handing me the set.

I looked down and realised that what I held in my hand was a set of dildos. How heavy they felt, how cold against my palm.

'When you're lying in bed at night, relaxed, start with the small one and insert it gently. If that feels uncomfortable, you might even try a pen and move gradually up from there.'

'A pen?'

'Yes, a pen, a biro, a pencil. You're a student, you must have lots of pens.'

I think this was meant to be a joke.

'Thank you,' I said, and dropped the set of stainless-steel dildos into my satchel.

When I got back to the house I tried inserting a dildo and it was painless. After that I laid the biggest dildo on its side on the mantelpiece in my bedroom and stuck pens in it. Every time I looked at it I would think, Still Life with Ballpoint. I don't know why, but I found this funny. There was something about the dildo that was perversely cheerful. It signified a belief that to every problem there was a practical, an engineered, solution.

After Dr Dildo, I knew I would have to think of some other strategy. Some kind of catalyst was needed, something involving risk and, more importantly, fear. I must find myself someone to love, someone to lose myself in. I must find a way to become *sick with longing*. I had read that phrase somewhere as a schoolgirl and the shock of it had left me flailing. It seemed that all around me people fell in love, effortlessly and with abandon, but in my case I knew that it would have to be willed.

But first I willed my body to do what I needed it to do. The dildo had shown me the way, and the next man who paid me attention I had penetrative sex with. It was dull and uncomfortable but otherwise okay. He was diffident and polite, and I didn't tell him I was a virgin because I didn't want him to treat me like a freak. I wanted him to think that I was ordinary, just like anyone else.

And as if nature had decided to collude with me, I didn't bleed. I was without trace.

18

When I had my first appointment with Lindsay, I wasn't at all nervous. I had seen him in the corridors and admired him from a distance, not least because he had that quality of characterless beauty that seemed to me then to be the very essence of normal, like those men and women in TV commercials — calm and complacent, but in a remote, even Olympian, way. And he had that same sheen of the cathode tube, only he was flesh. I could see the pores of his skin. I could see hair and sinew and bone.

But when I sat beside him, up close, of all things it was his hands that compelled me; those large, well-formed hands resting so comfortably on his knees. Tanned, with a fine down of bleached hair on the back — those hands were so at home there, and so at home with themselves, that suddenly I felt a tidal surge in the cavity of my chest and I wanted to grasp hold of those hands and cry. Instead I answered his questions with a series of calm, clever replies. But all the while my mood was sinking into the soles of my black lace-up boots, and in my head a shrieking whisper of a voice cried out to him, Help me, save me!

Night after night I lay awake imagining his hands massaging my hips, my belly, my thighs, my feet. Out of some deep pit of unease I conjured this man up as my rescuer. He would do, he was the nearest thing. And it was not just his hands. He was clever, polite, not bad looking, full of a kind of amiable certainty, and, above all, inaccessible. Not the kind of man to fall for a girl like me.

So I wrote the first letter. My initial drafts were absurd, almost comically clumsy, and I screwed them up and threw them away. But the impulse returned to me, again and again, and while my housemates wrestled in the kitchen, while they knocked and thumped and sent cups smashing to the floor, I sat at my table and I found my rhythm.

For days I became absorbed in the materiality of the letter. What kind of paper? What colour? How absorbing these questions were. Mauve? Pale yellow? In the end I settled on pink; it seemed the most ... *invasive*. That night, when I carefully inscribed my name, Sonia, I felt a heady rush of fear and adrenalin. As I laid down my pen I heard the whirr of some remote engine moving towards me and it took my breath away. I realised that I could, if I wanted, write these letters to anyone.

I had found my vocation. I was an erotic terrorist.

On the morning of our second meeting I spent hours in front of the mirror, trying to arrive at the right reflection. At last, exhausted, I wriggled into a brown suede miniskirt and a silver lurex top from a second-hand shop. I lipsticked my mouth, cleaned the smear from my glasses, and anointed my neck with a flowery perfume even as, despairingly, I knew that no matter what I wore, the surface me was a lie.

He greeted me, indicated a chair and asked me how my research was going. And all the while I was thinking of how and when I would give him the next letter. I could press it into his hands and leave quietly. I could hover at the end of the corridor, wait for him to leave, and slip it furtively under his door. I could, I could...

I was listening to his pleasant, even voice. I was smiling up at his golden skin and his cropped dark hair. I felt myself aligned demurely within the set of his broad shoulders, his broad thighs, like a moth caught in a headlight, my wings in a humming stasis, hovering...

It was a warm and windy autumn afternoon in the city. I don't know why, but it never occurred to me that I might run into him in the street. I was browsing in the window of a bookstore when suddenly I looked up and there he was, only metres away, and walking towards me. When he saw me he stopped.

'Where are you going?' he asked, as if it were natural for us to stop and chat like this, to pass the time of day. I couldn't say anything. I just stood there. He said, afterwards, that away from the campus – 'from all those enclosed rooms' – I seemed different. 'There was some subtle change in you,' he said, 'as if the light were catching you from a different angle.' All I remember is the cloth bag hanging limply from my shoulders, and how the wind blew my long cotton dress around my ankles. And beside us a junk shop, and in the open doorway a Grecian pedestal, painted in gilt and mounted with a stuffed galah that had a tape implanted in its chest so that it squawked unintelligibly out into the traffic. The smell of diesel wafted over from the road, and at the end of the block a low-flying helicopter fluttered darkly across the sky. I just stood there, gawping up at him with a gnawing feeling of hunger.

'I'm going to see a movie,' he said. And then, 'You want to come?'

In the small dark theatre with the sloping floor I waited on his direction and he led me to a far back corner. The theatre was almost empty, the movie already underway. I felt strange, like an automaton, as if someone else had moved into my body. He was clearly nervous, but I was suffused with a kind of electric calm. Almost immediately we were settled in our seats, he leaned over and kissed me. I responded without hesitation. As the kiss deepened I began to tremble, and he steadied my shoulder with his left hand. After a while, he loosened my dress so that he could stroke my breasts, and then he put his hand under my skirt. Instinctively I raised my buttocks off the seat so that he could drag my pants down to my ankles where, with a rub of one foot against the other, I flicked them off onto the floor. There is no need for graphic description here: with his hand he stroked me quickly to orgasm. It was fast and it was quiet. Then I bent my head to his lap.

When we both had caught our breath, though the movie was scarcely halfway through, he stood, drawing me up by the arm and indicating the exit.

Outside, when the light hit us, it was as if it hadn't happened. 'Well,' he said, 'I'll see you later.'

'Okay.' I couldn't move.

He nodded, smiling inanely, continuing to stand there for a moment. Then, raising his right hand in a half-wave, half-salute, he turned and walked on up the street.

The next day he looked up my address on his student files and, as he half expected, half knew, I lived close by to him. At eleven that night, having convinced himself that he was in need of a stroll, he was banging with his fist on my door. 'You are,' he told me with a blunt, even aggressive irony, 'all too accessible.' But faced with the act in full — considered, premeditated — I was awkward and unresponsive. I sat on the edge of the bed and trembled, until at last he whispered into my ear, 'Who was that girl in the cinema?'

An hour later we lay spent. And then, abruptly, he sat up. I remember how carefully he smoothed his hair, and how he complained about my grimy sheets. His great hulking body exuded a powerful male smell. 'You should wash your sheets more often,' he said.

I knew then he was going to be a disappointment.

After that first, convulsive visit, empty-handed, he brought gifts of food with him, luxury items that I had no stomach for: rich terrines and heavy red wines that made me ruttish, and then sick.

Once I dreamed we were gorging ourselves on pheasant pie, and that thick shards of greasy pastry protruded from our ears and noses and clung in buttery stalactites from our chins.

He was surprised to find that I was vegetarian; gave a soft, derisory laugh when I told him. His demeanour towards me was a strange, disorienting force-field of tenderness and something that felt uncomfortably close to contempt. One night he confessed to me that he was drawn by what he described as my mesmerising passivity. He seemed to feel that with me he was in a space where he would not be judged. The truth was that I judged him constantly.

Then followed a period of mania when he spent the middle of almost every day in my bed, and there was one reckless session on the floor of his office when we were disturbed by an insistent knocking on the door, followed by someone rattling the handle.

We went nowhere together. I saw almost nothing of him outside the house. We existed entirely within the capsule of my dark little room. He remarked again on my passivity; it seemed to both infuriate and arouse him. One afternoon he came so violently he told me later that he thought he was going to lose control of his bowels. I think he told me that to test me, but I just lay there and smiled up at him. 'Your eyes are a syrupy glaze,' he said. 'They stick to me. When I go home I have to wash them off.'

It wasn't long before I began to see that everything about my strategy had backfired. There was no space for yearning; there was no space in which I could be sick with longing. He had foreclosed on this space and there was only instant consummation, followed by a sense of the walls closing in. He was a big man and my bedroom was small, so that he seemed to occupy the whole of it, like a bear in a cupboard. When he moved, his skin brushed against the walls.

But this was before I fell in love. With his wife.

How strange the outcome of my few letters. How conducive to a feeling both of triumph and disappointment. How ruthless the romantic discovers herself to be.

I had thought that this man would not be interested in me. That I would have to plague him with letters and that these would lead ultimately to a painful confrontation. That I would be humiliated, mortified, left with an agonising wound. But he had caved in almost immediately!

Suddenly all the promise of my terrorism had imploded, and with that the momentum of my yearning stalled. Within weeks of our encounter in the movie theatre his glamour had evaporated. He began to turn into someone who was ordinary in the dull sense, rather than the mysterious, with the inevitable result that he was not as interesting to me as before. For one thing, he was not as normal as he had appeared; on the contrary, he now seemed possessed, and when he was not manic he was banal, chewing toast and scratching his chest. Raiding my fridge and complaining that it was empty, going out for late-night take-away. He had an enormous appetite, and with his big frame I could see that one day he would run to fat. Already the phantom of his future self disappointed me.

This was not what I had planned for. Secretly I was beginning to tire of him. Yet he was all I had.

One rain-sodden evening, early, when I was sitting in the

library, my eyes dry and my head stuffy from the airconditioning, I felt an urge to spy on him. On impulse I stood up, leaving my books open behind me, and walked out of the library and into Swanston Street in a kind of trance. And I walked. A long, long walk down Johnson Street, all the way along Brunswick Street, up St Georges Road and across to High Street, walking through a fine drizzling rain until I was damp through. I had walked past his house before and I knew that a narrow lane ran beside it, an almost concealed walkway covered in thick ivy, and I knew somehow that there would be a window and that I would look through this window. The thought of this propelled me through the wet streets, oblivious to the rain, and all the while anticipating the double thrill of seeing and not being seen.

At last I arrived, panting, at the top of Ruckers Hill. But I missed the turning into the lane and, confused, had to retrace my steps until I found it. Halfway down, when I was sure I could not be seen, I rested for a moment, leaning against their side wall. Then I approached the window. Standing on my toes, I could just see into the kitchen, and because the lights were on there was no reflection on the glass. A woman, her back to the window, was at the bench performing some task, a slight, busy movement that could have been peeling, or chopping. She wore faded jeans and a long, loose cotton shirt and her hair was pulled back in a dishevelled knot. Of course, this was exactly how she *would* look in her kitchen – and at that moment I felt a jealous stab of anger. It was not that this woman – she must be his wife – possessed her husband, but that she was so effortlessly at home in her world. And a terrible envy, a sense of exclusion that was half nostalgia, half sadness, suffused me with pain and spite.

Walking home, I thought of how easy it would be to burn that house down. With them in it.

That night I couldn't sleep. The pain bore in on me as never before.

But then, not long afterwards, I saw her face to face. It was early evening, and my friend Ruth and I were walking along Punt Road on our way to a club. And there they were, in their car, stalled in traffic, and I saw her turn and look out the window, directly at me but through me. She had no idea who I was, and with that thought I felt a strange quiver in my spine. Then, just a few days later, I saw them both get out of their car on High Street and walk a block from their parking space until they reached a chemist shop. From that moment, I was smitten. How beautiful she was! Not with a conventional beauty, which might only have sharpened my envy, but with some other quality that even today I couldn't define. She had an aura. There was something electric in her field.

In such a short time it stunned me, I found that a peculiar

shift was beginning to take place. I was beginning to think less about him and more and more about her.

Once again I returned to spy on their house, only this time it was her I wanted to see, not him, and I chose a time when I knew he would be in a seminar and she would be arriving home. For what seemed an age I stood under the overhang of a pepper-corn tree at the end of their street. When she turned in at the wheel of their nondescript white sedan I recognised her instantly, and watched as she parked with a kind of angled, abrupt jerk of the steering that spoke of an impatient temperament.

This time I saw her clearly, and without malice. When she got out of the car I saw that she was statuesque, with a strong, compact body and a certain kind of loveliness, allied to physical strength, that is the opposite of delicacy. In her muscularity was a secret vitality, a forceful tenderness, the source of some potential that in my own ephemerality I lacked. My body appeared as a mirage; only my thoughts were real. But she seemed to have a power that surged right through her, from her bright, unruly hair to her strong chin. And she looked like the sort of woman who always knew what to wear, as if her clothes were a careless second skin. I could see it in the way she was dressed that late afternoon. Tan leather boots, stone-coloured moleskins and a loose, navy poloneck sweater. I told myself that she probably got up in the morning and slipped the lot on without a second thought.

Unlike me, stranded in front of my mirror.

I watched her. I watched her open the iron gate, which creaked loudly, felt the heaviness of the cluster of keys dangling from her hand (so many keys on the one ring), saw her lean on the gate for a moment, as if winded, and then walk the short distance to the front door where she set down her bag and, peculiarly, rested her forehead against the door. At that moment I stifled an impulse to come forward and comfort her.

From then on, I felt an overwhelming compulsion to know her, to know her from the inside of her skin. It wasn't so much that she was beautiful as that she was solid and material, whereas I was slight. Her skin glowed. Her body was strong but in proportion, no part of it too long or too short, or in any way exaggerated or prominent. There was something pneumatic about her, something buoyed up and resilient. She had the irresistible allure of someone who cared about her appearance but didn't care all that much, just enough to move through the world with complete conviction. I had no conviction. I was always trying myself out for fit.

Making my way absentmindedly along Clarke Street, I meditated on how I might get to know her, and I thought of how I could break into that house up on the hill. It would be simple. First I would raise the subject of security with Lindsay, some pretence or other, my own fears about a break-in at night, and get a sense of where the house could be entered. In *his* intimate things I now had no interest. His glamour was waning. The spell of the letters, of my own words, had been broken. Now I was beginning to feel trapped. I needed some new object of desire. I had wanted to be found, and now that I was found I wanted to be hidden again.

But *she* was inaccessible. She was even more inaccessible to me than he had once been.

I imagined her in the shower, over breakfast at the kitchen table, always, and no matter in what surface disarray, looking essentially the same. Recognisably herself. No glance in the mirror could disconcert her. Some essence of her self was beyond challenge. She wore no discernible makeup and almost no jewellery, only gold studs in her ears and a loose gold watch. It was as if every action, every gesture, was uncorrupted by doubt.

I wanted her naturalness, I wanted that conviction. I wanted her aura to bleed into mine. I began to fantasise about being in her company. I wanted her to make sense of me. I wanted to look into her eyes and see my own face mirrored there. I wanted to be her child. I wanted to be *her*. I wanted to get inside her body, to become her tame vampire. When I made love to Lindsay I imagined I was her, not with her but *in* her body. I wanted to crawl up into her womb and start again.

I thought of the rooms of her house and how they must be

arrayed with magical objects, the outer signs of her essential self-hood. What kind of music did she listen to? What kind of books did she read? What kind of lingerie did she wear? What perfume? What odd mementoes of her past were lying just then in a drawer in her bedroom? If I could see those things, could *know* them, then some essential knowledge of what it was that I, Sonia, was lacking might be revealed.

The next time Lindsay called I surprised him by asking how he'd met his wife, and he sank without resistance into a long and detailed recollection of their courtship. I knew then that he loved her.

That made two of us.

One afternoon I followed her to a café, crossing the threshold of separation for the first time. It was a Saturday, around four, and she was reading the weekend papers. She rested her chin on her left hand and I noticed she wore a perfectly plain wedding band. I glimpsed a mole on her neck and a fine, golden down on her arms. Though for much of the time she frowned, I felt enlarged by her presence. On impulse I got up and stood by her table, alert and ready to pass through the membrane. To cross over. When she looked up, all I could think of was to ask for a section of the newspaper. 'Sure,' she said, extracting with one deft gesture the piece I had asked for. 'Will this do?' She smiled and a river of warmth flooded my body.

Another day I saw her in High Street and followed her into a supermarket. Walking behind, plucking items at random off the shelves, I observed that she was pale, and swallowed continually, as if she were holding something in. At one point she turned and looked at me quizzically, as if she recognised me. 'Do I know you?' she said. I stood stock still and shook my head.

I began to dream about her, a recurring dream that was painfully vivid. It was as if, without warning, an old wound had opened up and some psychic ooze had begun to leak across my cornea. And yet the dream itself was innocent – it was the waking state that flooded me with grief.

In the dream I was lying, propped up on cushions, on a low punt. Kirsten was standing at the stern with a long pole in her hands, steering us down a narrow river. It was late afternoon and on either side of us were thick mangrove trees with silvery-green foliage that hovered just above the dappled surface of the water. In the middle of the punt, sitting on a velvet cushion, was an engorged placenta, wine-red and liverish. The boat glided on, and all the while I was lazily at ease, trailing my left hand in the phosphorescent water, while on either side birds rustled among the mangroves and fruit bats flew in overhead, homing their way to their night feeding grounds. Each time, just before I woke, the silver body of a fish leapt into the encroaching dusk.

Finally I could contain myself no longer and I resolved to break into their house. In the side lane there was a high gate that was overgrown but unlocked. Behind this I found access to their laundry through a louvred window, and somehow I managed to dislodge the louvres and just squeeze through, my feet perched awkwardly on the rim of an old sink. I did not, as I had feared, have to break something. Once in, all was well because she was at work. Lindsay, I knew, was in a two-hour seminar and their dog was at the vet having surgery on his ear. I knew, as well, that they never turned the alarm on because Lindsay had complained to me that the merest thing would activate it at all hours of the day and night. And in any case, no-one in the inner city ever took any notice of alarms.

To begin with, almost nothing surprised me, certainly not the well-stocked cupboards in the kitchen, which were clean and orderly, despite the silverfish that scurried between glass jars of pasta and rice. On the fridge were photos of children and a cluster of souvenir magnets attached to bills and lists. But in daylight (what little there was of it) the kitchen was surprisingly scuffed and worn, in need of renovation and not at all how I had imagined it; not at all how it had looked when I stared through the window that first time, when the room was softened by lamplight.

Somehow I'd pictured them surrounded by surfaces of marble and stainless steel, but the formica was peeling and the chipboard was stained, though they did have an expensive set of knives sheathed in a block. Still, you could almost smell the ordinariness of it, so banal I had an impulse to just walk out the front door, except it would be deadlocked. So this was the homeliness, the wholesome space of the domestic that had both attracted and repelled me all my life? There must be more to it than this. More, perhaps, in the bedroom upstairs?

The stairs were steep, with a sharp turn at the top. The first bedroom was almost completely full of books and the second was much bigger and spacious — a long rectangular room with two high windows and dusty calico blinds, crookedly furled. If my heart had not been beating so hard (a kind of admonitory thud that kept me on course like a guided missile), I might have moved absentmindedly across, to where I would be visible from the street, and realigned them. I stared at the bed, which was huge (he was, after all, a big man) and covered with some kind of peasant throw that looked vaguely Mexican. There was a wicker armchair with a high back, draped with shawls, and a small coffee table made of cast iron and wood. I looked closely at the bedside tables. No surprises there. Frustration began to pinch at me even before I moved to rifle through her drawers. The top one was full of underwear, unremarkable, neither worn nor glamorous. What did I expect? A diary? A cache of letters? There wasn't even any interesting jewellery.

By now my heartbeat had slowed, replaced by some other discomfort, an ache of disappointment. There were no secrets. There could be no revelation of the ideal. Here in the crevices of their being they were merely pedestrian. There were no idiosyncratic riches, only the pathos of their possessions. No glamour, no special trace.

Only the bathroom was left. In desperation I opened the mirrored door of the cupboard above the basin and rifled among the pharmaceutical blah of cotton balls, unopened bath gels, painkillers in silver foil, shaving cream, mouth wash and boutique soaps. I was looking for their drugs. The phone rang and I hesitated, listening as his voice, not hers, breathed a disembodied message. When the beeps had finished (no message from the caller) I peered into the cabinet and along the glass shelves – there must be something, some talisman I could steal. And there was: a small white plastic container, flat and circular, like a powder compact only more clinically mundane. Levering the top off with my thumbnail, I saw a cream rubber disc, in diameter the size of a small cup rim. Its strangeness was repellent until ... yes, I had seen something similar in a book somewhere, or was it on a video? It was a diaphragm. *Her* diaphragm. Replacing the lid, I lifted my shirt and slipped it into the cup of my bra.

At that moment the alarm went off.

I froze.

If the neighbours rang Lindsay, they wouldn't reach him because he was in a seminar room. If they rang her, she had a forty-minute drive home. Then again, a key might have been left with a neighbour, in which case I would brazen it out, say that Lindsay had engaged me as a research assistant and I had left my bag behind and needed my things urgently. Not so calmly I walked down the narrow staircase and sat at the kitchen table, rigid. The alarm shrieked into the hallway from its cupboard under the stairs.

Then, just as suddenly, it stopped.

After twenty minutes I climbed out through the laundry window and fell softly into the bushes. Obscured beneath the overhang of a paperbark, I stood and adjusted my clothes. The lane was uncannily still. Once I was out onto the street, the mellow afternoon light filtered into my veins like a gift, and suddenly, as I walked down the hill, I felt unexpectedly unburdened, released. When I got home I put the diaphragm under my pillow and collapsed onto my bed in a kind of exhausted elation. I had broken into her house. I had broken into her body.

Not long after this I abandoned my studies and went away. Carl was driving to Darwin and I asked if I could go with him.

I did not return to finish my degree. I did not tell Lindsay I was leaving. I did not ring. I did not write him a letter.

19

Their house is number nineteen and it still looks the same. But the street is much altered. I remember a vacant lot here, with a single burnt-out terrace of charred eaves and overgrown stair-wells, where it was possible to do dope deals on a Thursday evening around dusk. Now the land is built over with new town-houses that are sharp and clean.

I can hear Lindsay's voice replaying in my head, a bland tape unreeling its cautious welcome. 'Yes, Sonia, Saturday afternoon would be fine.' Yes, I could come and visit him at home. Yes, I could tape our discussion. It was as if we hadn't spent that after-noon in the movie theatre, locked together in a dark corner. 'You can get away with anything in here,' he'd said as he handed over money at the box office, 'as long as you don't make a noise.'

Did he really say that? It doesn't sound like him. Maybe someone else said it. What else have I misremembered? Maybe I heard it in a movie; I've seen so many of them, sometimes three and four a week. Because some time after I abandoned my postgraduate research, I took up film studies, writing a paper about *that* movie, the one that had been running while we fondled one another in the back of the cinema. And, by an unlikely series of coincidences, the paper led me into my work in documentary filmmaking, as an assistant to the celebrated Eva Zawadski. So that impulsive decision to go with Lindsay into the darkened cinema changed me into someone else. Or did it?

I open the iron gate. Once, all those years ago, I broke into this house, and now here I am, back again, a respectable visitor, for whom they will tidy their rooms and make tea. I take a deep breath and knock on the door. What will she look like, after all these years?

The door opens and a woman is standing there, looking back at me. She is a thin woman, with short dark hair. Surely this can't be Kirsten? No-one could have changed this much. Kirsten was rounded, plump almost, and flushed with a kind of skin-bursting vitality. This woman is wiry, so that the tendons and sinews stand out. She has that tensile look, as if she fasts in between bouts of working out in the gym.

'I'm Sonia,' I say. 'I have an appointment to see Lindsay at three.'

'Come in.' She closes the door behind me. 'I'm Heather, Lindsay's wife.'

Heather? Who is Heather? I see that this other woman is

looking down at my black bag, the one I carry my recorder in. I say, 'I've come to talk to Lindsay about the heart.'

'Did you have trouble finding us?' she asks.

In the living-room all is perfect order, perfect calm. And there he is, sitting on a white couch. 'Hello,' he says brightly, and rises. 'Long time no see.'

He has put on weight, is an even bigger man now, and his dark hair is thinning, though he still has the same warm brown eyes. He does not move to greet me with a kiss. Instead he turns to this strange woman, his wife. 'Do you want to make the tea, darling, or shall I?'

'No, I'll make it,' she says, with just a hint of testiness.

Beside him on the couch are two children. He sees me staring at them and says, in his old, very precise way of speaking, 'This is my daughter, Lydia, who is six, and my son, Rollo, who's four. We've been reading a book, haven't we?' And turning in their direction he holds up a large illustrated book entitled *The Kingdom of the One-Eyed Giant*. 'This is my light reading these days, I'm afraid.'

I smile, one of those vague, unfocused smiles that are a visible sign of someone holding their breath.

With an almost imperceptible shrug of irritation, Lindsay tosses the book onto the coffee table. 'Run along and play, children,' he says. 'I'm going to talk to Sonia for a while.'

'Can't we finish the story?'

'No, not now. Later.'

'But we're nearly at the end.'

'Lydia, I said later, didn't I? So run along now.' The children stay exactly where they are.

I am immediately taken with Lydia, so like Lindsay with her dark brown eyes, her solemn self-possession, and the way a cloud of brooding intelligence seems to hover above her head.

'What have you got there?' asks Rollo, looking at my tape recorder.

'I've come to talk to Daddy,' I say.

'What are you going to talk about?' asks Lydia.

'I'm going to talk about his heart.'

'What about it?' asks Rollo.

'Now, come along, children, go upstairs and play for a while,' says Heather, who has returned from putting the kettle on. She turns to me. 'Orange Pekoe all right?'

'Fine.'

Lindsay looks over his shoulder. 'I'd like Lapsang,' he says.

'You want me to make *two* pots?'

He gives her his winsome smile, to which she appears impervious. 'Oh, all right, Orange Pekoe will do.'

'Mummy,' asks Lydia, 'why do we have to go upstairs?'

'Because we're going to have a conversation and we need to

think clearly and be quiet for a while. So run along.' Shepherding them ahead of her, she ushers them out into the hallway, returning some minutes later with a tray. On the tray is a large whimsical teapot in bright swirls of yellow and red and green, three intricately patterned cups and saucers, and a plate of chocolate biscuits.

I have spent the last five minutes setting up the tape and making small talk with Lindsay about the weather. What happened to Kirsten? I want to ask, but the words won't come. Now I am sitting on the couch opposite, facing him, smiling back at his broad, beaming buttery face, always so genial, so polite. Heather bends across the coffee table, blocking my line of sight, and lifts the teapot. 'Weak or strong?' she asks.

'As it comes.'

I see myself adjusting the sound levels on the recorder and hear myself saying, as if on automatic pilot, 'We'll just do a general rave around the subject, and then I'll go away and play it back to Eva so she can get a feel for the material, if that's all right.'

'Fine, fine,' he says.

'Perhaps we can begin,' I say, and he nods assent over his cup of steaming tea. 'Okay with you?' I ask Heather, and she also nods.

I press the record button.

'I'm wondering if there is such a thing as a male view of the heart,' I say to Lindsay. 'What do you think?'

'Well,' he begins. He is confident, assured, leaning back against the couch with one leg resting across the other. 'Men tend to rely more on reason...'

Heather is sitting on the edge of the couch, nursing her cup in both hands. 'They like to think they do,' she says. 'They like —'

'Can I finish my sentence?' says Lindsay good-naturedly, but with a hint of sardonic politeness. And she looks down into her cup and is silent. 'Men are more likely to at least attempt to think through a problem in logical terms,' he continues. 'For example —' He stops. 'You're drinking out of my cup,' he says to Heather.

'Does it matter?'

'Well, your cup is there, look.'

'Fine, I'll swap you. Here.'

There is an awkward moment, a hiatus, during which Heather shuffles the porcelain about on the glass-topped table.

'As I was saying,' resumes Lindsay.

At this moment the door opens and Lydia's plump figure appears in the doorway.

'Yes?' Heather says this loudly, so that we all stop and look in Lydia's direction.

'I'm trying to play with my tea set in the doll's house but Rollo keeps annoying me.'

'Tell him to come down here and I'll speak to him.'

Lindsay waits for her to close the door. 'I'll start again,' he says. 'Maybe we males are kidding ourselves for much of the time, but I think men have a certain detachment.'

I can't believe he's saying this to me.

'It's not that they don't care, but it's almost something to do with their greater spatial orientation; they see the whole picture.'

'Oh, yeah?' This from Heather. 'How come, if they're so detached, they account for the vast majority of cases of physical and sexual abuse in families, not to mention violent crime generally?'

'That's aberrant behaviour.'

'It's not aberrant behaviour, Lindsay. I don't see how you can say it's aberrant behaviour when there's so much of it.'

From upstairs comes a loud thud, as of something – a small body? – falling to the floor, followed by the sound of a child crying.

Heather sighs heavily. '*I'll* go,' she says.

Lindsay: 'Do you want me to go?'

'No, *I'll* go. You talk to Sonia.'

I hear her steps ascending the stairs, then her voice, at first remote, but coming closer as she descends back into the front hallway. She enters the room carrying Rollo, who is sobbing. 'He says Lydia pushed him off the bed and he fell on the floor and hurt his shoulder.' She kisses the top of Rollo's head where his black hair sits in damp, sweaty curls.

'You've been jumping on the bed, haven't you?' says Lindsay.

I look at my tape recorder, upright beside the whimsical tea-pot, which has a porcelain raspberry on top of the lid, not unlike an engorged nipple. Slowly the tape winds on.

'Can you take him?' says Heather, holding the disconsolate, semi-limp Rollo out to her husband. 'I'll freshen up the tea.'

'There, there,' says Lindsay, settling the boy on his large cor-duroyed thigh, 'you sit here for a while, quietly, while I talk to Sonia.'

Rollo looks out at me shyly from under wet lashes. His cheeks are pink. He sniffs.

'I think men take their hearts for granted a lot of the time.' Lindsay raises his voice authoritatively, as if to project it over Rollo's head. 'Unless they're in the throes of a new infatuation, they think it will more or less take care of itself. Unlike women, who, well, I get the impression that women are always holding theirs up to the light, you know, examining it for holes.' He breaks off, his voice dropping a notch. 'What is it, mate?'

Rollo is murmuring something into the folds of his shirt.

'What *is* it? I can't hear you.'

Rollo murmurs again.

'You want a biscuit?'

The boy nods. Though he looks away from me, he is self-conscious, acutely aware of my presence.

'Well, go on, help yourself. Just one, mind.' Rollo climbs down from his father's knee and almost in slow motion extends a chubby palm to encompass a biscuit.

'All right, run along now and see what Lydia's doing upstairs.'

The tape is winding on. Already we are almost halfway through and nothing of consequence has been said.

'Right, where were we?'

'You were talking about men compartmentalising their emotions.'

'Was I? I suppose they do.'

'Do what?' The door opens and Heather is back with a steaming kettle.

'Can you keep the kids out?' he says irritably. 'We're getting nowhere here.'

'You shouldn't have sent Rollo upstairs, it'll only start them off again.' She settles herself on the white couch next to her husband.

'Where am I supposed to send them? It's wet outside.'

'He could stay here, as long as he's quiet.'

'And then Lydia would want to come in.'

I attempt to resume our conversation. 'Your own heart,' I say, 'how do you see it?'

He hesitates, adjusting his glasses on the bridge of his nose. And that's when he gives me the look, a look that almost sends me spinning. 'That's an old question, Sonia,' he says quietly, as if prepared, at last, to acknowledge the past. The moment is almost intimate. And then he recovers, rubbing his nose and pretending to absentmindedness. 'I don't know that I *do* see it.'

I, too, recover myself. 'Well, imagine it then. In your mind's eye. Is it a Valentine heart, you know, Cupid's arrow and all that? Or is it a powerhouse, all pumps and pistons and valves?'

'Now, that's a very male image,' says Heather.

'Is it?' I ask. 'That's what I'm wondering. Do men see it primarily as a machine that propels them through their destiny, or –'

'Surely,' says Heather, 'it will depend on the degree to which they have been exposed to cultural influences. For example, the mechanical medical model –'

'Excuse me,' Lindsay interrupts her, 'who's being interviewed here?'

'Well, I was just pointing out –'

'I keep being interrupted by the children as it is.'

'All I was trying to say –'

'I know what you were trying to say.'

I fear an argument coming. I feel that suddenly this room and everyone in it will disintegrate into dust and only the small black recorder will be left running and still I won't know what happened to Kirsten. I intervene, perhaps too hurriedly. 'Let me ask you both this: What is the connection between reason and the emotions? And where does, say, intuition come into it?'

Heather is quiet, deferring at last to her husband. Lindsay leans back against the couch once more, his hands clasped behind his head. 'Intuition is all very well,' he begins, 'but what happens when you have to defend your intuition to others? In rational argument? Intuition is something that reason has to capture, or it is of use only to a single individual, and even then, of limited use. Intuition cannot be made instrumental or persuasive, that is, an instrument of policy, unless it is harnessed to reason.'

Heather can't help herself. 'That's true to a degree,' she says, 'but Lindsay tends to talk as if everything in life happens in committee. There *are* other spheres. Take, for example, Jung's famous anecdote about the scarab beetle and the Cartesian subject –'

Lindsay cuts her off. 'My point exactly. You're talking about a therapeutic discourse of doubtful validity in –'

There's a gush of air as the door is flung open. This time it's Lydia. 'Rollo's got a biscuit!'

'Well?' Her father's voice has a sharp edge of impatience now.

'Well, I haven't had one today.'

Lindsay throws up his hands. 'For Chrissake!' he mutters. 'This is hopeless!' Leaning forward, he picks up a chocolate orb and tosses it in Lydia's direction. The child makes a half-hearted, fumbling attempt at catching it, misses, and the biscuit falls to the floor and cracks. Lydia just stands there, staring down at the pieces.

'Pick it up.'

Lydia goes on staring.

'I said, pick it up, Lydia.'

With mute indignation, Lydia picks up the three pieces of biscuit and puts them down on the coffee table. 'Can I have another one?' she asks.

'No, you cannot!' exclaims Lindsay. His buttery face is flushed red and he's gone beyond impatience into anger. 'For goodness, sake, Lydia, just go upstairs and get out of the way!'

Lydia begins to cry.

'Lindsay!' Heather frowns at him.

'Well, for God's sake, it's impossible to have a conversation here at all.'

'Well, it *is* a wet Saturday afternoon and you have to make allowances.' Heather rises and goes out into the hallway where Lydia is grizzling.

I'm stymied. 'It's hard for them when they can't go out into the backyard,' I venture.

'We should have gone to the pub,' he mutters.

And we lapse into silence. I've been here over an hour and he hasn't asked me anything about myself, not a single polite enquiry. Am I married? (Yes.) Do I have children? (No.) Where do I live? He just sits there, with infuriating self-absorption. Married couples, I am reminded, are like a mysterious, opaque box, and you are either in the box or you are out of the box.

At that moment we hear Heather's voice ring out from upstairs. 'Rollo! You naughty boy! Look what you've done!' And then the sound of a loud smack and the sudden bawling of Rollo, far louder than his sister's and with an edge of hysteria. Lydia is quiet now. Through the open door of the living-room I can see her in the hallway, her eyes wary, her ear cocked for the sound of her brother's raucous sobs.

Lindsay is impassive on the couch. A darkness has come over him and his eyes stare away into some distant space of frustration and suppressed rage.

I am cool in my self-interest. I am prepared to wait.

Heather can be heard coming down the stairs. She reappears in the doorway. 'I'm sorry about that,' she says, 'but he broke the crystal dish on my dressing-table. It was my mother's and I was particularly fond of it.'

'I've got to make a call,' says Lindsay vacantly, to no-one. He leaps up and is gone from the room.

Heather sits in a light, almost formal way on the edge of the couch. She is very still, with her hands folded on her lap. 'It's hard to believe how destructive children can be, how careless,' she says. 'How something valuable can just suddenly cease to exist.'

I gaze at her. I wait for the silence to do my work for me.

'When I was pregnant with Lydia,' she continues, 'Lindsay and I had many discussions about how we would go about implementing discipline. We decided we'd never hit our children. But there you are, they get the better of you.'

'Does Lindsay ever spank them?'

'I probably smack them more, overall. You know, just a light tap. Most of the time he's almost unnaturally patient with them, but every now and then he explodes.' She picks up her cold tea and removes a bug that has fallen into it. 'It can be quite frightening. Once he picked up Rollo by the shirt collar and shook him. The children were terrified.'

Lindsay reappears at the doorway. He seems calmer now that he's made his phone call. Upstairs, all is quiet.

'I told the children I'd take them to the park,' he says to Heather. And then to me, 'Feel like a walk on the grass? We could continue our conversation there.'

He says it so casually and I think, Ah, he has just been biding his time.

We stroll to the bottom of the street, across the road and on down to a small park. On the eastern side of the park is a major road, choked with traffic, but the park is an oasis, its iron railings softened by a large plane tree. At one end is a playground with a loose surface of woodchips, and at the other a long, wire-caged cricket net where a small boy is sweeping his bat with practised ferocity. The sun breaks out from behind grey cloud, the air smells of wet earth, and suddenly I am suffused with nostalgia for my life back then, for this dreamy urban ambience that is a fusion of Edwardian houses and white winter light.

The children run from him in the direction of the playground, breaking away in a sudden rush, as if he is forever irrelevant and they may never return. When they are at a safe distance, clambering over the climbing tower, I turn to him and at last I am able to ask, 'What happened to Kirsten?'

He looks at me shrewdly. 'Don't worry, it was nothing to do with you.'

But before he can say another word, Rollo is running back across the grass towards us with an aggrieved frown. 'Lydia won't give me a turn on the slide,' he growls.

Lindsay peers into the distance, waving his right arm high to get Lydia's attention. 'Give Rollo a go,' he shouts. And then, turning matter-of-factly to me, 'Kirsten left me.'

'Oh.'

'She had a second miscarriage. Worse than the first. She haemorrhaged, nearly bled to death. It . . . it took her a long time to get over it, mentally as well as physically.' He folds his top lip in and under so it disappears.

'But she did get over it?'

'It wasn't just the loss of the baby. She found it hard to accept that her body could let her down. She was always a strong person, never got sick, could always get by on little sleep.' He sighs. 'So she developed a real thing about it. That was supposed to happen to other people.'

'What about you?'

'What about me?'

'You must have been upset.'

'I felt guilty. I didn't want children, not then, anyway. Just before the first miscarriage, I bought her a dog.'

'I remember.'

'A dog instead of a baby. That was the plan.' He smiles, and I feel more than a pang, I feel my ego bruising under the weight of his pain, which is not for the loss of me.

'At first she wouldn't look at the dog, and then, in one of those sudden moves that Kirsten could always make, she seemed to become obsessed with him. Every morning, early, and every night after dinner, she'd walk him.' He looks across to the plane trees. 'In this park.'

Now it's Lydia who has a grievance. She is walking towards us, her little face stony. She holds up her arm to reveal a small graze below the elbow. 'Rollo pushed me off the swing,' she says. 'He should be smacked.'

Lindsay leans forward slightly to rest his hands on her shoulders, and he looks into her eyes. Then he turns her gently around and back towards the playground. 'I'm not smacking anyone now,' he says. 'Sonia and I are having a talk. We'll be over in a minute, and then we'll go home.'

She looks at me grimly and walks off.

'Lydia was an empress in another life,' I say.

'At least one.' And at last he smiles, one of those handsome, sardonic smiles that so beguiled his students. For the first time he has spoken to me as if I am a friend.

'When did you and Kirsten separate?'

'Just over a year after the second miscarriage. She met a guy who used to live around here, just across the way in that house over there.' He points to a large, freestanding stone house at the end of the park. 'A refugee from the stockbroker belt who was slumming it for a while. Used to walk his dog every morning, right here, at the same time as she did.'

'Really?'

'Yes, really.' He says this bemusedly, without sarcasm.

'So they live around here?'

'No.' He shook his head. 'They're somewhere over in Albert Park, I believe.'

'Did you ever tell her about me?'

'Of course not.'

A white sports car turns out of a side street and roars off into the traffic. For a moment it appears to distract him. Then he turns sharply to me and says, 'So where did *you* piss off to, Sonia?'

At last he has brought himself to ask.

'I went north with Carl.'

'Carl?'

'My brother.'

'I didn't know you had a brother. You always seemed to live in a world of your own.'

'I did.'

He shakes his head, as if it means nothing to him now. He is dismissing me. He is putting me back in my place. Looking away and down to the end of the park, he whistles to get the attention of the children, waving at them to join us.

I think of how I stole her diaphragm, of how I might in some way have been responsible for her second miscarriage.

'This second marriage of Kirsten's — does she have any children?'

'A boy. About Lydia's age. I ran into them once in the city. The boy looked just like Kirsten, the living image of her.' For a moment he's almost wistful.

By now it's beginning to grow dark. He whistles again to the children and they look over and wait for their recall. As we stroll across the grass to collect them, I look up at him in shadowy profile, and all the while I am thinking that this is the man who one afternoon gave me an experience of blinding intensity, of luminous spontaneity that I have never been able to recapture since; an experience that seemed, at the time, curiously innocent.

At the corner of the park I stop and say, 'I'll walk up to the station from here.'

'Okay,' he says. No 'Nice to see you, Sonia' or 'How's your life?' No peck on the cheek, no shake of the hand.

I watch him take each child by the wrist and cross the zebra lines of the pedestrian crossing. Just as they reach the other side, the children break from him again and skitter across the kerb and onto the footpath. It's Rollo who leads the way, and in chasing after him Lydia loses her balance and stumbles into the overhang of a tree. She squints, and puts her hand up to her eye as if something is lodged there. Lindsay bends to examine her face and then, dropping to one knee, he takes hold of her shoulders and holds her still, looking into her eyes with a long and scrutinising gaze. I see him frown and shake his head, and then, in one small gesture of heart-wrenching tenderness, he strokes her cheek. Lydia smiles, and in that moment they are like lovers. It's then I see that his irritation with his children is surface. Lydia is the love of his life: she has him in her thrall. A few metres away, on the corner, Rollo is swinging by one arm around the pole of a traffic sign, flinging his elfin body out over the gutter in mock flight.

Something compels me to change direction. I wait for several minutes and then, instead of turning off to the station, I continue on down the street. When I get to his house I stop and peer shamelessly through the window.

There he is, sitting on the big couch with the children beside him. It's almost six, and the dark of evening has settled comfortably around them. Rollo has already crashed at one end, his face innocent in sleep, one small arm dangling over the side, his feet on Lindsay's lap. Lydia is beside her father, entwining her arm with his. I see now how extravagantly and with what abandon the children meld with him, when only a few minutes before they had been so resolutely separate. Lydia, at last, is at rest, her face a study of complacent anticipation. She hands him the picture book he abandoned when I rang the bell. With one hand he takes the book and rests it against his knee, while with the other he smooths her hair back from her face. Then he kisses her on the forehead. She yawns and nestles into his ribs. I see him open the pages to where he left off. I see his lips begin to move as he takes up the story again.

Torque

20

This story has a coda, and it concerns a cardiologist named David Goodman.

Some time after my meeting with Lindsay, I had reason to interview Goodman at his home in Albert Park. In the course of my earlier research I met him one evening at a fundraising dinner. We were seated at a round table in a vast, emporium-like room at the Sheraton and he was midway through an anecdote that caught my attention. I stopped listening to the man next to me and tuned in to what was apparently an uproarious account of Goodman's hobby, aerobatics, otherwise known as stunt flying. Goodman was describing a recent occasion when he had put his small plane into a dive manoeuvre directly over a camp of school cadets. Looking up, the boys had assumed the plane was about to crash into their campfires and bolted in panic into the surrounding bush.

After the general mirth had subsided, I waited for a lull in the conversation and made eye contact. 'Why do you do it?' I asked him.

He looked at me shrewdly, as if summing me up. 'It's fun,' he said.

Had he ever had a heart condition? No, he replied, he was as fit as a fiddle. 'Wouldn't fly a plane otherwise.'

Something about him stayed with me, and when Eva began work on a series of documentaries on the history of aviation I rang Goodman and asked if I could interview him about his stunt flying. There was a silence at the other end of the phone, and then: 'It's not stunt flying,' he said quietly, with a hint of reproval in his tone. 'It's precision flying.'

We agreed to meet on the Saturday afternoon at his house. He was busy but he would 'make time'.

I arrived at Goodman's house at two p.m. It was one of those sharp winter days in July when a greyish yellow light filters through the dense, evergreen foliage of old gardens and the effect is pleasantly surreal. I was nervous, as I always am when I interview someone. It's like the beginning of a love affair that one knows will be short-lived but intense.

On the front verandah of the house was a dog, a handsome animal with thick golden fur and a massive leonine head. I saw at once that this animal was deformed, and that one ear had a lazy droop, as if the cartilage had been damaged. I stiffened. Could it be the same dog?

This dog, which I sensed was elderly, waited soundlessly and with some dignity for me to make a move, staring at me with a quality of uninterested intelligence, a kind of haughty custodianship. When at last I stepped up onto the verandah it simply turned away, having evidently decided that I was harmless, and looked out at the street.

I rang the bell. Goodman opened the door in jeans and a light shirt. He was smaller than I remembered, squarely built, with receding dark hair. We shook hands and I noticed that his were surprisingly large and blunt. I complimented him on his dog.

'This is Chicka,' he said. 'He's a chow chow.' At the mention of his name the dog wandered over. 'Sit,' said Goodman.

Chicka sat.

'Shake hands.' The dog proffered a paw and Goodman shook it in a formal manner.

'Now shake hands with Sonia.'

The dog sat pat, eyeing me with suspicion.

'Shake hands with Sonia,' he said, even more quietly than before. He was a man who lowered his voice to make a point.

Finally, the proffered paw, and my unenthusiastic handshake, after which the animal retired to its post on the verandah.

Goodman shut the door behind us. 'I've trained him well,' he said. There was a hint of precision in this.

I followed him down the long hallway, past formal salon

rooms to the back of the house and a large, light-filled extension, hung with exotic wooden masks. One of them was huge, with grass hair the colour of terracotta, a fierce, grimacing mouth, and cowrie shells for teeth. For a moment I stood there, transfixed by its empty, hollow-eyed gaze. And then I became aware of Goodman standing close behind me.

'Sepik River,' he said. 'They were my mother's. She grew up on a plantation in New Guinea.'

He asked if I would like a drink and I said yes. Quietly, and in a deft way, he made two cups of instant coffee in delicate porcelain cups and saucers and put out a plate of macaroons. I liked the macaroon touch: it was considerate. His manners approached the courtly.

We sat at a white marble table beside French doors and looked out over a huge wooden deck. Outside there were lemon trees in pots, and a line of flowering pink camellia trees along a high fence. Beyond the gate, magpies pecked in the grass beneath a colonnade of wintry trees.

Inside there was an almost unnatural stillness to the house. I remarked on how quiet it was.

'Yes,' he said. Just yes.

I observed that he was comfortable with silence, more comfortable than I.

'Would you like to see a video?'

I looked out through the glass doors and saw the dog looking back in at me. That dog – how many chows in Melbourne
had a lazy ear?

We moved to a TV area at the other end of the room where
there were comfortable cane armchairs. Goodman located the
video he wanted from a wall of shelves that were neatly stacked
with upwards of three hundred boxed and labelled tapes – I did
a quick calculation based on the count for one shelf – and
inserted it in the slot beneath the giant screen. Then he activated
the remote control. At first it wouldn't work; although there was
a buzzing sound, the screen remained blank. But he was unfussed,
calm and methodical in the way he went about correcting the
problem. He had a stillness, almost a woodenness about him
which was hard to read. Was it dullness, or control? Lack of
imagination, or years of disciplined restraint? Here was a man,
I reminded myself, who could thread a catheter through an
artery: every move he made must be precisely calibrated.

Eventually he got the video recorder to work and the bright
image of a red plane flared suddenly on the supersize screen.
Then, without warning, we were inside the plane, in flight, and
the earth was spinning away below.

I watched politely but the video was jerky and chaotic – the
view kept dropping below the window of the cockpit to the instrument panel. This, he explained, was because under the pressure of

aerobatic manoeuvres the camera was four times heavier than normal and it was hard to keep it held high enough to capture the view outside.

When the video was over he stood up. 'Would you like to see a photograph of the plane?' he asked. And disappeared into a side room.

When he came back and handed me the photo I saw that it was a fierce little machine, bright red and so streamlined, of such high gloss, that it looked almost cartoonish. Airbrushed.

I turned on my tape recorder. 'Okay, tell me about the plane.'

'Well, it's called the Ferrari of the air. It's about eight metres long and it's got a nine-metre wing-span, so it's actually wider than it is long. And at the back here, unlike most ordinary planes, it's got what's called a full-flow stabilator so that the rear tail-plane is not fixed with a flap on the back – the whole tailplane moves, and that gives you a lot of authority.'

Authority. It seemed a strange word to use about a plane. 'What do you mean by authority?'

'Control. Control in terms of angle of attack on the wind. And then this very large rudder, here,' he pointed, 'means that you have a lot of stability, like a knife cutting through the air.'

'And it's a single engine?'

'Single engine, that's right.'

'And if the engine cuts out, can you glide in it?'

'Basically, the principles of flight are that the engine is the thing that takes you forward, and it's the angle of attack of the wings on the air that allows you to, as it were, skid along the air, in the same way a water-skier skids along the water. Only what the wings are doing, by angling slightly upwards on the way in, they're skidding on the air, which tends to make them climb. But at the same time, because of the weight of the craft, they're falling through the air and skidding upwards. So if you ever have a close look at a plane, you'll see that it's going straight ahead but it's also moving up, and it's actually a combination of climbing and falling.'

'Climbing and falling at the same time?'

'Yes.'

'Quite poetic, really.'

'I'm not into poetry. I wouldn't know.'

'But can you glide it in to land?'

'Oh, yeah, no problem at all. The only thing you need for lift for this particular plane – if you've only got one person aboard – is to be travelling at at least forty-three knots. That's called the buffer zone, or the stall speed. The idea is that there's an envelope, a limit beyond which the plane won't fly. And many of the aerobatic manoeuvres that I do are beyond the limit, outside the edges of the envelope. Which means that the plane does not fly. In other words, it's just falling. You're passing through the air, but that's not the same thing as flying.'

Climbing and yet falling, passing through the air but not flying – it was like everything he said was in another language, a kabbala of concealed meaning.

'Flying means that the angle of attack on the air is less than sixteen degrees, and this means you're developing low pressure above the wing and high pressure below the wing. Therefore you're flying. Once you get above sixteen degrees, the angle of attack is so steep that the plane won't – can't – fly. Not this plane, and not most planes either. That's because they develop turbulence above the wing, and won't develop an increasing pressure underneath the wing. So if I do a manoeuvre called the Falling Leaf, which is a series of incipient spins, it's full backstick and the plane comes up to above the sixteen-degrees angle. Then it's power off, so it drops below the stall speed and begins to go down. Like a leaf falling out of a tree.'

'And you're just falling?'

'Dropping like a stone. Not only does the engine stop, but the propeller goes stationary as well, because of the load on it. In the middle of a spin you're looking at a stationary propeller.' He grinned, and took a measured sip of his coffee. 'But the plane falls very quickly, so it gathers speed, and if it gathers speed above about ninety knots, you have to butt out of the manoeuvre because you're exceeding the extremities of the plane's tolerance to stress. Now, the recovery –'

'Is there much margin for error in that?'

'Sometimes, if you hit your own wind at the wrong angle, it can feel very violent in the plane, much more violent than it looks from the outside.'

'Unpleasantly?'

'It makes a lot of people feel sick.'

'How does it make you feel?'

'Doesn't affect me.' He said this quietly, without bravado, and I believed him. 'Now, the recovery –'

At that moment the phone rang. 'I'm sorry,' he said, and got up out of his chair and moved across to the phone that sat on the black granite bench in the kitchen.

'Hello, darling,' I heard him say. 'Yes, yes, she's here ... Sonia Bichel ... Yeah? Yes, okay, I'll tell her that ... Oh, about halfway through, I imagine ... Okay ... Okay ... See you then.'

'My wife,' he said, returning to his chair. 'She's got some crisis at work.'

'On a Saturday?'

'Not uncommon.' He adjusted himself in his chair. 'Where were we?'

'The recovery.'

'If I'm doing a ten-tonne spin my eyes become affected and the whole world becomes blurry. After about three or four turns, five mostly, everything outside becomes a complete blur and you actually lose track, you can't find your bearings – say, a local dam or radio tower – at all. So there's no point in looking out, you have to look in at your own instrument panel, look at the controls and see five thousand feet come up, make sure you're not accelerating beyond eighty knots per hour, and then, at five thousand feet, commence the recovery.' He leaned forward, arms resting lightly on his knees. 'First of all, you confirm the direction in which you're travelling. And then – and this is the most frightening thing about it – then you let go of the control column. Let go the stick completely.'

'Why?'

'Because you don't need it. What you do is concentrate on the rudder. As hard and as fast as you can, you put the rudder in, because the force on the rudder is very strong and you need to be *very* authoritative and push that foot in. And when you boot that rudder in, the frightening thing about a spin for a non-pilot is that you angle down, you're looking straight at the ground, and your rate of rotation actually speeds up from one time a second to three times a second.'

'To come out of a spin, you speed up?'

'Yes. It gets worse before it gets better.'

'So you go out of a spin into a spiral dive, then you take the rudder off and climb out?'

'Yes. And you generally recover from five thousand feet to three and a half thousand feet.'

'How long does it take?'

'About eight seconds.'

'That must be a long eight seconds.'

'Oh, no, no, it all happens pretty quick.'

'Are all these exercises crisis manoeuvres for getting out of problems?'

'No, they're just fun.'

'Just fun?'

'Yes.' He grinned. 'But they are crisis manoeuvres as well.'

'So, when you're doing this – when you're dropping like a stone – do you feel safe?'

'Absolutely.'

'Absolutely?'

'Yes.'

'Why?'

'Firstly, because I always do a very methodical check on the plane before I go up. I check everything. It's easier to fix it on the ground. And then, if for some unforeseen reason the engine fails, as long as I've got two wings then I can skid to the ground. There's a thing called a glide ratio, and providing you get your calculations right, you can glide your way out of trouble.'

'That's it?'

'Pretty much. But of course you take precautions. Before I start, I pick out my emergency landing spot, because when the engine stops in the middle of the aerobatics I don't want to have to worry about trying to find a place to put the plane down. I want to push the edge of the envelope as far as I can, while at the same time knowing exactly where I can land if I have to.'

I smiled. 'You want it both ways.'

'Wouldn't you?'

'And you never feel tempted to take a risk?'

'No, never take a risk.'

'You feel safe up there?'

'Always.'

'Do you believe in God?'

'Yes.'

'And when you're up in the plane, do you feel closer to God?'

'Oh, no, you don't feel closer to God at all.'

'Not even a bit?'

'Not really.' He paused for reflection. 'Well, God is always on the margins, I suppose.'

'But not in your face, so to speak?'

'No,' he said solemnly. 'You're very much in your own face up there.'

'Because flying is a purely technical exercise?'

'Yes. Absolutely.'

At that moment we seemed suddenly to reach a hiatus, some

cul-de-sac of silence. He stood up and flexed his shoulders. 'Another coffee?'

'No, thanks.'

'I'll just get some water. I'm not used to all this talking.'

He returned with a jug and two glasses and set them down on the coffee table between us. Then he looked at me intently, waiting for my next question. I sensed that he was enjoying himself.

'And all this — you do all this on instruments?'

'Absolutely, the instruments are everything.'

'You can't use your instincts?'

'On the contrary, if you rely on your instincts you'll crash. The inner ear, for example, which creates instinctive balance, is neutralised by the motion of flight.'

'So you can't rely on instinctive balance?'

'The opposite. And in bad weather, especially, it's very easy to become disoriented. A plane could be momentarily upside down and the passengers wouldn't know. And when a plane banks, for example, all the senses are fooled. The body feels it has turned when it hasn't. You have to believe your instruments. Nothing else.'

'Really?'

'Yes, really. It's a science.'

'So the whole time you're up there, you're just doing one

calculation after another? Your mind never wanders, there's no time for daydreaming?'

'Oh no, no, you don't think about anything.'

'It's full-on concentration the whole time?'

'Absolutely. Full-on.'

'For how long? On average?'

'An hour. You're pretty tired after an hour.' He paused. 'And also, it's very hard, very heavy on the upper body. Because of the G-forces.'

'G-forces?'

'The increased loading caused by inertia during a well-flown turn is felt within the cockpit as additional heaviness. Pilots measure it in Gs, as a multiple of gravity's normal pull. What happens is that when you experience four times the force of gravity, or five times in some of the manoeuvres, every part of you experiences this extra weight. So whatever you might weigh now, you effectively weigh four times as much. The most obvious way people feel it is when the blood runs out of their head. Because the heart is a little slow, it's two or three seconds behind the effect, and so when your blood starts to run out of your head – and your heart hasn't started to beat faster to keep the pressure up so that you've got blood to your head – then what happens is that people start to what's called "grey out". They lose the ability to see colours and then they start to get tunnel

vision. All the peripheral vision goes and then eventually the tunnel vision comes together and they black out.'

'How do you prevent that?'

'When you lose colour, you let go, let the Gs off. In other
words, stick forward – wherever you are – stick forward and get
out.'

'How long have you got when you start to lose colour?'

'Well, there's a thing called G-loc, which is loss of consciousness as a result of Gs. The general view is that seven Gs
inside seven seconds will knock you out, or five Gs for seven seconds will knock you out. That's the general view.'

'What's it feel like?'

'You feel your heart pounding. It can get up to two hundred
beats per minute.'

'Is it exhilarating?'

'Oh, a lot of people get hooked on Gs. It's not a bad feeling,
it's pretty good actually.'

'So you get a high from all this?'

'A high?'

'Like joggers. A rush of endorphins.'

'Oh. It's pretty . . . it's a bit of a buzz. Yes.' Again there was a
long pause, but it didn't seem to matter. We seemed to have
arrived at a rhythm in our conversation. 'But you know, the biggest high is not in the flying, it's in the landing. A really smooth

landing, just . . . a nice touch.' And he waved his hand across a line in the air.

'Really? After all that? You go up and throw yourself around in the air just so you can have the pleasure of a smooth landing?'

'Yeah.'

'So you get high by coming down? That's a paradox, isn't it?'

'Yes, it is. But landing is not that hard, actually.'

'It isn't?'

'No. Just the bit where you flare out at exactly two feet above the runway.'

'Flare out?'

'Yeah, you have to flare. You increase the angle of attack so you're getting more lift at lower speed, and you just sit above the runway and gradually go down a couple of inches at a time on that last two feet and just touch it on. Don't forget that when you're landing on the runway, you're *colliding* with the earth – at something like, well, you're doing certainly a hundred and sixty clicks, so you want to get it right.'

'You want to collide with precision?'

He gave me that focused look again. And then laughed. It was the first time. 'To do anything perfect is hard,' he said.

We talked on. Goodman described a number of manoeuvres in unwaveringly precise detail: varieties of spin, the loop, the flick roll, and others I can't recall. The biggest thing about aerobatics, he insisted, was that it took you out of your comfort zone, so that your general ability in everything became stronger. 'You become a more confidant person overall.' He was adamant that anyone could do it, and when I expressed surprise, if not incredulity at this assertion, he reiterated his belief. 'Anyone without a phobia or a physical disability can do what I do. Within one hour, I could have you using the control column of the plane, flying a loop and roll, and recovering level flight. I guarantee it.'

When I protested that some people must have a better spatial sense than others, he agreed that you had to have some kinaesthetic sense. 'You've got to know where you are when you're upside down. If you know that, you can deal with anything.' He spoke of how he saw himself outside the plane, but also how the plane was an extension of his body and he felt as if the wings were his.

'So you're never disoriented?'

'Never, not ever.'

Just then, the phone rang again. This time I couldn't hear so well, though I heard the word 'darling' and assumed it was his wife. And then the words 'Okay, okay, I'll meet you there.' When he was seated again, he grinned. 'Always some drama,' he said.

'Drama?'

'With my wife.'

'I would have thought there was a fair bit of drama in your own line of work.'

'Different.' He shook his head and said it again. 'Different,' as if indulging her in her absence.

'What does your wife do?'

'She's the director of a correctional facility for delinquent boys.'

And then I knew that it must be her. First the dog and now Rundle House. And I heard the sound of my voice drifting on the air as if I were listening to myself from a distance. 'Rundle House?'

'Yes. You know it?'

'I've . . . I've heard of it.' Breathless. 'I used to know someone who worked there. What's your wife's name?'

'Kirsten. She's worked at Rundle House for a long time. She might know your friend.'

'She might.' I paused, and took a sip from my glass of water. 'Will I have a chance to speak to her?'

'Why would you want to speak to her?'

I shook my head, that little shake of a head that accompanies a lie. 'Just to get her take on this. She must worry about you when you're up there?'

'Kirsten? No, she doesn't worry at all.'

'Does she go up with you?'

'Went up once. Didn't have a problem with it, just couldn't see the point of it.' He smiled, as if, oddly, this were something in her favour. 'Mind you, she doesn't like the idea of me taking the boy up.'

'The boy?'

'Luke. He's six.'

'You take your son up?'

'No, but I will. When he's old enough to do all the calculations for himself.' He leaned forward intently. 'You know, my wife said your name was familiar to her.'

'Really? Did she say why?'

'No.'

'Well.' I took a deep breath. 'I've interviewed a lot of people in my work . . .' And couldn't finish the sentence. It occurred to me then that if I kept him talking long enough, maybe Kirsten would come home. The question was, did I need to see her again? 'Let me ask you perhaps the most important question, which is why you took it up. Why did you take up stunt flying?'

'Uh-uh.' Waving his finger at me. 'You're doing it again. Not stunt flying, remember. Precision flying.'

'Okay. Why did you take up precision flying?'

'That's very interesting.' He seemed to have stopped in his tracks. 'That's quite an interesting question. You know, no-one's ever asked me that before.'

'No-one?' I could scarcely believe this.

'No. And I don't know that I've ever wholly admitted why I took it up, so you're getting it for the first time. But . . .' Another pause. 'There're two levels to this decision. Like many kids, when I was younger – I'm talking about ten years old – I had dreams that I was in a plane, it was going down, the pilot was dead, and I got into the cockpit and landed the plane.' He smiled. 'That sort of thing.'

'So you were living out a fantasy?'

'You could say that.' And then he gave me a long, appraising look, as if calculating whether he should go on. 'And I think that, probably . . . It's true that very often you need a setback to push you forward, and . . .'

'Yes?'

'I was at a point where I'd had a string of successes, my career was on track, I'd done some exciting things, and then, very surprisingly, for the first time in my life I had a setback. My wife . . . That setback was that my . . . my wife died.'

'Oh.' I waited for him to continue but he seemed stunned. 'How many years ago was that?'

'Eleven.'

'An illness?'

'Head-on collision.'

'You were driving?'

He shook his head. 'She was alone. The other driver was drunk.'

I waited.

'And out of that . . . out of that I thought, Well, you know, *now's* the time when, if I want to do this, I'm least going to affect anyone else. I can fall out of the sky and it won't matter.'

'So the idea was always in your head?'

'No, it wasn't in my head but, but I think I probably had the view – my self-esteem was somewhat low and I thought this was a way of regaining my self-esteem, which indeed it did for me, in very large measure.'

'Your self-esteem? Why? Your wife's death wasn't your fault.'

'It wasn't my fault, no, but I felt . . . It sounds odd but I felt that I had been victimised. Victimised by fate. Something that was mine had been taken away from me. Without just cause.'

'But as a doctor, you must see that happen all the time?'

'Yes, but it's different when it happens to you. And after that I wanted very much to move on and do something new, and I guess I saw the flying as good therapy, and somewhat of a challenge.'

'You don't think there was a self-destructive impulse in all this?'

'Oh no, no, not at all, absolutely not. But there was the thought that I wanted to, as it were, break out of the traditional conservatism that had seen me do all the right things in my life – only to lose what I most cared about, all gone up in smoke.' His voice was hoarse. 'And also, I think, it made me . . . I don't know. I can't define it. It'll come to me in a minute.'

But it didn't. I saw my opening. 'And how did you meet your current wife?'

'After Judy – my first wife – died, I sold up and moved out. A friend was being posted overseas for a year and he was looking for someone to live in his house and look after his dog. The kids were out on their own, in flats, so I offered. I moved to Northcote. It was very different from where I'd lived before and I thought it might . . . Anyway, every morning I'd take this dog for a walk in the local park and that's where I met Kirsten.'

'With Chicka?'

'Actually he was called Chuang then. Silly name. I dubbed him Chicka and eventually it stuck. He was a wilful dog. Hopeless, really. It took me a long time to train him.'

'So fate brought you and your wife together?'

'Yes, I suppose it did.'

Fate had taken away one wife and replaced her with another. Fate had propelled him into a dangerous form of consolation, and fate had kept him alive to enjoy it. But fate had no just cause, either way.

'And you never think, That's it, I've done enough of this,

I've pushed my luck far enough?'

'No, absolutely not. No, you don't put thousands of dollars into building a skill and then throw it away. It's an investment in yourself.'

'But when you remarried —' I almost said her name, and checked myself. 'When you married again, you didn't feel, Well, that's it, I've proved something, I can stop now?'

'No, no. As I said, it's an investment. You've taught yourself the skill, you don't want to lose it.'

'Why not? You've proved you can do it.'

'I still enjoy it.'

'So you're still having fun?'

'Absolutely. Still having fun.'

The afternoon was drawing in, the room was growing dark, and I knew now that she wasn't coming home. I asked if I could ring a taxi.

'Where do you live? I'll drive you home.'

'You must be expecting your wife.'

'No. I'm meeting her at a function later.'

Of course. The phone call.

As we walked down the hallway to the front door, he paused at the entrance to a large salon room on the right. 'Have a look in here,' he said. 'We've just had all this front area redone.'

'It's lovely.'

'Yes, we're very pleased with the renovations.'

'Can I look at the photos?' I asked, gesturing at the mantel-piece.

'Sure.'

And there she was, next to a small boy, beside a river, and she had her arm around the boy, who was grinning back at the camera with an expression of shy triumph. In one hand he held a fishing rod while in the other he brandished a small speckled trout. Kirsten was sturdier now, more matronly, and her golden halo of hair was cropped into a sensible bob. I saw at once that she was herself, the same self she had always been, but somehow she was no longer magical. At least, not for me, even though there was still that fullness of bloom that once suggested to me an incandescent promise of wholeness, some indivisible space of potential that could not be disabled. And it hadn't been; she had survived. And so had I.

We drove across town in heavy traffic. It wasn't a route he knew, and I'm a poor navigator, but he was calm and okay with my late signals. Not surprisingly, he was a very good driver, and piloted the silver Audi with the quiet authority with which he had patiently explained the force of gravity, G-loc and the hammer-head effect. I asked him if he had read the Tom Wolfe book about the first astronauts, and whether he thought there was such a thing as the right stuff. Yes, he replied, he'd read it, but in his view it was a bit of a wank.

'All that macho stuff, that isn't what it's about. It's a precision thing. You do your sums and you get your result.'

I asked him how many children he had from his first wife and he said two. The girl lived in Perth with her boyfriend and he hadn't seen her in a while. His elder son, Ned, who he'd always thought he'd got on with pretty well, was now refusing to see or speak to him.

'He's got in with some cult, one of those Japanese outfits.' He looked across at me – that appraising glance again. 'Do you know anything about them?'

'No.'

'It's pretty weird stuff.' He hesitated, as if weighing up whether to say more.

'How did your son get into this?'

'He fell in with a girl whose family are all into it. Now he's gone to live with them out at Moorabbin and he doesn't want to have a bar of me.'

'Why not?'

'Because I challenge him on it. It's not rational. It's all a form of mind control and I want him to see that.'

'What do they believe in?'

'All sorts of mumbo-jumbo. That there's an invisible world full of spirits that get a hold of you and won't let go.' He waved a pedestrian across the road. 'You have to perform all these rituals, turn round three times in a circle and clap, and so on, and if you don't, bad things will happen to you.' He shook his head. 'All sorts of things. It's about mind control, pure and simple.'

'How old is he?'

'Twenty-two.'

Twenty-two. I remembered what that felt like. Desperation could take you anywhere.

When he dropped me off at the corner of my street I thanked him for being so generous with his time.

'Thanks for listening,' he said. And he touched me lightly on the arm. It wasn't a sexual touch, it was a human touch – friendly, making connection. Suddenly I felt like the stiff one, opportunistic, calculating, guarded. And I felt I should offer some reparation.

'Don't worry about your son,' I said, 'he's got a long way to go yet.' I opened the door and climbed out of the car.

As I bent to window height to say goodbye, he leaned across to the passenger side, one hand resting on the handbrake. Looking up at me intently, he said, 'Now, don't over-dramatise what we've talked about. None of that beat-up stuff about stunts. It's not stunt flying, remember. It's precision flying.'

'Yes,' I said. 'I'll remember.'

That evening I sat out on the sundeck at the rear of the house, wrapped in a blanket. I couldn't get the photograph of Kirsten out of my mind, the way her son had stood there, nestled safe within her aura. There was a surplus in that aura, a breadth of field, and this, I saw, was what had drawn me to her all those years before. We construct ourselves out of our mother's surplus, and to a lesser degree our father's, and where there is too little, or none, we find it in the surplus of others: we attach ourselves to their lodestar and suck up the sparks. We draw succour into a painful vacuum. These others shimmer on the horizon of our dreams like pillars of consciousness, and their vibration carries us through the days, even though they themselves may be mundanely unaware of our existence. It may happen that they do this for only a short time, but even in the short time that we love them, that experience of love, however bent out of shape, is crucial to our survival. Once the heart is opened, it can begin to recover.

At the time of my interview with David Goodman, my husband and I were temporarily separated. He was living in Montreal, having left two weeks before to take up a six-month contract that would enable us, at last, to put down a deposit on a house, a house not unlike the one we were renting then. That house was small and run-down, with a neglected backyard, and it had an odd feature: a rough-hewn sundeck with no railings, a blunt platform that jutted out abruptly from a door at the top of the stairs.

Since my husband's departure, I had taken to sitting on this platform at night and thinking of him. On the night before he left we had made love, and since then I had become possessed by the idea that I had conceived a child. On the morning of the day that I interviewed Goodman, I rang and made a booking to see my doctor for a pregnancy test, for I felt certain that something in me was no longer latent, was beyond readiness and already expanding. That night, on the sundeck, I thought of Kirsten's diaphragm, and how for a time I had slept with it under my pillow. Did I still have it? All around me were boxes, unpacked, and somewhere in one of them, along with the detritus of my student days, it might well be lying in an envelope – dry, rubbery, without anchorage. Did I feel the urge to look for it? No, it was the idea of the diaphragm that was important: a talisman of her body, the maternal body. And now that body was morphing into my own.

That night, I dreamed I was in a light plane heading east, towards a dense bank of cloud. At the controls was a stranger, a black man, tall and thin with delicate wrists.

'I am your pilot,' he said. 'We must find a space beneath the cloud or we will be unable to fly above the mountains and we'll have to turn back.'

As we approached the mountain, a hole opened in the clouds, the size of a playing field, and steadily we rose up through the gap into the clear blue space beyond. But when I looked down I saw that the hole had closed behind us and we were stranded above an endless quilt of white.

My pilot turned to me. 'I had better radio in and get a signal.'

But by now the radio was dead. Not only this, the plane had suffered a complete instrument failure. We had no means of fiinding our way home.

It was then that I heard an odd flapping sound and looked behind me. On a small bucket seat at the rear of the plane was a pheasant.

'There's a pheasant on the seat behind us,' I said.

My pilot's gaze was fixed. 'You'd better nurse it,' he said, 'until we find our way out.'

Not now, I thought, and perhaps not ever.

And so we flew on, blinded by dense white cloud. After a

while my pilot turned to me again. 'You'd better check on that pheasant,' he said.

But when I looked behind me the speckled bird was gone. In its place, sitting upright on a velvet cushion, was a baby, plump and naked save for a thin strip of gauze around its middle. I opened my mouth to speak, but before I could say a word I heard a cry from my pilot.

'Look, the hole is still there, the hole we came up through. The cloud has moved but the hole remains. We can find our way out of this.'

I looked to the baby.

The baby smiled.

The plane banked, and in that turning I knew that the infant was my own child, and that I had dreamed its coming. I looked down, into the welcoming abyss, and there beneath us was the earth, a great luminous egg hovering in space.

Headlong we began our descent.

Acknowledgements

This book was produced with the assistance of a grant from the Literature Board of the Australia Council and a fellowship at the Varuna Writers Centre in New South Wales.

I am indebted to the following books: *Descartes: An Intellectual Biography* (Stephen Gaukroger, Oxford University Press, 1995); *From Beast-Machine to Man-Machine* (Leonora Cohen Rosenfield, Octagon Books, 1968); *Minds of Their Own: Thinking and Awareness in* Animals (Lesley J. Rogers, Allen & Unwin, 1997); *Should We Have a Baby?* (Candida Peterson, Rigby, 1982); *Without Guilt and Justice: From Decidophobia to Autonomy* (Walter Kaufmann, Dell, 1973); *Dr Miriam Stoppard's New Pregnancy and Birth Book* (from which the quote on page 169 is taken; Dr Miriam Stoppard, Viking, 2001); *The New Pregnancy and Childbirth* (Sheila Kitzinger, Transworld, 1997). I also acknowledge William Langewiesche's essay on flying, 'The Turn', from *The Best American Essays 1994* (ed. Tracy Kidder, Houghton Mifflin, 1994).

My grateful thanks to Sally Pryor, who alerted me to the story of Descartes' doll in her paper 'Thinking of Oneself as a Computer' (1990); to Stephen Muecke, who translated the recipe for *confit* of duck from the *Larousse Gastronomique*; and to the intrepid Philip Myer, for his patient discourse on aerobatic flying. Any errors are mine. Thanks also to Clare Forster and Meredith Rose at Penguin, and to Debra Billson for her design; to Lyn Tranter at Australian Literary Management; and to Fiona Place, Margaretta Pos, Judith Lukin-Amundsen, Jason Lohrey, and Andrew and Cleo Lohrey.

Extracts from this novel have been previously published in *The Best Australian Stories 1999* (ed. Peter Craven, Black Inc., 1999) and in *Scorched: Penguin Australian Summer Stories* (Penguin, 2004).

This work deals with the dilemmas of fictional characters and is not intended as an argument either for or against any kind of medical testing.

Three Dog Night

Peter Goldsworthy

Is it possible to be too much in love? After ten years in London, Martin Blackman returns to Adelaide with his wife and fellow psychiatrist Lucy, blissfully happy. But then he introduces her to his old friend Felix, once a brilliant surgeon, now barred from practising and changed beyond recognition. In the complex triangle that develops, Martin must decide how far he's prepared to go for Felix. So begins the darkest of journeys for all three of them . . .

Confronting, unpredictable, richly sexual, *Three Dog Night* is a lyrical page-turner from one of Australia's finest storytellers.

'Goldsworthy's most ambitious novel thus far . . . and his best'

JM Coetzee, Nobel Prize-winner

'An intense and brilliant novel about the fathomless human capacity for self-deception . . . a work of concentrated formal elegance that confirms Goldsworthy's status as one of Australia's best novelists.' James Ley, *Sydney Melbourne Herald*

'Lyrical, sexual and highly involving, without a single false note and charged with that pervasive Goldsworthian disquiet.'

Robert Drewe, *The Age*

The List of all Answers

Peter Goldsworthy

Ranging from the early comic sketches to the disturbing brilliance of his recent stories, this outstanding collection reinforces Peter Goldsworthy's reputation as a modern master of short fiction. Simultaneously light and dark, unsettling and amusing, his stories leave indelible traces in the memory. A writer's writer, he is also never less than compellingly readable.

'No Australian author has written more convincingly about the power of hormones or the fear of death.'

Bruce Bennett, *Australian Short Fiction: A History*

'Each story is a polished miniature . . . fluent, shapely, eminently readable . . . We are moved in turn to laughter, tears, embarrassment and horror.' Katharine England, *The Advertiser*

'These stories are tinged with irony and delectable wit, running the gamut of emotions from envy to despair. Goldsworthy's ear for dialogue is as exceptional as his inner eye for character is exquisite.' Ali Lavau, *Who Weekly*

'In some ways Goldsworthy is the Chekhov of his time and place . . . poised, controlled, acute, funny, mean, miserable.'

Heather Falkner, *The Australian*

Memo for a Saner World

Bob Brown

Over the years, Bob Brown has been assaulted, jailed, vilified and shot at for his stance on the environment and human rights. This is his account of the defining moments in that life of activism, from the famous Franklin River blockade to his parliamentary protest against George Bush — a few minutes that gave voice to what many Australians felt but had no way of saying.

By turns inspiring, compassionate and outraged, this personal story of being green makes the key issues easily understood. If you're someone who avoids reading about the world because you think it's too depressing, here's the good news: it's worse if you don't know. While some of the facts Bob presents are less than cheerful, his message is powerfully hopeful.

With Bob Brown and the Greens set to become even more influential in Australian life, *Memo for a Saner World* is an essential record of what he stands for.